Fed Up!
A Relatable Memoir

By:

C.P. Henderson

Copyright © 2016 by C.P. Henderson

ISBN 13: 978-1530968183
ISBN 10: 1530968186

All rights reserved. Without limiting the rights under copyright reserved above, no part of this publication may be reproduced, stored in or introduced into a retrieval system, or transmitted, in any form, or by any means (electronic, mechanical, photocopying, recording, or otherwise) without the prior written permission of the copyright owner.

This is a work of fiction, with some truth. The names have been changed to protect all parties involved. The author acknowledges the trademarked status and trademark owners of various products referenced in this work of fiction, which have been used without permission. The publication/use of these trademarks is not authorized, associated with, or sponsored by the trademark owners.

This book is licensed for your personal enjoyment only.

Acknowledgements

I'd first like to thank God for allowing me to write this book, as well as, overcome many of the obstacles that were placed in my thirty-six-year journey called life.

Secondly, my spectacular husband, he's been my biggest supporter and cheerleader.

Third, my amazing sister, who not only heard these stories first hand but read them over and over again until I got everything just right.

Lastly, Meaghan Kelly, she asked probing questions that allowed me to really make the characters and stories come alive on paper.

Introduction

If only real life could take a screenshot from reality TV. A lot more smacks, hits, and table flips while spewing every explicit word known to man would liven up any situation. As much as I would have loved for any of those options to be my reaction to the many upsetting situations I experienced while working for the feds, I knew better. *Orange is not the new black in my world; it washes me out.*

Reality TV is far from most people's "reality," however, we still find ourselves drawn to watch. How much weight is the biggest loser actually going to keep off? Who really has hundreds of thousands of dollars sitting around to flip a house in California? Don't get me started on the people who like to be yelled at by a raging lunatic in a kitchen full of knives!

Working for the federal government has been an experience I will never forget, no matter how hard I try. I have met some really cool people along the way and experienced things that probably only happen at federal agencies. Let me rephrase that, I have experienced things that are probably only tolerated *because* it's a federal agency.

Though I've never worked for private industry long enough to reap the benefits, I know there are perks: bonuses, expense accounts, fabulous Christmas parties. Don't get me wrong, working for the feds has its privileges, ten federal holidays a year (a few extra if the President decides to be generous), being able to pretty much tell your boss what you will and won't do, and up to two weeks off a year. *Can you tell I like to be away from work more often than not?*

As you are reading, I hope you'll see my experiences as entertaining, comical, and most importantly relatable. I have changed the names to protect the innocent and not so innocent. The chapters are named after reality shows that either depict a main character's personality or are fitting for the story. Enjoy!

Locked Up

In two short hours, my life was completely going to change. No longer would I be working night shift for two days, then evening shift for three days with no health insurance in crappy Del Rio, Texas. Unlike most twenty-three-year-olds fresh out of college, I had a plan to join the United States Air Force. A year and four months prior, the United States was rattled like it had never been before. We were attacked on our own soil. I had known since middle school that I wanted to join the military and follow in my grandfathers, father, and sister's footsteps. That dreadful day solidified my decision.

"You have way too much mouth to be enlisted," my mother told me repeatedly. "Rank has its privileges. You need to go in as an officer."

There aren't many times I can say this, but I'm extremely glad I listened to my mother's advice.

"Raise your right hand and repeat after me," Colonel Shawn Grant instructed shortly after I arrived at his office in San Antonio, Texas. I had been communicating with Colonel Grant over the last three months. He'd always been extremely cheerful and laid back on the phone. I was nice to finally meet him and put a face to a voice.

He was exactly how I had pictured him. He was one of the main reasons women loved men in uniform; his uniform fit like a glove. His pants were tailored perfectly and rested with a slight bend on the top of his shiny shoes. His long sleeve shirt was pressed to the nines, and his cufflinks had the Air Force emblem on them. He didn't have the typical 'military' haircut, where the sides are shaved low with a patch of longer hair on the top. Instead, his salt and pepper hair was about a quarter of an inch all the way around, a look most couldn't carry off.

I raised my right hand and repeated after Colonel Grant, "I, Carol Pugh, having been appointed a second lieutenant in the United States Air Force, do solemnly swear that I will support and defend the Constitution of the United States against all enemies, foreign and domestic; that I will bear true faith and allegiance to the same; that I take this obligation freely, without any mental reservation or purpose of evasion; and that I will well and faithfully discharge the duties of the office upon which I am about to enter, so help me God."

"Congratulations LT!" Colonel Grant said with a faint British accent as he shook my hand. "You will start commissioned officer training (COT) February 8th, at which time you need to check into the temporary living facility (TLF) at Maxwell AFB, Alabama by 1600 on the 7th. I highly encourage you to get some of your uniforms while you are here or once you return to Del Rio. That will save you some time once you get to Maxwell."

"Yes, sir," I answered.

"You won't see your one-time clothing allowance of two hundred and fifty dollars until you get your first check." *Two-fifty? My service jacket alone is two hundred dollars.* "Do you have any questions for me?"

"Where are you from? I detect a slight British accent."

"I'm originally from Winchester, England. My parents and I moved to the US in the seventies. Once I finished college I applied for American citizenship, joined the Air Force, and the rest is history." *OMG, his accent is amazing. Focus, Carol!*

"Wow. That's cool. My mom said once I finished college they wanted to move back to Europe. I finished school in September of last year and they moved to England in December."

He let out the sexiest laugh. "Looks like they weren't playing around."

"No. They weren't."

Colonel Grant rattled off a list of other things I needed to take care of before I made the two-day drive to Alabama. I only heard half of what he said because I was so caught up in his bright blue eyes. All I knew was I had two weeks left in crappy Del Rio. Once I hit dusty Interstate 90 I wasn't going to look back.

I arrived at Maxwell AFB at noon on February 7th. It was exactly how I remembered it as I was looking out the rearview window after picking my sister, Ann, up from her basic training graduation eight years earlier. The grass was still brown and in desperate need of water and fertilizer. The buildings needed a makeover, scratch that, they needed to be demolished. *Asbestos galore.*

I checked into what was going to be my home for the next four weeks and was instructed to meet in the lobby at 0700 the next day. The room had a very basic motel feel, imagine Bates Motel but set in the 1980s. The first thing I noticed when I entered the room was the dingy maroon bedspread with a checkered stripe pattern, and the faux oak wood headboard that looked like it had been hot glued to the wall. I chuckled at the failed attempt to spice the room up with numerous Bob Ross paintings on every wall. *I always thought the military was about minimalistic living. Whoever decorated this room must have had stock in Bob Ross' work!*

COT was very different from traditional basic training for line officers. For starters, people who went through COT were already officers, while those that went through traditional basic training were referred to as 'recruits.' The instructors were enlisted and could yell at and berate the recruits. They couldn't do that with my class because we out ranked them. *Good thing because I didn't want anyone yelling at me to run faster or march straighter.*

Once I got settled into my room I decided to give Ann a call. We talked via email, text, or phone several times a day. Even though we are seven years apart, we are extremely close. So close, that we often say we are twins because we can finish each other's sentences and even have sympathy pains when the other one isn't feeling well.

"Hey. Did you make it there safely?" Ann asked.

"Yea. I'm here. This room seems kinda run down."

"Do you have to share it with anyone?"

"No, thank goodness. I do have to share a bathroom."

"Girl, you just don't know how easy you've got it."

Ann had been in the Air Force slightly over eight years. Her basic training experience was a nightmare compared to my little four-week training. Whenever I would complain about anything she'd say, "suck it up buttercup."

"Have you met anyone in your class yet?"

"No. You know I'm not leaving this room until the morning."

"Don't be anti-social." After a few seconds, we burst into schoolgirl giggles. We both had the ability to post up in our own little worlds for days and be completely content not talking to a soul.

"And on that note, I'm about to let you go."

Once we hung up, I began to settle into my room. Knowing I was only going to be there for a few short weeks, I thought it was pointless to unpack all of my clothes, especially since I would be wearing a uniform for the majority of the day. I placed my toiletries in the bathroom I would be sharing, locked the adjoining door, and flipped on the TV. I zoned out for a few hours and before I knew it was 10 pm. I turned the TV off and shut my eyes for the night. *I had to be bubbly, happy, go lucky Carol, not why are people talking to me before I get my cup of coffee Carol.*

Having heard the old saying 'if you're on time, you're late' numerous times when I was in Junior ROTC in high school, I made it a point to be in the lobby by 6:50 am.

"Good morning ma'am," said one of the drill sergeants. *This guy has got to be a little younger than my dad, and he's calling me ma'am. Ha!*

"Good morning," I replied as I shook his hand.

"As soon as everyone gets downstairs, I'll give a briefing on today's activities."

"Sounds good. Looks like I'm the first one down here."

"Yes, ma'am. You must have a military background. That handshake was pretty firm and you're on time aka early." *Glad I came down early!*

"Oh yea. I have heard the saying plenty of times about being on time vs being early. My dad is retired Air Force and my sister is currently active duty."

"Nice."

We chatted until the next person in my class arrived in the lobby. Once everyone arrived, the drill sergeant informed us that we would be marching to the auditorium where class was held daily.

We formed four rows and then were sized. I took my rightful place in the back row, where the short people always end up, and watched as the madness ensued. I'm pretty sure most people learn the difference between their left and right feet around the age of three. *Not these folks!* Only a few people were in step with the drill sergeant's cadence, while the rest of the group sounded like a colony of penguins shuffling to the beat of a nonexistent drummer. *Thank goodness I'm in the back because I would hate for the back of my heels to be scuffed due to these folks lack of coordination.*

Once we arrived at auditorium, and were seated, the drill sergeant explained what the next four weeks were going to look like. I expected to be in class eight hours a day and have mandatory group workout and study sessions. I only got one of those things right, the eight-hour class days. We didn't have to work out or study as a group. *Hallelujah!* The evenings were ours to do with what we wanted, so in true military fashion that meant we drank! And then drank some more.

About halfway through the training, I received an urgent message from a gentleman by the name of Sergeant Dunkin, who worked at the Office of Personnel Management (OPM) in San Antonio.

"Hi Lieutenant. How are you doing? This is Sergeant Dunkin from OPM. I'm calling to talk to you about your orders."

"I'm doing well. What's going on with my orders?"

"Right now we have you going to Offutt in Nebraska. I got a call from the commander there, and he said he didn't need an additional lab officer at this time."

"Really? So what does that mean?" My leg started shaking. I didn't want to end up somewhere crappy, like Grand Forks, North Dakota.

"Well, the commander said if there aren't any other lieutenant slots anywhere else, you could still come, but you wouldn't have very much to do or a place to sit."

"That's not good."

"There is a base in need of a lab officer - Andrews."

"Where's that? DC?"

"It's technically in Maryland. About 30 minutes from DC." A smile slowly spread across my face. I'd wanted to go to Howard University, but that idea was quickly shot down when my parents saw how much out-of-state tuition would cost.

"Ok. Well I guess I'm going to Andrews. Doesn't make sense to go somewhere I'm not needed."

"Great. I will fax a copy of your new orders to you ASAP. Call or email me if you have any questions."

"Ok. Thank you." *Looks like I'm going to the east coast!*

My class consisted of doctors, nurses, and chaplains. Like life, everyone can't be the best at what they do, and I think a few of those not so sharp tools decided to join the Air Force. *Excluding myself of course. I was very sharp.* These same people were stressed about our final exam. Military history and different types of aircraft weren't my favorite subjects, but the board exams most of us had to pass to practice our craft were way harder than any military test. I overheard study group sessions that went on for hours because people couldn't 'grasp' a concept. I figured if I knew at least 80% of the material I'd pass the test. *How hard could it really be?*

The final came and went. I am extremely glad I didn't succumb to the nightly study sessions and worrying. I studied the night before and passed with an 85%. *If I were to have to take that test today I'm pretty sure I'd get a 40% and that's being generous.* Everyone passed but one lady. She had managed to fail the final exam not once, not twice, but four times. I honestly don't think she ever really 'passed.' Because she was a nurse, and nurses were in high demand, they let her squeeze through the cracks.

When graduation day came, everyone was excited about leaving Maxwell and heading to their respective bases to begin their career as a butter bar (for some it was a silver clover. Our class commander came in as a Lt Colonel! Most people will be in the military at least fifteen years before seeing that rank.)

My dad, who served twenty-four years in the Air Force, was beyond excited for me. So excited that he flew back to the states to be there when I received my certificate of completion and to help me drive from Alabama to Maryland. After I introduced him to a few people I had gotten to know, and some of the instructors, we headed to my room to pack up my belongings.

"Thanks dad for coming all the way back over here to help me drive."

"No problem. You know I'm proud of you and Ann. I love to see how successful my girls are becoming." His chest was puffed off more than when I graduated from college.

"I'll take the first leg of the drive."

"Sounds good."

We gassed up my silver Toyota Corolla and started the twelve-hour journey. Luckily, he was driving when we arrived in Maryland. I wasn't prepared for the traffic. Ann had been stationed in Maryland for a few years, and I always came to visit during my summer breaks, but we never really were on the road during rush hour. I sat in the passenger seat feeling a bit overwhelmed. *How am I going to navigate I95 by myself?* My heartbeat quickened, and I could feel my hands getting sweaty. I didn't have much time to work myself into a tizzy before my dad slammed on the brakes and laid on the horn.

"Idiot," his brow was furrowed. My dad never got mad in traffic. Matter of fact, he rarely got mad at anything. *Oh no. I'm a very aggressive driver! I'm going to be mad all the time.*

Once we navigated through the madness of the Woodrow Wilson Bridge, Andrews AFB was a mere twenty minutes away. We checked into TLF and called Ann to let her know we had arrived safely.

The next day, I reported to Malcolm Grow Medical Center's laboratory to meet Lt Eddie Santos. Lt Santos had sent me a welcome letter and pamphlets on things to do in the Maryland, DC, and Virginia area while I was at Maxwell.

"Good morning," I said to the airmen at the front desk. "Is Lieutenant Santos in?"

"Yes, ma'am. Let me call him for you." A few minutes later, Lt Santos came through the door that led to the lab.

"Hi, Carol. It's great to meet you." Lt Santos said with a bright smile as he shook my hand. "We're so glad that you're here."

"Thank you, Lieutenant Santos," I said as I took in his scent. He smelled like a mix of coconuts and Hershey's chocolate. "It's good to be here." Lt Santos and I had played phone tag several times while I was at Maxwell. We were never able to speak due to his hectic schedule.

His Dominican accent was beautiful on the phone but sounded even nicer in person. *Yes, I have a thing for accents.*

"You can call me Eddie. I'll introduce you to everyone and then walk you upstairs to the orderly room so you can turn in all your paperwork. After they go over everything with you, you'll be able to start your house hunting leave." *Amazing! I just got here, and I'm already going to be on leave.*

"Great."

As we walked through the lab, I couldn't help but check Eddie out. He was probably in his early thirties and in great shape. His biceps were so big the buttons on the cuff on his battle dress uniform (BDU) looked like they were going to pop off at any moment. He literally looked like the sun had kissed him because he had the smoothest caramel skin I'd ever seen in real life. And that smile, perfectly straight white teeth and a lone dimple in his left cheek. I tried my best to look him up and down inconspicuously. I quickly got my thoughts in check when I saw the bright silver ring on his left hand. *Dammit!*

"This is the core lab," Eddie said. "Core lab consists of hematology, chemistry, urinalysis, and coagulation. The microbiology and blood bank departments are located in the basement. All routine patient samples are run on the right side of the lab and STAT samples are ran in this small area." I nodded as he was talking.

The lab was in immaculate condition. Compared to the lab I worked at in Del Rio, you could eat off the floor here. *Granted I'd never do that. Just the thought of eating in a lab makes me queasy!* There were no blood or urine stains anywhere to be seen. Even the sink used to wash your hands was clean. Most of the time, those sinks would have globs of soap caked on the soap dispenser or rust stains around the drain.

Once we exited the lab we walked past Major Armando Gonzales' office, the officer in charge (OIC) of core lab.

"He must have stepped out for coffee or went to a meeting. I'll introduce you to him later."

"Ok."

We kept walking down a long hall where several higher ranking enlisted military personnel and civilians had offices. Each office was truly unique in how it was decorated. I could definitely tell the difference between a civilian's office versus a military person's. The military people had all of their awards and certifications donning the walls, while the civilians had pictures of their families and the different leadership they had worked with over the years. Situated at the end of the hall was the lab commander's, Colonel Lynn Nolan's, office.

"Morning, Colonel Nolan. I want to introduce you to the new lieutenant," Eddie said.

"Good morning, ma'am," I said I as I reached to shake her hand.

"Morning," was her gruff response as she squeezed the life out of my hand. She wasn't at all what I expected a commander to look like. She looked like she had just stepped out of *Little House on the Prairie*. She had a messy bun at the nape of her neck, and her uniform looked about two sizes too big. Not to mentioned her shirt was beyond wrinkled. Most officers are known for being cheap, and she didn't disappoint. She was rocking the infamous military issued BCGs (birth control glasses. If anyone wore these it was guaranteed they wouldn't get any) most people wouldn't be caught dead wearing. These glasses had to be about five centimeters thick. *I better stop thinking mean things because I'm pretty sure she can read my mind with those things on.*

"Glad you're here. Once you get back from house hunting leave I want to sit down with you and discuss where you'll be working."

"Sounds good."

"I hope you have some goals in mind of what you want to accomplish at Andrews. This base can make or break your career." *Those words were probably the most honest thing anyone ever told me while I was at Andrews.*

"I will have some by the time we meet again." *Ok, think of some BS to impress her.*

"Good. Eddie, once you finish showing her around, can you tell Maddie to come up here? I need to talk to her about her upcoming temporary duty yonder (TDY)."

"Yes ma'am," Eddie replied.

As we were walking downstairs to the part of the lab that housed the microbiology and blood bank departments, Eddie offered me some advice. "When you meet with her, make sure you have one thing that you are confident to talk about in detail."

"What do you mean?"

"Before you came in, did you work in a lab?"

"Yes. I was a generalist in a small lab back home."

"Ok. Whatever department you liked best, talk about that one. Maybe she'll make you the OIC of that department. We have five officers including Colonel Nolan and four departments in the lab. I'm over point-of-care testing, Captain Ocampo is over microbiology and blood bank, and Major Gonzales is over core lab. There is talk about breaking core lab up, so if you like chemistry or hematology tell her which one you prefer. That way she may make you the OIC of that section."

"Ok. Thanks for the advice."

By this time, we were standing outside of Captain Ocampo's office. She was busy typing away on her keyboard when Lt Santos knocked on her door.

"Hi Captain. I want to introduce to Lieutenant Pugh Carol this is Captain Ocampo."

She stood up and came to the door. She was a petite Filipina woman in her late thirties. Her uniform had to be the best fitting uniform I had ever seen on a woman in the medical field. Most medical personnel, lawyers, and chaplains were known for looking sloppy. Her dark hair with honey brown highlights was cut in a tapered bob that fit the shape of her face perfectly.

"Good morning, Lieutenant. We're glad you're here," she said with a raspy thick Tagalog accent.

"Thank you. It's good to be here."

"Where are you coming from?"

"Texas."

"I love Texas. I used to be stationed in San Antonio." Her face lit up.

"Cool. I'm from a really small town about two and half hours west of there. Del Rio."

"Oh. I've heard of that place. Not much out that way, right?" She raised her perfectly waxed eyebrows.

"Not at all," I replied with a shake of my head.

Eddie interjected, "Captain, Colonel Nolan wants to see you. She said she wanted to talk about your upcoming TDY."

"Oh. Ok. Excuse me. I need to get up there."

She grabbed a notepad from her desk. "Nice meeting you Lieutenant," she said over her shoulder.

Eddie continued to show me around the rest of the lab and introduce me to the enlisted personnel. I was truly amazed to see such a diverse work environment. This wasn't at all what my dad's office looked like when he was in the Air Force. Nor was it what Ann's office looked like. They were usually the only two black people in their units.

After all the introductions were made Eddie said, "Let me walk you upstairs so you can turn all of your paperwork in and get started on finding a place to live."

"Ok. Do you have any neighborhood recommendations or places I should avoid?"

"Well, my family and I live on base. The cost of living here is ridiculous, but you will get a nice little chunk of change for living off-base. If you can find a place that is cheaper than your basic allowance for housing (BAH) you can actually make money. It all depends on what's important to you. If you like the idea of living in a 'city' get a place in DC. If you like history and posh living, I'd suggest Northern Virginia. Maryland is the cheapest out of the three places to live, unless you get a place in Montgomery County. That's one of the most expensive places to live in the US."

"Montgomery County is out of the picture then. Thanks for the information. I'll keep it in mind while I'm looking."

"Here is the orderly room. They'll tell you the next steps you need to take. Here's my cell phone number if you need anything." He gave me his number on a sticky note.

"Thanks."

I was in the orderly room for about forty-five minutes. During that time, one of the airmen who worked there went over the physical standards I must met yearly.

"Ma'am, please step on the scale."

"Ok." *I know he is going to have something smart to say, but I'm holding on to my purse. I need the extra weight.*

"Looks like you're at one hundred thirteen. Wait, you are holding your purse. You can set it in that chair." *Man!* I set my purse down.

"Looks like you're at one hundred eight. Wow, you are a frail body." I didn't want to hear that. I had heard it all throughout college. *I guess people think only fat people are insulted by weight comments.* "You have a long way to your max weight, which is one hundred forty pounds."

I threw my head back and let out a deep belly laugh. "I can't imagine myself gaining that much weight."

"Don't get pregnant then. That's how most skinny girls like you pack on pounds quick." He said as he smacked his lips. *It's a good thing the 'don't ask, don't tell' policy is in play, even though no one has to ask this dude anything. He's all about the boys.*

He also went over when my deployment window would be and the names of my squadron's leadership. Once he gave me the spiel I was sent on my way to look for my new place. I was given strict orders that once I found a place I needed to return to work immediately. *I technically had two weeks to find a place so guess how long it took me to find an apartment?*

"The address is two fifty-one South Reynolds Street, Alexandria, Virginia," I told Ann. She was meeting me at the place I had decided to rent.

"Ok. My GPS says I'm about two minutes away. I'll see you in a second."

I talked to Ann after I'd looked at four apartment complexes. I gave her the rundown of what some of the amenities were and asked if the price was fair for the area. This one was the first she said sounded good. Once Ann got there we took a tour of the model home and then of the actual apartment I was going to lease.

"Are you sure you want to stay here?" She questioned. *I could see that she wasn't really feeling the place, but it was $995 all bills included!* "You described this way better than it actually looks."

"It's fine."

"Why don't we go look at some of those apartments?" She pointed to a couple of high-rise buildings that were a few blocks away.

"Nah. I'm good."

"Ok. You still have seven more house hunting days left. I think you should look at a few more places."

"You know how much I hate looking for apartments. This place will be fine. Besides, if I don't like it, I only signed a year lease." *Boy oh boy, I should have listened to her and looked at a few more places.*

"Ok. I won't say anything else. Do you want to get some lunch?"

"Sure. I need to stop by TLF and get some clothes cuz I'm coming to stay with you the rest of my time I'm off." I had the same smile a Cheshire cat had.

She just shook her head. She knew I was technically supposed to go back to work since I had found a place. I knew if I signed the lease this early, I took a chance of getting in trouble if someone wanted to see a signed copy. That's why I told the leasing office I would be back to sign a lease in six days. *Smart!*

When I returned to work the air was very somber. "Lieutenant, are you aware of what's going on right now?" Captain Ocampo said before I could even get my foot into the door completely.

"With regards to?" I replied. *I wasn't a mind reader.*

"The President just announced we are going to war with Iraq. You should have your BDUs on."

"Would you like me to go home and change?" I opened my eyes very wide.

"No. But you should be better prepared." *Prepared for what? The war isn't happening in this hospital lab.*

"Ok," I said in a dismissive tone as I walked to Eddie's desk

Eddie pointed to a desk that was littered with stacks of paper and junk. "Good morning. This is where you're going to be sitting. This is Sergeant Miller's desk. She is out on convalescent leave for the remainder of this week and next week." *That entire conversation with Sgt Dunkin about me not having a place to sit if I went to Offutt was a lie.*

"What should I do with all of her papers? I don't want to mess anything up. She may have some sort of system going on here." *Doubtful.*

"Don't worry about it. All of us are going to be moving out of this cube farm at the end of the week. This is going to be the new conference room. So don't get too comfortable." *Why would I get comfortable in a desk that's not mine?*

I was a bit disappointed that I didn't have my own desk. I didn't like sharing anything that touches my face, like a phone, with other people. The thought of having my ear on a phone that multiple people used grossed me out. Once I disinfected the phone and got the desk organized the way I liked, I went upstairs to see if Colonel Nolan was available to talk. I knocked on her door.

"Good morning, ma'am."

"Hi Carol. Come in and have a seat. I have a mentee coming to see me in about ten minutes, but you can sit in on the meeting. I had planned on talking to you about similar things later today. For right now let me tell you a little bit about me." She leaned back in her chair and put her hands behind her head before she started talking. *Here we go.*

"I always knew I wanted to be in the military from a very young age. When I came in the nineteen-seventies, there were no women lab commanders. Women were nurses. I don't have the bubbly personality that many nurses have, which led me to –," She continued talking for what seemed like an eternity. As I listened to what was like a roller coaster of her life, I found it harder after each blink to stay focus. I could feel my eyes beginning to cross as I tried to keep up with her rapid pace of such a boring life. I jumped a little when there was a knock on the door. *Hallelujah!*

"Good morning, Colonel Nolan," a perky African-American woman said.

"Hi Althea. This is Carol. She's a brand new butter bar like you. Althea works on the other side of the base in communications. We meet weekly and discuss ways she can be proactive in advancing her skill set to get promoted earlier." I nodded to acknowledge Althea.

"Ok ladies. The best piece of advice I can give you is get out there and get involved. Don't ever let a man tell you that a woman can't do something. If they do, that's when you prove him wrong by doing it. It'll be like a kick in the nuts when he sees you excel." *Ok. She's a bit of a feminist.* Colonel Nolan continued to tell us how, as women, we need to strive for perfection and not to get bogged down by a society that's controlled by men. *This is too much for me! I just want to come to work and get paid.*

Thirty minutes later, she finally changed the subject. "I have a really important event happening this weekend that I would love for both of you to participate in," Colonel Nolan sounded like she was going to explode. *Umm, I don't know about this. My weekends are mine.*

"Sure what is it?" Althea asked with a little too much enthusiasm.

"One of my many passions is participating in Civil War re-enactments. I have an authentic Confederate soldier uniform I purchased off eBay a few years back that fits me amazingly. I would need the two of you to help with the setup of the field." *Did she really just say she does Civil War reenactments as a Confederate soldier and wants two black women to participate in this mess? You've got to be kidding me?*

"That sounds like fun. Count me in." Althea exclaimed. *Girl, you're taking brown-nosing to a whole other level right now.*

"I won't be able to attend. I have plans this weekend," I quickly said.

"I do them twice a year. Next time you can participate, Carol." *Ummm, that's not a no, but a hell no. Guess what, Colonel Nolan? THE SOUTH LOST! How many times do you need to reenact that?*

"What time do you need me there?" Althea asked.

"Well, I'm going to set up mid-morning on Friday. Come to my office around ten-thirty in some clothes you don't mind getting dirty." *She's doing this mess during duty hours? Rank does have its privileges.*

They continued talking for a few more minutes before Althea said she needed to get back to her office.

17

"Nice meeting you, Carol," she said as left the office.

"Ditto."

"Carol, I would like to discuss what your duties are going to be. As a new lab officer, you should be familiar with what everyone does in the lab. With that being said I would like for you to do a rotation through each section of the lab."

"Ok. I worked as a generalist in a small regional hospital before joining the military for about six months."

"Ok. That's good. It shouldn't take you long to get through the sections." *Is she expecting me to run patient samples? No way, officers don't do that. They shuffle papers all day.*

"Do you want me to start shadowing Major Gonzales?"

"No. I want you to start in the drawing room with Airmen Birds. Draw patients for the rest of the week." *You've got to be kidding me! I didn't go to college to be a phlebotomist.*

"Ok," I said as I crossed my arms. I was pissed! *Did all of the other officers have to come in and start in the drawing room? I bet not.*

As I was heading to the drawing room I ran into Major Gonzales.

"Hi. Carol?" He extended his hand. He was a cheerful round Filipino man in his fifties.

"Yes. Hi Major Gonzales."

"You can call me Major G. Come in my office. Eddie told me you arrived a week or two ago. Sorry, I missed your first day. I was at a hospital meeting repping the lab. So how are things going? Where did you end up finding a place?" *No he didn't just say 'repping.' Guess he's trying to be hip. Ha.*

"Alexandria."

"Most of the young people live in Virginia. Have you met with Colonel Nolan yet?"

"Yes. That's where I was coming from when I ran into you."

"Did she assign you to a section yet?"

"Not yet. She told me to go to the drawing room for the rest of the week."

"For what?"

"She said she wanted me to familiarize myself with what everyone does in the lab. I was assuming she wanted me to get with each of the officers to learn what your roles were. I guess she had other plans."

Major G got up from his desk and shut the door to his office. "I can't believe she's pulling this bullshit. I'm going to go talk to her when we're done here. Let me just tell you something. She is probably the most racist person I have ever met in my entire Air Force career. You'd think that she'd be more aware of her surroundings considering ninety-five percent of her staff are people of colour." *Did I just walk into some sort of racial conflict? Offutt is looking better and better by the minute.*

"I'm not trying to stir anything up."

"Don't worry. I'll say that I saw you in the drawing room and was wondering why you were in there versus shadowing me. Go talk to Airmen Birds. He's the best I have up front. I'll come get you once I talk to Colonel Nolan."

"Ok. Thank you by the way."

"No problem. I remember what it feels like coming in and always being the minority. I never want anyone to feel like they're less than someone else because they're not what's considered the 'right' race." *I know that's right!*

I headed to the drawing room to meet up with Airmen Birds. "Hey Lieutenant. What can I do for you?" Airmen Birds eagerly asked.

"Teach me everything you know," I said as I placed my hands in the prayer position.

"You're kidding, right?"

"Nope. I want to learn how specimens move through the lab, and since this is the first stop for patients, I figured this would be a great start."

"Ookk. You're the first officer to ever come up here and do this."

"Oh, so that means I can't go ask Lieutenant Santos if you're telling me the right thing or not," I said with a wink.

"I'll tell you the right way, ma'am," he said with a smile.

Airmen Birds showed me the ins and outs of checking a patient's orders, collecting the right tubes of blood, labeling the tubes, and distributing them to the right sections of the lab. He was only nineteen years old but was very professional. *I had to make sure to tell Major G how great this kid was.*

After observing the process several times, I figured I would give drawing blood a shot. The drawing room had a total of eight chairs which were all filled. Because it was late afternoon most of the patients were retirees who still received care at the base. Next to each chair was a cubby that had seven small sections. Each section contained either tubes that were used to draw patient's blood depending on what tests were ordered, fresh needles, alcohol wipes, gauze, fresh tourniquets and band aids. Everything required for a successful blood draw.

"Who's next?" I called out as I pulled a fresh pair of small purple nitrile gloves out of the box that was attached to the wall near the entrance of the drawing room. An older gentleman raised his hand. "Can I get your full name and last four of your social, sir?" I asked as I looked at his labels to verify I was drawing the correct person.

"No, you may not. You look too young to be doing this? I want someone else to draw my blood." *Really? I'm about the same age as these airmen. Direct patient contact sucks! This is exactly why I decided to go to college.*

The other two airmen in the room stopped what they were doing to see how I was going to respond. "Ok. Who's next after this gentleman?" I said. Another man raised his hand. I verified his name and social with the labels that he handed me.

"I think you're a cutie. I don't mind you drawing my blood at all," he said. I lightly touched the gentlemen's hand and giggled.

As he was walking out he turned to the other man who had refused to let me draw his blood and said, "She did a great job. Next time don't be such an ass." I took a small bow as I threw the pair of gloves I had used when I drew his blood in the trash.

"Who's next?" I called out. *I'm only doing this because I have younger troops watching. After today, I'm d.o.n.e. drawing blood forever!*

The next day Major G came down to where I was sitting to talk to me about the meeting he had the previous day with Colonel Nolan.

"Morning Carol. Would you like to go get a cup of coffee?"

"Sure."

Once we got to the cafeteria, Major G told me to take a seat. "How do you like your coffee?"

"Cream and extra sugar," I replied.

"Ok. I'll be right back." As I was waiting for Major G to return with the coffee I saw Colonel Nolan and Captain Ocampo heheing it up. Captain Ocampo was headed to Maxwell AFB for squadron officer school (SOS) soon. I figured Colonel Nolan was prepping her Very few officers in medical fields got the opportunity to attend the six-week course in person. Most did the course via correspondence classes.

"Here you go, kiddo," Major G said as he handed me my coffee.

"Thank you." I blew in the cup to cool it off.

"No problem. First things first, I want to let you know that you will be working with Eddie from today on. When I spoke with Colonel Nolan about you being in the drawing room, she wasn't too happy. I was able to spin it by saying it could later cause problems because the younger airmen might consider you a peer versus a superior." *Superior? Only difference between us is I decided to go to college before coming in the military.*

"I don't think anyone knows my age."

"Ha. It's not hard to find out things around here. Trust me when I say they know how old you are. As long as you set boundaries up front, you won't have any problems. I know it's going to be hard because they're your age, and us officers are all married with kids. No fun for a single girl like yourself." *Amen to that!* "Just remember, don't fraternize. You have way more to lose than they do."

"Ok."

"I don't know if you are aware or not, but Captain Ocampo is going to be gone for the next six weeks to attend SOS. She's leaving Monday. I don't know what Colonel Nolan did to get her a seat in that class but –," He stopped himself from saying anything else.

"I knew she was going. I didn't realize it was next week."

"That's why you'll be working with Eddie. Eddie is going to hand over point-of-care testing to you. While Maddie is gone he'll be handling micro and blood bank, as well as learning what my job entails because I'm going to be doing a permanent change of station (PCS) to Nellis AFB in about a month." *NO! This guy seems super cool and he's already leaving.*

"I've never done point-of-care testing before."

"Don't worry. He'll go over all the details with you. The program is already established so you will basically make sure new nurses and technicians are trained on the equipment. You'll also maintain the equipment. I think it's going to be a great opportunity for you. You will get a lot of exposure to different people in the hospital. You'll also get to network."

We discussed a couple of other personal things while we drank our coffee. I had only known Major G for a short period of time, but he left a lasting impression on me of what a true mentor should be.

****

Six months into the job I'd forged several good relationships with people throughout the hospital. About 80% of those were with enlisted. I found it really hard to relate or bond with the officers. For starters, most of them were married with kids. Secondly, the ones I encountered on a daily basis were out for themselves or were so caught up in rank they couldn't see anything else.

Major G had left, and Eddie had moved upstairs to take over the core lab. One dreary Monday morning, I walked passed Colonel Nolan's office, and it had been completely cleaned out. *I could have sworn all of her belongings were there when I left Friday afternoon.*

"What's up with Nolan's office?" I asked Eddie.

"She was fired."

"What? You can't get fired in the military." I shook my head in disbelief.

"Well, she got sent to Bolling AFB to ride out the rest of her time until she retires. Someone found out she was using government vehicles and personnel to haul her Civil War reenactment equipment around." *Ha! Why do people always think they're too smart to get caught?*

"How long does she have until she can retire?" I asked.

"Two months."

"Had that been anyone else, they wouldn't have let the person retire. They'd be trying to demote them or kick them out altogether."

"Very true."

"Please don't tell me that Ocampo is going to be in charge." My whole face went limp.

"You know she is. Should be interesting."

****

I didn't have much faith in Captain Ocampo's leadership abilities. She tended to wig out and publicly shame people into submission. While she was the micro OIC several troops kept making minor mistakes. Rather than single the two individuals out, she decided to hold a Saturday training session for the entire section.

"Lieutenant, I think it would great for you to come in on Saturday with the rest of the troops even though you don't work in micro. They'll see it as a morale booster that you took time out of your weekend to come in and support them," Captain Ocampo said to me the Thursday before she announced the mandatory training.

"I guess I can come in." *I sure as hell didn't want to, but I could see where she was coming from. Plus, if I ever get to be the OIC of micro the troops would remember this.*

"Great."

Saturday rolls around, and the training literally consisted of MSgt Bryant, the highest ranking enlisted person in the section, reading standard operating procedures (SOPs) for each test performed in the department. *There were 60!*

"Do you guys want to keep going or would you like to break for lunch?" MSgt Bryant asked. Everyone was looking with heavy lids at one another, yet no one said a word.

"Let's keep going," I said with a clap of my hands.

"Lieutenant, you are merely here to observed. You have no opinion on how this training session will progress," Captain Ocampo snapped. *What the --? This bitch has lost her mind.*

I could feel the blood rushing to my face, and my ears instantly felt like they were on fire. Here I was coming in on my day off to sit here and be supportive but she's going to talk to me like I'm an idiot. I can't believe the gall of this woman. I had my hands under the table and could feel my nails digging into my palms as I clenched my fist tightly. One of my buddies sitting to my right rubbed my back and whispered calm down. Someone finally spoke up and said let's just go to lunch, probably to break the awkward silence.

As I packed up my belongings because I couldn't stay a minute longer, I said, "I hope you all learn what is wanted of you so you can get out of here and enjoy the rest of your weekend. I'll see everyone on Monday."

I went to my car and screamed! I was livid. How dare this wench try to shame me in front of people who are supposed to respect me? I decided to call Ann for advice. Ann always had this way of calming me down when I was upset. After a five-minute conversation, she told me to tell Captain Ocampo, in a respectful way, that I didn't appreciate the smart comment, and it wasn't very professional or appropriate. *Hummmm respectful. Better make sure to say ma'am after everything. This heffa doesn't deserve an ounce of respect.*

"Hey, Captain Ocampo. Can I speak to you for a second?" She was still in the conference room gathering her belongings.

"Sure. Let's go to my office so I can eat my lunch."

We walked to her office and she told me to have a seat. "This won't take long. I just wanted to say that I don't think it was very respectful for you to say what you said to me in front of all of the enlisted troops."

"What did I say?" she asked. *Really? She has amnesia now!*

"About me being here only to observe."

"Oh." She started to giggle in a dismissive manner. "I didn't mean anything by that. I've been under a lot of stress with the massive amount of mistakes that are happening in micro. I want to make sure patients are taken care of." *Ok what does that have to do with you being a bitch to me in front of everyone?* "I want to make sure the troops understand what they need to do. I don't want to rush the training."

"With all due respect, ma'am, most people's eyes were glazed over. Reading to them like they're in elementary school may not be the best training method." I started to stand.

25

"This method has worked in the past." *Obviously not if you're doing it again.* "I apologize if you took what I said the wrong way." *BS apology. Let me get out of here before I say something I can't take back.*

I could feel my heart start to flutter faster each second that passed. "I hope you enjoy the rest of your weekend. See you on Monday."

"Ok. Have a great weekend," she said with the fakest smile I'd ever seen.

****

"Ocampo knows how to play the game," Eddie said one day while we having a cup of coffee. "She knows who to kiss up to."

"I saw that when Nolan was here. She'd always be in her office sucking up," I stated.

"She made sure to get in with the right people before Nolan got the boot. Her being the commander while we wait for a new one will look good on her performance report, but it's not going to get her promoted any faster."

"Yea. I'm hoping that we'll get someone here sooner versus later."

About a week later, Colonel Mars, the squadron commander, came down to the lab to make the inevitable official.

"Hello everyone. We are looking to have someone replace Colonel Nolan ASAP. In the meantime, I'm pleased to announce Captain Ocampo will be the acting laboratory commander. This is a tremendous responsibility for a junior officer to step up to, but if anyone can do it, she can." *Omg, I want to barf. If Colonel Mars says one more thing about how great Ocampo is, I swear her head is going to explode.* "I know everyone in the lab is going to support all the decisions Captain Ocampo makes while she's in this leadership role."

Colonel Mars continued to talk for another ten minutes about how important the lab is to the hospital as a whole and some other fluff. As soon as Colonel Mars was finished, Captain Ocampo latched on to her like a leech as they walked out of the lab together.

Two hours later, Eddie, Olivia (the newest second lieutenant that had arrived a month prior), and I were summoned to Captain Ocampo's office for an impromptu meeting.

"Hi guys. So I just wanted to go over some things. Since I'm now the commander, I'd like to change things up a bit as far as who's going to be in charge of what." *Stop rolling your eyes, Carol! Stop rolling your eyes!*

"Eddie since you are my most senior officer, I want you to remain the OIC of core lab. Core lab responsibilities will take up a lot of your time, and I know you're still learning what needs to be done so I'm going to take the phase two student program off your plate. Olivia, you have civilian experience in blood bank so I'll give that over to you. We can talk offline about what you'll need to do on a daily basis and what my expectations of you will be." Olivia exhaled loudly when she said they were going to get together. *Ha. Looks like Olivia isn't an Ocampo fan either.* "Carol, I want you to continue doing point-of-care testing. I also want you to start handling all of the phase two students."

She continued, "I will remain the OIC for micro, but Carol you can be my backup if I'm on leave or TDY."

"Do you guys have any questions for me?" She leaned back in her chair and folded her arms.

Eddie spoke first, "When do you plan on telling the troops the new arrangements?"

"Well, I will tell everyone downstairs later this afternoon. Since you're already upstairs in core lab nothing is going to change so if you want to tell them what's going on down here you can. I really don't see the purpose." *Everyone should be made aware of what's going on in each part of the lab since we are one unit. Who cares that we are on separate floors!*

"Does that mean that you're not going to have a meeting with the entire lab?" I asked to make sure she was really as dense as I supposed.

"I don't really see the purpose. Like I just said to Eddie, Carol, nothing upstairs is going to change." *Yep, she is!*

"I guess," I said under my breath.

The next morning Captain Ocampo called a meeting with the entire lab. Guess she had to go home and get a second opinion from her husband about what to do. He was also an officer but had way more experience than her.

"Good morning, everyone. I called this meeting to explain how the lab is going to be setup under my leadership. Lieutenant Santos will remain the OIC for core lab. Lieutenant Green will be in the new OIC for blood bank. And lastly, Lieutenant Pugh will remain the OIC for point-of-care testing. She will also be taking over the phase two program. In the event that I'm not in the office, Lieutenant Santos will be the acting commander, then Lieutenant Green, then Lieutenant Pugh." I could feel myself about to blow AGAIN! *How is Olivia going to be next in charge, and I outrank her?*

"Does anyone have any questions?" Captain Ocampo asked with her fake smile.

"Shouldn't Lieutenant Pugh be acting commander if you and Lieutenant Santos are out?" I looked around to see who had asked the question.

"I'm not sure who just asked that, but it is my decision on who will do what in the lab. That's final."

You could literally hear a pin drop after she said that. She made it seem like I was the most incompetent person she had ever worked with and didn't have an ounce of leadership ability in my body. I had managed to get a Women, Infant, and Children (WIC) program established at the hospital in the small amount of time I had been there. This program greatly helped younger troops who were single parents and even those who were married, but on a tight income. Captain Ocampo was dead set against it, but I managed to meet with several higher-ups and got the program pushed through. A few months after I had gotten everything into place, Captain Ocampo had gone to Colonel Mars behind my back and said she'd single-handedly done everything. Luckily, I had spoken to Colonel Mars about the program so she knew I had done all of the work.

I was approached throughout the day by several enlisted troops about the meeting. Even though I was upset Ocampo had blatantly disrespected me yet again, I didn't let it show like the first time. At that moment, I decided I needed to start keeping a written record of her antics.

Once I had learned everything there was to know about point-of-care testing, I decided to start an online accelerated master's degree program. Each class was six weeks long, yet the amount of work for each was equivalent to a full semester class.

One morning Captain Ocampo came to my office and said, "Lieutenant Pugh, there is a training in San Antonio on a new polymerase chain reaction (PCR) method I want you to attend. Everyone who works in the micro department must attend this training. If you deploy, this is the methodology used to identify a pathogen in the field."

"Ok. When is the training?"

"It's in two weeks. The training itself is a week-long. I need you to get all the paperwork filled out so I can approve it." *Damn. I'm going to have to take schoolwork with me.*

"All right. I'll get everything together by close of business (COB)."

The training was a breeze, but it was hectic trying to log on to my class to chat and turn in assignments. I knew I didn't want to go on another TDY while I was in school. Two months later, Ocampo approached me about another training opportunity. This one was a professional military education (PME) class for new lieutenants.

"LT, I want you to attend the new lieutenant training at Maxwell in three weeks."

"Ma'am, I've had friends attend that class. They said it really wasn't worth the time. They learned much more from the officers they worked with." *Hummm, maybe I should go!*

"I wish I would have gotten a chance to attend it. I figured you'd want to get some military classes under your belt. Plus, Olivia and Eddie said they weren't able to attend due to a scheduling conflict." *So I'm the last choice?*

"I'm actually in school so it wouldn't be easy for me to attend either. When I attended the PCR training it was hard to get all my assignments turned in on time."

"Lieutenant Pugh, your graduate classes shouldn't affect your PME. You are an Air Force officer. That should be your first priority." *Really? This is a job for me. The Air Force owes me this degree after having to deal with this broad.*

"I understand I'm an officer, but it was my understanding that the training was optional since Olivia and Eddie declined."

"I really think you should reconsider. It could really help your career." *She is really pressing this stupid three-day class.*

"I honestly think a master's degree would have more clout than a three day PME class, ma'am." I rolled my eyes.

She stood in the doorway of my office for a few seconds before huffing and walking back to her office. *So dramatic.*

A few minutes later she sent me an email asking how long had I been in school and when I anticipated being done. I provided the information to her. A few days later I overheard her on the phone with the base's education office. She was asking what were the necessary steps involved in getting started on a graduate degree. *Jealousy is rearing its ugly face.*

Once Eddie handed over the Phase II program I started to develop a close bond with the students and the young twenty-somethings in the lab. I always thought it was funny how I had to give a 'safety' briefing to everyone twenty-five years old and under. They would have to sign a document stating they'd be careful in whatever activities they decided to partake in over a long weekend. As they were forming a pile of the signed papers, I was busy signing my own safety briefing sheet.

Ocampo started to notice how the younger troops would come to me for advice or to vent about their personal problems.

"Carol, I have noticed you seem to be extremely close to the enlisted personnel. It's borderline fraternizing, and I highly encourage you to back off." She had one hand on the door frame of my office and the other on her hip.

"Excuse me?" I stopped looking at my computer screen and snapped my neck around.

"I've noticed how the troops from upstairs come down here, and you talk to them with your office door closed."

"I never knew having an enlisted person ask me about how to start a bachelor's program or talking about their personal life was 'fraternizing.'" *She's just mad because no one comes to her for advice.*

"The perception is you have your favorites." *You've got to be kidding me! She really needs to get the hell out of my office.*

"I have sent out multiple emails offering to help anyone who is interested in starting or finishing a degree. I volunteered to go to the education office with them, help them fill out financial aid paperwork. It's not my personality to turn away someone who asks for my advice or help. If it appears that I'm showing favoritism, I think whoever told you that should look up the meaning of the word. If certain people keep coming to me for help, I'll keep helping them. For those that don't show any interest, I'm not going to approach them to do something they've shown no interest in doing."

"I've gotten your emails about the school stuff. I think we, as officers, should encourage the enlisted folks to focus on their military education." *Seriously? Not everyone is gung-ho military!*

"Ma'am, not everyone is going to make the military a career. Even those who decide to make it a career should get a free degree while they're in. I can't push people to stay in the military for twenty years. I try to encourage them to have a plan b. Their military career has a definite end to it. A degree will always open doors."

"Carol, it's your responsibility as an officer to lift the enlisted up and be a good example. Do you understand what I'm saying?" *What the hell is she talking about? I'm living what I preach. I'm getting a second degree.*

"I understood you the first time you said officers should encourage enlisted folks. That's what I have been doing. I'm not pushing them to do what you want them to do." *Maybe if you built better relationships with people they'd listen to you.*

At this point, she gave me a look that memed, 'I can't believe you just said that to me.' I was so tired of talking in circles with her I turned back to my computer to finish up what I was working on – a paper for one of my classes.

A few weeks later I was approached by one of the airmen that worked in the core lab in the hallway between my office and Ocampo's. "Hey Lieutenant. Do you have a second?"

"Sure, Torres, what's up?"

"I was wondering if you'd like to go out sometime."

"Umm, what did you just ask me?" My eyes opened to the size of eggs as I placed one hand on my chest in utter disbelief.

"I'd like to take you out to lunch." *No this fool isn't trying to ask me out on a date. And he's doing it in front of the wench's office!*

I made sure to say it loud enough for Ocampo to hear because I knew she had set this up, "That is absolutely inappropriate of you to ask. Don't ever do that again. If you need help with something work related, I'm more than willing to help you. But if you cross this line again, there will be repercussions."

I guess he wasn't expecting me to respond in that manner because his facial expression went from slick to oh shit! I wanted to say don't let Captain Ocampo get you into a predicament she'll deny any involvement in.

"I'm sorry, ma'am."

I turned around and walked to my office. I looked back and saw Torres go into Ocampo's office and shut the door. *HA! Her little plan didn't work. She should have at least got someone cute to ask me out if she was trying to set me up. A 5'3 slightly pudgy Filipino guy is not my type!*

Shortly after my run in with Airmen Torres, I made it a point to leave the building during lunch time. I was tired of getting interrupted during my lunch hour with, "I know you're eating, but can I ask you a quick question?" Ocampo had taken notice that I would leave my office each day around 12:30 pm. One day I forgot my wallet in my office. When I walked back into the building to get it, I saw her coming out of my office.

"Is there something I can help you with?" I said down the hall.

"Oh. Lieutenant, I thought you had stepped out for lunch," she stammered. She nervously rubbed her hands on the side of her slacks.

"I did, but I forgot something. Do you need something from me?"

"No. I didn't see what I was looking for."

"And that was?" I was about three inches from her face.

"Umm, I'll talk to you when you get back from lunch. And in the future, I need you to let me know each time you leave the building, and how long you'll be gone." *Are you kidding me? I know I'm in the military but this is ridiculous.*

"You're kidding right?" I questioned in utter disgust. I didn't care that I had my hand on my hip.

"No. I am responsible for all the personnel in this lab. I need to know your whereabouts at all times." *Yeah right. You just want to know so you can snoop and not get caught.*

Our new commander finally got to the base about eight months after Colonel Nolan got the boot. Everyone could now breath a huge sigh of relief. Captain Ocampo really gave having a Napoleon complex a new meaning. I guess because she was small, she felt that she had to be the biggest bitch possible. With the start of our new commander, things had to look up. I couldn't take reporting to Captain Ocampo a day longer.

"Good morning, lab staff," Colonel Mars started off. "I'm so pleased to formally introduce you all to your new commander, Lieutenant Colonel Bartholomew Price. He's coming from Luke AFB out in Arizona. Let's give him a warm welcome." Everyone joyfully clapped. He had to have been thinking wow, these people are really excited to have me here. We were ecstatic!

"I know that Captain Ocampo has kept the lab running like a well-oiled machine. Please give Captain Ocampo a round of applause for her hard work." She got a few claps, mainly from her flunkies, while everyone else looked around avoiding eye contact with Colonel Mars, who had a very perplexed look on her face.

"Maddie, please get Bart up to speed," Colonel Mars said before leaving the lab to return to her office on the fifth floor.

"Yes, ma'am," Captain Ocampo replied with her infamous fake smile.

Once Lt Colonel Price got settled into his new role, he called a meeting with all of the officers.

"Good morning, everyone," he began. "I want to commend you all on the great job you've done since Colonel Nolan's retirement." Lt Colonel Price made it a point to look at each of us directly in the eyes. Ocampo was beaming with pride.

"Thank you, sir. I have a great group of officers here that really stepped up to the plate. I couldn't have run this lab without them." She smiled at us like an adoring mother would look at her children. *If that mother had been Joan Crawford.*

"One of the reasons I joined the Air Force was to experience different things. I like my officers to be versatile and know something about each part of the lab. I have worked in labs where my supervisor never allowed me to supervise more than one area during the entire time I was stationed there. I feel like that really does a person an injustice. Each job you have should prepare you to run your own lab. I want you all to be confident about what each section in the lab is responsible for." We all shook our heads in agreement.

"With that being said, I'd like to change up the assignments. Captain Ocampo, I would like for you to take over the daily operations of core lab. Carol, I want you to continue working with the students and oversee microbiology. I will give point-of-care testing to a senior enlisted person. Your records, Carol, are in awesome condition. Olivia, you will remain in blood bank, but I also want you to take over the quality assurance (QA) program. I have reviewed your work, and you keep very meticulous records. I know that you'll take our QA program to another level. That leaves Eddie, where should I place you?"

"Um, sir, I'm ready for whatever assignment you have for me," Eddie said a little unsure of why he hadn't been given a section to oversee.

"I'm so happy to hear you say that. Your assignment is going to be a little more challenging than what the ladies have in front of them." Lt Colonel Price opened up his desk and pulled out a folder. He handed it to Eddie.

"I don't know what to say," Eddie stammered.

"What? Tell us!" My legs were shaking. *He better not be PCSing.*

"I'm PCSing. To Okinawa, Japan!" *NOO!!!!* My shoulders went limp. I thought I was going to pass out.

"I hope you're pleased with your next assignment," Lt Colonel Price said. "I was stationed there many years ago. I'm sure things have changed tremendously, but my family and I had a great experience."

"Sir, you have no idea. I'm beyond excited. My wife and I were just talking about where we would love to go next. It was either Japan or Europe. She's going to be elated when I call and tell her the good news."

"I'm sure she will be. Eddie will be leaving us very soon, but his replacement should be coming in about a week and a half. Her name is Lieutenant Katy Brisk. When she gets here I want her to shadow you,

Maddie. I'm not sure yet, but I think I may have two officers run core lab since it has the most personnel and the biggest budget."

Ocampo was fuming. She crossed her arms and sat there like a spoiled brat. She was not into 'sharing' responsibilities because that would entail her having to also share praise when things went well.

Rumor had it that Ocampo's husband had gotten orders to San Antonio and would be leaving soon. I didn't want to get my hopes up because even though San Antonio is a great place for couples who are both in the military to be stationed, there was no guarantee they'd get a joint assignment.

"Really?" Ocampo said into her cell phone. She was so loud I could hear her from my office as she was making her way into the building and up the stairs to the core lab. "That's great news. Thank you so much. I can't tell you how much I appreciate it this." *I hope she is leaving soon!*

Ask and ye shall receive. Hallelujah, Ocampo was leaving. Due to the fact her husband already had orders to go to San Antonio, she was able to pack up her office and was gone within two weeks. She had somehow gotten a special duty assignment as an assignments officer. That meant she was responsible for staffing all the Air Force labs around the world. I had signed a thirty-six-month commitment when I joined the Air force. Her transitioning into this new job sealed my fate of getting out once my commitment was up.

"Why the long face, Eddie?" I asked about two weeks after Ocampo left. "You should be happy. You know who is gone and you're leaving soon."

"I'm not going to Okinawa after all." Eddie had the grimiest face I'd ever seen him have.

"What! Why?"

"Price caught me before I left yesterday afternoon and told me my orders changed. I'm not leaving here for another month."

"That sucks, but at least your oldest will be able to finish the school year here with her friends. Where are you going now?"

"Minot." He cringed as the words escaped his beautiful lips.

"Oh no! North Dakota. I'm sorry."

"My wife was so upset. She said she thinks Ocampo had something to do with my orders changing."

"Most definitely. You saw how she was looking at you when you got the news about Japan. I bet if you had acted like you were disappointed about going to Japan she wouldn't have changed anything. She's got to be the most spiteful person alive."

"I never had a problem with her. Granted, I saw all the things she did to you, but I thought there was something going on that I didn't know about."

"Nope. She had it out for me ever since I said I didn't want to go to that funky new lieutenants' training. Funny thing is, she knew she treated me like crap. When my parents came to visit me a few months back she met my mom. The next day she was like 'I bet your mom was like oh so this is the bitch that's giving my daughter hell.' I laughed because she was dead on about being a bitch and giving me hell."

"WOW. She said that?" He stopped mid-sip of his coffee.

"Yep. I know you were really excited about going to Japan, but whatever you do don't let anyone know that you are disappointed about going to Minot. She still has her little spies around here. If they hear you complaining, I know it'll get back to her, and she'll think her evil plan worked."

"True."

"How are things going with Brisk? It sucks that you have to train her versus packing."

"Training her is ok. She's different. I don't know how to read her very well. Some days she seems to be ok and other days she's super moody."

"You know she's prior enlisted like you, right?"

"No, I didn't know that. How did you find out? I didn't think you two talked much."

"We don't. Sergeant Miller told me they went to tech school together. Small world."

"It really is. I told her that I would meet her in the lab at ten thirty to go over some preventative maintenance records so I need to head in there now."

"Ok. Remember what I told you, don't look bummed. Things are going to work out fine." As soon as he crossed the threshold into the lab he had that 100-watt smile shining. No one would ever have guessed he was upset minutes earlier. As I was exiting Eddie's office, Lt Colonel Price was coming out of his.

"Hey Carol. Come here. I'd like to talk to you for a moment."

"Morning," I said as I entered his office. He motioned for me closed the door. *Uh oh. What does he want to talk about?*

"I heard that you are planning on getting out when your commitment is up. How can I convince you to re-enlist?"

"HA. Sir, there's nothing you can say to get me to re-enlist. I've met some really cool people while being here. I've learned some life lessons about myself. I look forward to being a free woman."

He chuckled, "You make it sound like you've been locked up the last two and half years."

"With all due respect, sir, I feel like I have been."

"I really wish you would give one more base a chance. I've seen how you interact with the younger troops. They really look up to you. You could impact so many people's lives."

"I feel like I can do that as a civilian."

"Well, it doesn't seem like I'm going to convince you to stay in today. I'm not giving up on you, though. I have six months to change your mind." *Good luck with that.*

The next six months had to be the slowest six months of my entire life. Lt Colonel Price kept his promise and asked if I was sure about getting out at least four times a week. If he had come right after Colonel Nolan left, I probably would have had a different outlook on the Air Force. I couldn't get into the political ass kissing that Ocampo was so good at, and with her controlling what base I would end up at, I had to make a break for the hills.

"Lieutenant, it was such an honor to work with and for you," Airmen Jones, the class leader of my last Phase II class, said at my going away party. "Not only did you teach us things about lab work, but you also encouraged us not to settle. You have left a lasting impression on me and my fellow classmates. I wish you were staying in because I would love to work for you one day." *This kid is trying to make me change my mind and stay in. Nope! I see the light at the end of the tunnel.*

"Thank you, Lieutenant, for encouraging me to start working on my bachelor's degree," Sgt Blacksmith said. "I'm so glad you gave me that extra push of encouragement. I've never had an officer invest so much time and energy into my personal growth."

A few more people stood up and said kind words. This was what I was going to miss the most about the military. I loved having a positive impact on people's lives, but I couldn't get past the mandatory working out, zero dark thirty recalls, or someone telling me who I could and couldn't hang out with or date.

It was bittersweet to say, but I said it – Bye lock up, hello freedom.

Flipping Out

I'd been back in Texas for about two months when I received a call from a Maryland number I didn't recognize.

"Hello."

"Hi. Is this Carol?"

"Yes it is."

"My name is Baneka Jenkins. I'm calling from the Baltimore VA hospital. I'd like to extend a job offer for the medical technologist position you applied for." *If only she would have called me two months earlier, I would have still been in Maryland.*

"Extend a job offer? I haven't interviewed for this position."

Baneka exhaled loudly and said with an annoyed tone, "There's no need to interview. This call is to offer you the position. Are you still interested in the job?"

"Oh. Yes, I'm still interested."

"Ok. Can I get your email address? I'll send you an offer letter. You can review it and if everything is to your satisfaction, we can get the on-boarding process started."

I gave her my email address. About five seconds later, the message popped up on my phone. *A GS-11! I don't even remember applying for this job, but I'm glad I got it.* (GS stands for general schedule. It's the federal government's salary scale. The grades range from GS-1 to 15. Within each grade are ten steps.)

"I was able to skim the email you just sent. I have two questions."

"Ok. What are they?" Baneka asked. I could feel her rolling her eyes through the phone.

"I have since moved from Maryland and live in Houston, Texas now. Where can I get the required physical done at?"

"There is a VA hospital in Houston. I'll call and ask if they can do us a favor and let you can have the physical done there. That's common practice when we have people coming from different parts of the country. What's your second question?" She rattled off.

"I just signed a lease on an apartment and have to give two months' notice. With that, I wouldn't be able to start until the end of May. Is that going to be a problem?"

"No, that's not a problem. We understand that people can't just up and quit a job and start in two weeks. Besides the on-boarding process will probably take about a month."

"Ok. Sounds good." I jumped up out the chair I was sitting in and did a fist pump in the air.

"Please respond back to the email letting me know that you are accepting the offer and when you'd like your start day to be."

"Will do. Thanks." I smiled from ear to ear.

"If you have any additional questions just shoot me an email." Her tone was slightly less annoyed.

"Ok." And with that we ended the call.

Hot dog! I got a federal job without having to interview. I called my parents and told them the news. They were both federal employees and were just as excited about the job as me.

"Coming in at GS eleven is great! You are going to be making close to sixty thousand dollars a year," my dad said.

"Yea I know. I'm glad that I didn't have to interview. It sucks that I just made that long drive from Maryland to here and now I have to do it again."

"Maybe you can ask Ann to help you make the drive," my mom suggested. *Good idea. That would be so much fun.*

"We are so proud of you, sweetie! You are really accomplishing so much," my mom gushed. We talked for a few more minutes, and I told them I would keep them posted via email. *Calling England is expensive!*

"Guess what?!" I screamed into the phone when Ann picked up.

"What?" She answered in a groggy voice.

"I am moving back to Maryland."

"After all that noise you made about being sick of it, you're going back?" *Yeah, I did bitch about being sick of Maryland, but being back in Texas wasn't all that I had hyped it up to be. Plus, Maryland was where the money was at!*

"I just got a call from the Baltimore VA. I got a GS eleven position in the lab. Didn't even have to interview for it."

"Dang! That's good. Congrats."

"Thanks. You should come to Texas and drive back with me. We can make it a girl's trip, and you can help me look for an apartment." Ann had left Maryland and was now stationed in Germany.

"That sounds fun. When do you plan on going back?"

"My first day of work would be the Tuesday after Memorial Day."

"Cool. I'll price some tickets and get back to you."

"Ok. I just wanted to tell you the good news. I'll let you go cuz I know it's late and this call is going to be expensive."

We ended the call, and I headed straight the leasing office to give them my two months' notice. Despite my sister living overseas we still talked on a regular basis. While I was active duty, we were able to talk on the Uncle Sam's dime for free. Now that I was a 'civilian' we managed to talk via email and text. *What in the world did we do before texting existed?*

Two months never passed so quickly. Ann arrived the day before I was scheduled to leave Houston. As luck would have it, her flight arrived earlier than anticipated. I dropped the remote when her text came through saying she had just landed. I hopped into my Toyota Tacoma and sped to the airport. I was so excited I was able to make what normally takes an hour in thirty-five minutes. *Thank goodness I didn't get a ticket!*

"Hey," I said as I hopped out of my truck and squeezed her in a tight bear hug.

"Whew, that flight was long. I'm glad to be off the plane," she said as she climbed into the truck.

"I'm going to swing by my place since this will be your only opportunity to see where I lived for the last couple of months. Then I'll drop you off at Auntie's house. I won't subject you to having to pack anything."

"Thank you. After that long flight and the long drive we have ahead of us I need to just rest."

The next day I swung by Auntie's house before the sun had a chance to make an appearance. We were up so early we had to wait in the Starbucks drive-thru, not because of a long line, but the baristas hadn't even had a chance to get their head pieces on yet. Loaded up on caffeine goodness we commenced our 21-hour drive.

Ann had recently started dating a doctor and couldn't stop talking about him. "John has got to be the best guy I have ever dated," she gushed.
I'd never seen her so smitten with a guy. She talked about John to the point that I dared her to talk about something or someone else for an hour. That was the quietest hour of the entire trip. *Cute!*

After twelve hours of driving, we decided to stop in Chattanooga, Tennessee, to give our weary bodies a break for the night. We indulged in some sinfully delicious bar-b-que before crashing at a Holiday Inn Express.

We decided we'd wait until the rooster crowed before we got up and started the last leg of the trip. We arrived in Owings Mills, Maryland, just as the hellish rush hour had died down.

I'd never lived in northern Maryland before. All I knew was I didn't want to live in Baltimore. I wanted to be in a quaint suburb like Owings Mills. I was only familiar with the area Ann had lived in while she attended medical school at John Hopkins. I didn't want to end up in a craptastic apartment like I had in Alexandria, which entailed me looking at over ten apartment complexes. *Whew!*

After hours of hunting, I finally decided on a place. It was beautiful. It was located in a gated community and had a lush swimming pool that looked straight out of a Las Vegas resort. *Granted I don't swim, but I figured it would be nice when people came to visit.* Inside the apartment was just as nice. I was on the fourth floor overlooking the pool. It had a fireplace and the biggest walk-in closet I'd ever seen in an apartment.

By the end of the day, I was able to lay my head down on the comfy plush pillow at the Hampton Inn feeling very confident this apartment was going to be amazing.

"Thanks again for flying back so I wouldn't have to make that trek on my own. And for helping me find a place." Tears started to well up in my eyes. *I'm not going to cry. Not going to do it!*

"Of course. I had fun." A lone tear rolled down Ann's face.

"Don't you dare start that." We embraced each other and laughed. "I can't wait to meet this John guy. He sounds amazing. I've never seen you this happy about a dude."

"He is great. I'm hoping we can get stationed at the same base because he's going to be leaving in about eight months."

"It may not matter because if we don't get along you'll have to dump him," I teased.

We ended up breaking down and embraced for another two minutes. I stood at the entrance of the international terminal door and waved goodbye.

The first weekend in my new place was a whirlwind. When the moving man came he saw that I lived on the fourth floor, with no elevator, and decided to charge me extra. When I refused to pay the additional $200 he said he wasn't going to unload the truck. *Dude was holding my furniture hostage!*

To make matters worse, he came solo, which meant I had to help him lug all my stuff up four flights of stairs. Thankfully, I didn't have much furniture, but needless to say I was beat. I wasn't looking forward to getting up early the next day and driving an hour to orientation.

Luckily, I didn't have to deal with any traffic as I was going away from downtown Baltimore. When I arrived at Perry Point I thought I had taken a step back in time. The property looked like an old Army post. Come to find out the entire campus had been a large ammonium nitrate plant and village with three hundred homes that housed its employees. I was shocked that people still worked in the buildings because they looked like there were on the verge of being condemned and infested with asbestos.

I had no idea what to expect of this orientation. For the last three years of my life, I was told what to wear, where I needed to go, how to get there, and not to ask any questions. Prior to that, I was under my parents' rule so it was basically the same setup. Thankfully, my parents had been in the federal system their entire careers, and briefed me on which health insurance to get and which TSP (that's the government's 401k plan) to sign up for.

About halfway through the third day - once all the formalities were completed - we were told to report to our respective duty stations. *Wow, that kind of sounds like something that would have been said in the military.* I was going to be working in Baltimore, not at Perry Point. I figured by the time I had lunch, drove back downtown to Baltimore, I'd be sent home so I went home. I figured I'd start fresh the next day. *How much work really gets done late in the day?*

Thanks to Ann's advice, living in Owings Mills made my commute a breeze. My apartment was literally a two-minute drive from the last stop on the train line. I'd never rode the metro in Baltimore, but it was way easier to navigate through than the metro in DC.

I'll never forget my first morning commute. I pulled my truck into the parking lot and watched as people haphazardly threw their cars into park, made a mad dash to the turnstile where they stuck their monthly passes into the machine, and sped walked to the train's platform. Since this was my first time riding the train I wasn't able to go straight to the turnstile. I had a purchase a day pass.

"How much is a day pass?" I asked the hefty woman sitting in the booth.

She didn't look up from her book as she pointed to the sign. *Good morning to you too! Sheesh.*

I pushed a five-dollar bill through the opening. Again, without looking up she pushed a day pass through the window and continued reading her book.

"Day passes are four dollars," I spoke loudly into the booth's opening.

"My bad," she scoffed as she pushed a dollar through the window. *Welcome back to the east coast, Carol!*

Since Owings Mills was the last stop on the line there was a train already at the platform with its door open. I sat on one of the heavily scratched and graffitied orange seats near a window.

"Doors closing," chimed the automated voice.

We were chugging along at a nice speed, way faster than the cars that were parked on I695, which was located right next to track. *This was the best decision. I hate dealing with traffic.* About half way through my commute, the noise level went from pleasant to miserable. Because Baltimore City doesn't have a public school bus program kids ranging from middle school to high school rode public transportation. Kids would get on the train cursing and talking extremely loud. *Where'd they get all this energy so early in the morning?*

As I stood to get ready to exit the train, pretty much everyone else did too. Lexington Market was a popular stop on the line. When I entered the train station I swear I entered another dimension. Everywhere I turned I saw trash, food containers, rats, drug addicts, and panhandlers. I couldn't believe that at 6:45 am people were getting high in broad sight. The smell of urine made my stomach churn. I quickly walked out of the station to find the same madness in the streets.

The actual Lexington Market is the one of the longest running markets in the US. It opened in 1782 and smells like it hasn't been cleaned since then. It hosts a bunch of different restaurants, fish markets, butchers, etc.

Because it's located diagonally across the street from the VA hospital it was common practice to walk through it, especially when the weather was bad. I made it a point to avoid it like the plague. Walking through it I felt like I was playing frogger, but instead of dodging traffic I was dodging crackheads. I also hated the way my clothes smelled after leaving. Imagine the smell of fried food, mixed with curry while the temperature is 90 degrees. *Yuck!*

After that adventure, I finally arrived at the hospital. The building was in the middle of downtown and was connected to the University of Maryland Hospital by a sky bridge. It was quite impressive on the outside. The inside was a different story. I walked in through the emergency room exit where I was immediately asked for my ID by a security guard. I flashed it quickly and kept walking towards the elevator. As I looked around the lobby I noticed sixty-five inch TVs that were bolted to the walls and covered with shatterproof Plexiglas to prevent tampering. *What did I just get myself into?*

I rode the elevator to the fourth floor, where the laboratory was located. I stepped off and saw peeling wallpaper and scuffed floors. *This place needs a makeover stat!* I followed the arrows that indicated the lab was located to the right.

"Hi. Today is my first day. I'm looking for Sam Beckman." I spoke into the window.

"What's your name, hon?" asked the older heavy set lady who was sitting behind the lab's drop off window.

"Carol."

"Hold on, hon. I'll go get him for you. Walk around that corner and come in. Sam is going to be excited you're here." *I never knew people in Baltimore had such heavy accents.*

By the time I came around the corner, Sam was eagerly waiting for me. "Hi! It's so nice to meet you," Sam said as he extended his hand for me to shake. I shook his hand. *Who's talking so loudly at this hour? I need some coffee.*

"It's nice to finally be here," I said as I shook his hand. "I really appreciate you holding the job for the last two months so I wouldn't get penalized for breaking my lease."

"No problem. I figured that's why you wanted to start later. I knew you had to move yourself since there was no relocation package for this position. Let me show you around and introduce you to everyone."

Sam walked me around the chemistry department and introduced me to the five people I would be working with.

"Hey Aisha. This is Carol. She's going to be one of the new chemistry techs."

"Hey girl," Aisha said as we bumped elbows. "I have these nasty gloves on and don't want to touch your hands with them."

"Thank you!" I smiled.

"Aisha is my early bird. She gets here
preventative maintenance and quality contr
analyzers. That way by the time the phlebo'
ward rounds everything is good to go. She '
training you."

I shook my head acknowledging everythin

"Neal. Rashid. This is Carol. She's going to be one ᴜ₁ ⸗
chemistry techs." *Seems like we just interrupted their morning gab
session.* Neal gave me a slight grunt and head nod, and Rashid said hi.
They quickly went back to their conversation.

"You must be Carol," Emma said. She literally appeared out of
nowhere, but I recognized her voice as the one that was so loud when I
first came in the lab.

"That's me," I replied as I bumped her tiny elbow. *Man I feel like giant.
She's got to be like 4'8!*

"Carol, this is Emma. She'll also be training you on some of the other
analyzers." I nodded.

"I will make sure that you are trained properly. A lot of people around
here do not do things the correct way. You will see quickly." *Wow she
just called people out in front of the boss.*

As we were walking away, Sam said, "She's small but very outspoken."

"I can tell," I laughed.

"Last, but not least, this is Aiden. He just started about two weeks ago."

"Hi," I said and bumped elbows with him.

"Aiden! Come here, I need to show you something," Emma hollered
across the lab. Both Aiden and Emma were Filipino. Shortly after
Aiden walked to see what Emma wanted, I could hear her giving him
instructions in Tagalog.

e one more person due to start in two weeks. After she starts, the mistry department will be fully staffed for the first time in a year."

"Wow. That's good!"

After Sam introduced me to everyone in the chemistry department, he walked me around to the other departments in the lab. Once all the introductions had been made, Sam brought me to his office.

"Here is the combination to your locker in the women's restroom. You can store your belongings in there. I highly suggest you don't leave anything in the lab. Things tend to grow legs here." *What?*

"Ok." I said taken aback.

"Since all of the morning ward rounds are complete, I'll have you work with Bertha. She is the phlebotomist you spoke with this morning at the window. Normally, a chemistry tech covers the drop-off window, but she's on light duty because she hurt her back drawing a patient a few weeks ago."

"I'm going to go put my things in my locker and then get with her."

"Sounds good. I know no one would mess with your things in my office, but it's good to get into a habit of not tempting anyone." *Damn. Are there crackheads that work here? Little did I know...*

"Hi Bertha. Sam told me that you're going to be training me on accessioning samples." I extended my hand for her to shake.

"Yea, he just told me. My, you are so proper! Where are you from?"

"My dad was in the military, but I claim Texas. That's where I lived the longest."

"I'd never guessed that. You don't have an accent." *That's because I didn't live there my whole life.*

"Anyway, let me go over accessioning samples with you." I pulled out my notebook to take notes.

50

I breezed through the explanation on how to accept/reject specimens. After lunch, Sam came over to check up on me. "How are things going?"

"She's quick, Sam. This one is a keeper," Bertha said.

"Thank you for the compliment Bertha. I think I've got it."

"I was hoping you'd say that. Today is Bertha's last day up here. Tomorrow I am going to need you to be up here alone. If you have any questions you can always ask Aisha. I figured you wouldn't mind something easy on a Friday." *No I wouldn't. Thank you, Sam!* He continued, "For the rest of the day, you can help Bertha up here and start reading the standard operating procedures (SOPs) for our main analyzer. That's where you will be starting on Monday. What time would you like to come in, seven or seven-thirty?"

"I'd prefer seven."

"Great. How are you getting to work, driving or metro?"

"I ride the metro."

"Ok. Let me get you the forms to fill out for your metro pass. The VA pays for a monthly pass for those who use public transportation." *Awesome!*

I filled out the forms Sam gave to me and returned them to him later that afternoon. I wanted to get him everything he needed so I could get my pass for the next month.

"Good morning, Aisha," I said first thing Monday morning.

"Hey girl. I'm almost done with the preventative maintenance on this one analyzer. Give me a couple of minutes. Start reading the SOPs for this analyzer. Once I finish up we start going over everything."

"Ok." I went and sat at one of the workstations in the area. *I need to get some coffee because reading these SOPs was boring on Friday and doubly boring today.*

About fifteen minutes later Aisha came over. "I know you are bored to tears reading those things."

"Yes I am," I said as I let out a huge yawn.

"I forgot to tell you, you have to sign off on each one that you've read."

"I figured so I signed off on all of them."

"Great. Looks like you have common sense, which you'll see is rare around here," Aisha said with a giggle. I already knew Neal didn't have any common sense. He had a sandwich in his lab coat pocket and the bag wasn't even sealed all the way. *GROSS!*

Aisha went over the ins and outs of getting the two main chemistry analyzers up and running. Nothing was too complex. What took some time to learn was the lab's information system. There were so many steps needed to get through each menu. I made sure to take good notes.

Sam had me scheduled to train with Aisha for two weeks. By the end of the first week he came to me and said, "Aisha told me that you've got these two analyzers down. That's great. Do you feel comfortable moving on to the other instruments in the lab?"

"She's a great teacher. I'm ready," I tapped a pen on my notebook.

Over the course of the next month and half I learned everything I needed to know in the chemistry department. I had even started helping Sam get organized for an inspection the lab was due to have at the end of the year. *Sitting in an office for the last three years was paying off for something!*

Certain sections of the chemistry department required two people to partner up due to the volume of samples that passed through it. Sam tended to assign a hard worker and a person who tended to be a bit on the slow side - aka a lazy person. About six months into the job I was paired up with Rashid, the laziest person in the entire lab!

"Guess who I'm paired up with this week?" I asked Aisha.

"For your sake I hope it's not Rashid," she had her fingers crossed as she said that.

"Augh, YES, it's him," I said as I threw my hands up in the air. "Let me get both these analyzers up and running before he gets here. That way there's no chance of him breaking something."

"No. Let him set up the back-up analyzer. If you do it all, he'll come in here wanting to run his mouth about the Ravens and his daughter."

"True."

The first thing I did at the start of each day was wipe down all the countertops and phones. Rashid and Neal were notorious for not wearing gloves and dropping blood or urine all over the place. *Mental note...NEVER eat anything they bring in when we have potlucks.*

By the time Rashid arrived at 8:00 am I had the main analyzer up and running and was almost done entering all the ward round results into the computer.

"Morning," Rashid came in with a newspaper tucked up under his left arm. *Um, I know he doesn't think he's going to just sit here all day and read the paper while I do all the work.*

"Morning," I replied. "The main analyzer is up and running. You'll have to get the backup ready. I can handle all the patient samples while you're doing that."

"Why didn't you get both machines ready?" He had the nerve to have an attitude.

"Because what would you have done?" I replied sarcastically.

He walked off and threw his paper at the computer he would be using that day. Then I saw him walk to Sam's office. About fifteen minutes later, Sam came out to the lab and started working on the backup analyzer. *Are you kidding me? He just went and whined to the boss?*

"Hey, Sam. Are you about to do maintenance?" I asked. Sam was the end all be all when it came to troubleshooting and maintaining the analyzers we had. If he was going to do something new I wanted to learn.

"No. I'm just getting it ready for the day." *What?!*

I glanced over my shoulder to where Rashid was sitting logging into the computer. Once he had logged in he walked to a different part of the lab to talk to Neal. *This kind of BS could only happen at a federal gig!*

Thirty minutes later there was no sign of Rashid. We received a large amount of samples from one of the clinics that was about an hour away from the hospital. *You've got to be kidding me. This fool still hasn't come back from talking to Neal? I'm not going to do all of his work!* I continued to load samples onto the analyzer, but I was only reporting out STAT samples. When Rashid finally got back to his workstation he had a stack of results to put into the computer.

"I'm going on break," I said as soon as he crossed the threshold into the room.

"Ok."

I pointed to the printout of results that had collected on the floor, "All those results need to be verified. Also, all the samples sitting right here need to be diluted because they're lipemic."

"Ok."

As I was walking out I heard him say under his breath, "Lazy bitch." *Oh, so I'm lazy? Ok!*

Fifteen minutes later I returned and found the lipemic samples still sitting where I had left them.

"Did you dilute these samples?"

"No."

"I hope you didn't verify the results because they're not going to be accurate," I said as I rolled my eyes.

"I forgot."

"You forgot something I told you needed to be done fifteen minutes ago?" *You need to retire old man!*

"You ain't my supervisor. You can't tell me what to do."

"I didn't tell you want to do, I told you want needed to be done. Things that YOU are responsible for while working in this area." *This fool is going to make me really go off on him in front of the entire lab.*

"You can't tell me what to do!" *Senile and deaf!*

"For the second time, this is stuff that you're supposed to do while in this area." I walked off because I could feel my blood pressure starting to rise.

Knock, knock.

"Come in," Sam said.

"I think you may need to have a little conversation with Rashid. For some reason he thinks it's my job to do the stuff he's supposed to do." I was flushed with frustration.

"Oh Rashid," Sam said as he rubbed his temples. "I was hoping things would be different once he got the hang of this department."

"Looks like the only thing he's gotten a hang of is expecting others to do his work." This statement came after weeks of my observing how everyone took care of the things he should have done rather than confronting him.

"I'll speak with him this afternoon." Sam started to wring his hands together.

"Ok."

When I returned to my work area, Rashid still hadn't completed the dilutions. *These poor Veterans have no clue what kind of idiot is handling their blood work. I hope he never has to be in the hospital and gets care like he gives.*

"What time do you want to go to lunch?" I asked Rashid. Since we worked as a team someone had to be there to cover the section at all times.

"Eleven thirty." *You've got to be kidding me. He came in at 8, took about a 30-minute break, and now he wants to go to lunch that early?*

I just shook my head in disgust and said, "Ok."

A quarter to one rolls around, and Rashid waltzes back in rubbing his stomach. I'm seething! I lock my computer screen, wash my hands, and walk out to go eat lunch without saying a word to Rashid. When I return it looks like a hurricane had hit my workstation.

"Glad you finally came back," he smirks. *WTF, I was gone 30 minutes, the allotted time for lunch.*

"Finally? I wasn't gone for an hour and half. What happened here?" I pointed to the serum and urine drops that were on my workstation.

"There was a huge drop from the clinics right after you left for lunch." *That doesn't explain why you made a mess of my area.* "Then Sam talked to me about getting samples processed faster and correctly. Did you correct some of the results I verified earlier?"

"Yes."

"Why?"

"All those samples I told you that needed to be diluted were inaccurate. So I did the dilutions and put the correct result in."

"Great! Sam is mad because he said that there are thirty-five corrected reports now."

I shrugged my shoulders as I turned away to put my lab coat and gloves on. I started to spray my workstation down with bleach when I heard

Rashid say, "All these patients are going to die anyway. What difference does it make?"

I turned around so fast I got a little dizzy. "Are you kidding me? We all are going to die, but that doesn't mean you want to receive piss poor care before your time's up. I pray you never have to go into the hospital and have someone like you handling your blood work."

"I have been in this hospital before." *This man is truly an idiot.*

I turned around and continued what I was doing. *If he says one more dumb thing to me today, I'm going to lose it.*

The rest of the afternoon no words were exchanged between the two of us until twenty minutes before quitting time. I overheard him telling one of the phlebotomists who was covering the drop off window, "I can't stand Carol. She thinks she knows everything." *How could he possibly make that statement and he's known me a whole six months? And if I knew everything, did he really think I'd be working at a VA hospital?*

"What was that, Rashid?" I questioned loudly.

"Nothing," he replied. I could see him mimicking me asking the question.

"Oh no, I think it's something. If you are bold enough to say something that stupid be bold enough say it to my face."

"I didn't say anything."

At this point, if I could have lifted the table I was working at up, I would have flipped it over. "You're just embarrassed because I called you out. You always have something to say! No one respects you. People just tolerate you." *Oh no. I could feel so many more things bubbling up about to spill out of my mouth.*

"Bitch, do you want to take this outside?" *Really old man?! You want to fight me?*

"Nope. I want to handle it right here so everyone can see what a jackass you are." I tried to keep my voice calm and steady.

"I know that you walk to the metro every day."

"Is that supposed to be a threat, like you're going to have someone jump me?" At this point, several people were watching, yet no one said anything.

"What's going on here?" Sam rushed from his office to see what was going on.

"Ask Rashid," I said. "It's time for me to go home." I logged off of my computer, threw my gloves in the trash, and walked to the door.

"Oh, and if something happens to me from this point on while I'm walking to the metro, Rashid had something to do with it. All these people are witnesses." With that, I walked to the locker room to get my purse and left. I wasn't the least bit afraid of his idle threat. *Looking back, I probably should have been since a lot of his friends were dope fiends.*

The next day Sam called me in his office. "Good morning, Carol. Have a seat."

"Good morning," I said.

"I'm sorry that you had to deal with Rashid's antics." *Sounds like this wasn't his first time acting a damn fool!* "I need for you to write up a detailed statement about the events that transpired yesterday. If you can get it to me by the end of the day that would be great."

"I'll have it to you in thirty minutes." *I was a pro at documenting stupidity.*

"Great. Rashid has worked in every department of the lab. This is his last stop and with the stunt he pulled yesterday –," Sam trailed off. "The sooner you can get me that statement the better." *There sounds like there's more to this.*

I went back into the lab, cleaned up my work station, and logged on to the computer. Just as I was about to start writing my statement, Aisha came over.

"Hey, girl! I heard about what went down yesterday. I always miss everything since I leave so early."

"Rashid was on something yesterday. I don't know who he thought he was talking to."

Aisha shook her head, "Rashid has issues." *Really!* "Ever since his baby was born he has been off his rocker."

"Baby? Dude's got to be at least sixty-three."

"Yep. He was messing with this young girl, and she got pregnant. She didn't tell him she was pregnant until she was in labor. She had the baby and dipped. Turns out the baby was born hooked on heroin."

"That's horrible."

"Yeah, Miah has a lot of issues now. She's three years old."

"It sucks that he has to deal with a sickly child, but he needs to get it together. He's too old to be acting like he's 'bout that life."

Aisha threw her head back and laughed, "He had some serious health issues right before she was born and was admitted upstairs. That knucklehead came down here and said he didn't want anyone other than me handling his blood. I guess he was scared people were going to mess with him since he messes up so many other Vets' samples. After Miah was born he got shuffled around the whole lab because he was making so many mistakes."

"That's the government way - mess up and move him to a different area versus getting rid of him."

"He almost killed two people when he was working in blood bank." *Why am I not shocked that he didn't get fired? Oh yeah, key word, almost.*

"Man. Well, I have to write up what happened yesterday and give it to Sam. I want to get it done before dummy gets here."

"Ok. I'm glad you stuck up for yourself. Most people just say, 'Oh that's Rashid.' He's threatened Bertha before." I shook my head in disgust.

Twenty minutes later, I gave the statement to Sam.

"Thank you for getting this to me so quickly."

"No problem."

"Just so that you're not put back in a hostile environment I switched you and Emma. Go ahead and start setting up the immunoassays. I've already told her that she would be working with Rashid the rest of the week."

"Nice, but you didn't have to do that. I can take care of business. I don't care for him personally, but I do care about the Veterans he could care less about."

"I'm glad that you are able to handle this maturely, but I don't think the feelings would be reciprocated." *Senile, deaf, and immature!*

"Ok."

The rest of the week went by without a hitch. I overheard Emma yelling at Rashid a couple of times and chuckled to myself.

****

One day after work I started having excruciating cramps. The pain had been pretty bad while I had been at work, but I decided I would tough it out. Once I got home I figured I'd take a hot bath and soak my pains away. Unfortunately, that plan failed miserably.

I was never a big fan of being seen and treated where I worked, but I figured I might be able to get in and out of the VA emergency room faster than I would had I gone to the University of Maryland's ER. I think I made it from my house to the hospital in record time. *If this is anything like contractions I do NOT want to have a baby.*

"Hi. Can I help you?" the ER nurse asked.

"Yes. I need to get some pain meds. I'm cramping really bad." I had one hand on the counter and the other on my stomach. I could barely stand up straight.

"Ok. Can I have your VA ID card?" I passed it under the window. "Do you work here?"

"Yes."

"Where?" *Do I really look like I want to have a conversation right now? Just check me in!*

"In the lab."

"Ok. We will get you back ASAP. Here's your card. Just have a seat." I shuffled over to the waiting room and prayed they'd call me back fast. There was only one person in the waiting room, and he appeared to be waiting on someone. Five minutes later I was called to the back. *Hallelujah!*

"Hi. My name is Dr. Bernstein. What brings you in today, ma'am?" *Great, a resident from the University of Maryland. I'm going to have repeat myself several times.*

"I'm having really bad cramps. I have a history of adhesions," I said. As soon I tried to continue I started to cramp so intensely I began to tear up.

"On a scale of one to ten, with one being no pain and ten being the worst pain in your life, what is your pain level?"

"Eleven!" I was writhing in pain.

"What have you used in the past to treat these type of cramps?"

"Aleve, Motrin, Tylenol. Nothing over the counter seems to be working."

"I would like to perform an exam on you. I'm just going to palpate your stomach, and you tell me where it hurts." *Well, my stomach isn't hurting so ....*

First, he listened to my lungs. Then he asked me to lay down on my back as he pressed on my stomach. Of course I didn't jump off the table because my stomach wasn't the issue. All of a sudden I felt another wave of cramps hit. I drew up in a ball and started shaking.

"Ma'am, I need for you to lay flat so I can finish examining you."

"My stomach isn't the issue. It's my uterus. Or ovaries."

"Oh." *Really? That was his medical response!*

"I've come in here before with the same issue. The doctor gave me a shot of tramadol."

"That's a pretty strong drug for cramps. Let me go talk to the attending physician. I'll be right back." *Go! Hurry up!*

"Ok."

Ten minutes later, which felt like an eternity, both doctors returned to my room. I saw Dr. Bernstein with a syringe. *Finally, I'll get some relief.*

"Hi, Carol. My name is Dr. Welch. I'm the attending physician. Dr. Bernstein told me that you were experiencing some cramping."

"Yes. They are starting to get worse."

"Where is the cramping occurring?" I pointed below my belly button.

"Ok. Do you mind if I exam you?" *Yes, I do! What's the point of the resident doing everything when the attending comes behind him and does the same exact thing?*

Dr. Welch did the same routine Dr. Bernstein did. "Your lungs sound good and I didn't feel anything when I palpitated your stomach." *Duh!*

Nothing is wrong with those things. Lord, please give me strength because I'm about to lose it.

"Your blood pressure was higher than normal, which is probably due to the pain. I checked your records and noticed that this seems to be an ongoing problem. I highly suggest you make an appointment with the women's health clinic tomorrow. I tend to err on the side of caution when giving out narcotics for pain. Your record indicated that's what the previous ER doc gave you."

"Yes. The pain was bad, but this time it's far worse."

"I understand, however, because African Americans tend to have a higher incidence of addiction, I prefer to administer something that isn't a narcotic." *Did those ignorant words really come out of his mouth? I'm not one of these strung out dope fiends that come in here wanting a quick fix.*

"That was very insulting. Give me something for the pain NOW so that I can get out of here."

"I didn't mean to insult you but studies have shown –."

I cut him off, "Honestly, I don't give a damn about studies considering I'm sitting here in excruciating pain. Give me the Toradol so I can go home." *Liquid Motrin. I swear the VA thinks Motrin is the cure for everything.*

"Well, it seems like you knew what my other option was. Dr. Bernstein will give you the shot." Dr. Welch left the room.

"Put it in my left arm," I said impatiently.

Dr. Bernstein cleansed the area and gave me the shot. "I need you to stay here for about fifteen minutes just to make sure you don't have an allergic reaction. If you need anything else just ring the call bell." *Get out of my face.*

As soon as Dr. Bernstein left the room, I gathered my purse and left. *I just wasted an hour and half of my evening. Someone was going to hear about this.*

The next day I put my purse and sweater in my locker and headed straight to the patient advocate's office. *Dr. Welch had insulted the wrong person.*

"Good morning, may I help you?" the young lady sitting behind the reception desk in the patient advocate's office asked.

"Yes. I'd like to lodge a formal complaint on one of the residents that was working in the ER last night."

"Can you give me a brief summary of what happened?"

"Sure. I got to the ER around seven last night complaining of lower pelvic pain. When I told the doctor what a previous doctor had used to treat the pain, he told me that he doesn't prescribe those type of meds to African Americans because we have a higher incidence of becoming addicts."

"No, he didn't say that!" She stood up and put her hand on her hip.

"Unfortunately, he did."

"That's a damn shame. Excuse my French. Can you fill this form out? I will have my director speak to the ER Director immediately. This is unacceptable."

It took me twenty minutes to fill out the form. I was as specific as I could be. I wanted to make sure that no one else got treated the way I had. I had faced discrimination in the past but nothing this blatant.

****

The monotony of working in the lab was starting to rear its ugly face. I never understand how people could work in the lab for fifteen plus years doing the same thing day in and day out. I had only been in the position for a little over a year and was dying to do something different. I started looking for opportunities that would allow me to grow. I came across two programs and was extremely grateful Sam encouraged me to apply for both.

The first program was called Leadership Development Institute (LDI). This was a year-long program where thirteen individuals from a region met once a month to discuss hot topics going on in the VA. At the end of the year, each individual had to present a project on something they felt was a problem within their particular hospital.

The second program I applied for was another year-long program. Seasoned VA employees worked with the director of a Medical Center to see how a hospital is run from the top down. If I got the job, I would work at the VA hospital in Washington, DC.

Both programs required an interview. It was the first time I ever had a performance based interview. The questions focused on learning about a particular performance task, the action taken on my part, and the outcomes of my action. It was a bit nerve racking especially when I was asked to use experiences from my time at the VA. *I'd only been at the VA for a year and never got out of the lab.*

"Congratulations Carol," Sam said one morning when I walked in. "You got accepted into LDI. I got an email late Friday, and you were already gone for the day."

"Thank you," My jaw dropped with shocked.

"Your first meeting will be at Perry Point the week after next."

"Ok. Thanks again for encouraging me to apply."

"I know you're going to do great," Sam said as he handed me the printed email that stated I had been accepted. *Thank you, Jesus. It's only because of You that I got this because I didn't know what I was talking about in the interview.*

During the first LDI class, I was able to meet several people that worked in the hospital. One of them happened to be the Director of Patient Advocacy. She had a no-nonsense type of demeanor. During our morning break, she approached me.

"Hi Carol."

"Hi."

"I recognized your name when you introduced yourself to the class. I just wanted to let you know the status of your complaint." *Nice!* "I personally had a conversation with doctors Bernstein and Welch. I also spoke with the ER Director. He said he'd make all attending physicians attend a sensitivity training."

"Were you able to speak with Dr. Welch alone?" I questioned.

"I sure did. He seemed very entitled and wasn't too receptive to my constructive criticism. Oh well, he still got it. He's only been with the VA for a couple of months. I've heard rumors from ER staff about his inappropriateness, but no patients have ever complained about him."

"Wow," I was truly speechless.

"Thank you for coming forward. We want to make sure this type of behavior is nipped in the bud." Her brow was stern but caring at the same time.

"I appreciate you following up with me." *It really does pay to speak up!*

****

"Looks like we are working together," Neal said when I walked into the lab one Monday morning. *Dammit!*

"Ok," was all I could muster. Neal wasn't as lazy as Rashid, but he was nipping on Rashid's heels to claim that title. I had been partnered with Neal one other time. He did the bare minimum but was able to keep the pace I liked, until Rashid would come around wanting to talk.

"Hey man, did you see the game last night?" Rashid asked Neal as soon as he stepped into the lab.

"Yea, I saw it."

"Flacco pretty much made us lose the game!" *Us? I didn't know he played for the Ravens.*

"Um hum," Neal answered. I never quite understood why Rashid insisted on talking to Neal so much. Neal rarely said more than two words at a time, unless he was on the phone cussing out his wife.

While Neal and Rashid gabbed about the Ravens I decided to prepare some urine samples to load on one of the analyzers. As I was pouring a sample off into a tube that was suitable for the analyzer, I dropped the cup and some of the urine splashed on my face. I picked the cup up off the floor and went to the restroom to wash my face with soapy water. My hands were trembling thinking about catching something from that nasty urine sample. Nothing got in my mouth, nose, or eyes, but this was when I realized I gotta get out of the lab. Seventy-five percent of the patients were either HIV or Hepatitis C positive. *I looked up the patient's history and praise the Lord, he was clean.*

Each time I walked past Neal I would throw daggers like, "Come on man, are you going to work today or not?" After forty-five minutes of hearing each play and how the Ravens' coach could have done something differently, I exhaled loud enough for both Rashid and Neal to get the point.

"Man, Ray Lewis is the man," Rashid said as he headed to his side of the lab to get started on his work.

"Yep," Neal replied.

"Neal, I'm going to load the rest of these samples on the analyzer and take a quick break ok?" He nodded.

When I returned fifteen minutes later, Neal had all the results entered in the computer. I was shocked because normally he left everything for the person he was working with. I guess he saw my accident and felt bad for me. The rest of the week flew by. I didn't want to start my mini vacation in a bad mood. I was off to see Ann in Texas. She had finally moved back to the States, and I was beyond excited.

The four days I spent with Ann were a blur. Before I knew it I was on my way back to Maryland. I wasn't able to get a direct flight back to Baltimore and had to connect in Houston. Luckily, I didn't have to switch planes once we landed. As passengers were getting on the plane, a group of Africans got on and lit the plane up. They smelled like they have bathed in onion soup and curry.

"Ladies and gentlemen, this is a full flight so please start filling in those middle seats." *Oh no, one of them is stopping. I don't think my lungs can handle this smell for the entire flight. Whew! He kept walking.*

"Is this seat taken?"

I didn't say a word but shifted my legs to the right so the cutie could sit in the middle seat next to me.

"Thanks."

"Um hum." I opened the latest *Dexter* book.

"Ladies and gentlemen, once you have found a seat please step out of the aisle so that the people behind you can find a seat. On this flight, we will be serving complimentary soft drinks, coffee, and tea. We also have beer, liquor, and Monster energy drinks available for purchase."

"Those drinks are disgusting," the guy next to me said. I giggled and batted my eyelashes a little. *This guy is really handsome. I'm glad he wasn't with the tribe called funk sitting behind me.*

"Those aren't the best energy drinks," I said.

"Hi. My name is Adam."

"Carol."

Three hours later we touched down at BWI. It was the first time I talked to someone an entire flight. Adam had been in Houston celebrating his best friend's birthday from college. During those three hours, I was able to take in every detail of his face. I'd always heard how having a symmetrical face makes someone more attractive. It's true. Everything about his face was beautiful, right down to the mole on his right ear.

As we were walking through the jet bridge Adam turned around and said, "Hey, let me give you my number."

"You can give it to me, but I don't call men. Here's my number instead."

I gave him my number and in true guy fashion, he called me three days later. We talked on the phone for about a week before we decided to go out on a date. He picked me up, something I normally don't allow a guy to do when I first met him, in a black Dodge Charger. *Guys in Maryland were crazy!* We went to a romantic Spanish tapas restaurant and chatted the entire night. At the end of the night, he walked me to my door, on the fourth floor! He was even respectful enough to only kiss me on the cheek.

Too bad we hadn't met a few months earlier. He lived about two blocks away from the job. I was only going to be at this job for about two more weeks. Turns out I had gotten accepted into the health systems management (HSM) trainee position.

Bye bye Baltimore. Hello DC.

Cutthroat Kitchen

"Has the paperwork been pushed through yet?" I asked Lydia, the HR rep at the DC VA, for what seemed like the 100th time.

"I'm still working on it."

"The program officially started over a week ago so I'm already behind. Is it possible for me to speak with someone else who can handle this issue? I'm transferring from a VA literally down the street." *Baltimore was a little further than down the street, but I wasn't coming from across the country.*

"I'm working everything as fast as I can."

"Ok. Thanks." I hung the phone. I was beyond frustrated that things were moving at such a slow pace. I found out over a month ago that I had been accepted into the health systems management trainee program. Sam was well aware that I would be moving on soon. I had even given my apartment complex notice and secured a new apartment in Columbia, Maryland.

This weekend was going to be hectic because I had planned on moving most of my small stuff, like clothes, pots, pans, etc. to the new place. I wanted to start the new job the following Monday, but by the looks of things I wasn't going to be starting for another few weeks.

"Do you need any help hauling stuff to your new place?" Adam asked. We had started hanging out a lot since we exchanged phone numbers a month and a half ago. *He could be the 'one.'*

"Um. No. I hate moving. I don't really like asking people to move my things. Thank you for offering, though."

"Ok. If you need these muscles let me know."

"I appreciate it. Let me get off this phone so I can get over there and avoid some of the traffic on I95."

"Ok. Talk to you later."

"Bye."

Three days later I finally got a call from Lydia. "Hi Carol. I finally got all the information that I needed from the HR department in Baltimore. Can you start this coming Monday?"

"Sure. My boss knows I was waiting on this call so I will tell him that this Friday will be my last day."

"Ok. You can report to the HR office when you get here. We are located on the first floor."

"Great. See you on Monday." *Finally!*

When I arrived Monday morning Lydia was waiting for me at the reception desk with her hand on her hip. *I'm not late. Why does she have an attitude?*

"Good morning," Lydia said gruffly.

"Morning," I said. *The commute was horrible and today is only day one. I can do it, I can do it. Lord what I have gotten myself into?*

"Let me walk you over to the front office." The front office was literally fifty feet away from HR. *Why didn't she just tell me who to ask for? Anyway. I'm here.*

"Good morning, George."

I'd met George briefly when I came to the hospital for my face-to-face interview. He was one of half a dozen people I met that day. *Why in the world I had a three-hour interview with four different higher ups for a trainee position baffles me to this day.* I must say it was the toughest interview, not because of the questions, but due to the fact that I was hungover.

My best friend hosted a Miller Genuine Draft party the night before in Philadelphia and insisted I come. With Philly being a mere two-hours away, I wasn't going to turn down a good party or free drinks. I could have kicked myself the next day. Not only were my eyes slightly bloodshot, and my head was pounding, but I'm pretty sure there was a slight cinnamon smell of Fireball radiating from my pores. It got harder towards the end of the interview to keep a smile on my face.

"Hi Lydia. What's up?" He didn't look away from his computer screen.

"This is the new –." Before she could finish George looked up.

"Carol. Finally, you're here." *Finally? I would have started when all the other HSM trainees started had it not been for this one.* I smiled at Lydia.

"I'm in the process of booking a plane ticket for you to go to Nashville on Thursday," George rattled out quickly.

"This Thursday?"

"Yes." *That ain't happening. I have movers coming this weekend.*

"I'm not going to be able to do that. Because I got such short notice about my start date I was only able to get movers to come this Saturday. It's too late for me to try to reschedule, and I have to have everything out of my old apartment by Saturday at noon."

"Humph. You are going to be behind your fellow classmates and you won't get another chance to meet all of the other trainees until January when you have to go Utah." *Maybe next time you should tell to the HR rep to move faster.*

"Sorry?" I shrugged my shoulders. *Not sorry. Oh well.*

"Well, I guess it is what it is. Let me show you to your office. You will be sharing it with another person. She's in a similar program as you called the graduate healthcare administrative training program (GHATP). The only difference is her program is for new graduates with a public health master's degree."

"Ok."

As we walked through the larger office he introduced me to all of the executive staffs' secretaries. Everyone seemed nice enough.

"Here's your office. Ashley, I want you to meet Carol. Carol, this is Ashley. Bond." He left us alone in the office. *Did he really just say bond?*

"Hi Carol. I'm so glad they didn't cancel the position since you didn't start when everyone else did. One of my friends in New York said the HSM trainee wasn't able to start for three weeks after our first day so they canceled the position. It's going to be nice sharing an office." Ashley was speaking a mile a minute. She had the brightest, friendliest smile.

"Wow. HR took forever to bring me on."

"Did you move here from another state?"

"No. I was right down the street at the Baltimore VA."

"Oh so you know a lot of about the VA."

"Not really," I said. "I was only there for a little over two years and didn't venture out of the lab much."

We continued going back and forth getting to know each other. Ashley had just graduated from Catholic University. She'd been interning at the VA during her last semester to get 'real life' experience. *Real life experience with a government agency? That's funny!* When she saw the opening for the GHATP program she jumped at the chance for a paid internship.

After an hour and a half gab session, I started to get everything on my desk organized. I tried to log onto my computer to check my email but couldn't. I went to George for help because he was the go-to person for administrative issues.

Knock. Knock.

"George. I just tried to log onto my computer and it's saying that my username isn't found."

"I haven't had a chance to get with IT to get you set up with an account. That is on my list of things to do today." *What? Ridiculous, it's not like you didn't know I was starting over a month ago.*

"Ok. What would you like for me to do in the meantime?" *Great. It's going to be a long day with no computer access. I didn't even bring a book to read.*

"Get with Ashley. You can work with her on whatever project she's working on."

"Ok," I replied as I crossed my arms attempting to hide my annoyance.

"Oh by the way. You are meeting with Mr. Rodriguez at eleven. Since you don't have access to your calendar, ask me at the beginning of each day to see if you have meetings with the top four Medical Center execs you interviewed with." *Each day? How long is it going to take for me to get access?*

"Will do." I turned on my heels and walked out.

"Ashley, I know you've been here longer and have relationships with these people. What is your impression of George?" I asked when I returned to the office.

"He's a little brazen. Most people don't really like him. Mr. Rodriguez loves him. It takes some time, but he grows on you." *Yeah like fungus on you know what!*

"Hum. I guess I'm part of the most people crowd."

I entered Mr. Rodriguez's secretary's office at 10:50 am. *Crazy that he has a secretary and an executive assistant. I always thought they did the same thing.*

"Hi, Vivian. I have an eleven o'clock with Mr. Rodriguez."

"Yes. I see that on his calendar. He's still on a conference call with the hospital director in New Orleans. He should be off shortly. Have a seat."

"Thank you," I said as I sat in the soft leather lounge chair.

Twenty minutes after eleven Mr. Rodriguez opened his door. "Carol. Come in." I walked in and took a seat in one of the plush linen upholstered chairs. I placed my notepad in my lap ready for an assignment. Ashley told me he doesn't waste time. *I guess my time isn't important considering he had me waiting for twenty minutes.* "I'm glad that we were finally able to get you here. Is everyone treating you nicely?"

"Yes. Ashley has been a tremendous resource."

"Yeah she's good. She helped on a lot of different projects when she was just a volunteer. I really see her going places." He said in a reflective way as he sat back in his chair. "You really impressed me when you came for the interview." I nodded.

"Thank you."

"This program is an essential tool in the succession planning of the VAs future leaders. When I get new trainees in I like to tell them a little about myself. I graduated from Tulane University in New Orleans with a Bachelor's degree in Biomedical Engineering. After that, I got my Masters in Business Administration. I went through the same program Ashley's in when I graduated. That's how I was able to get my foot in

75

the door with VA. I was the acting Medical Director of the VA hospital in Biloxi until Hurricane Katrina hit. Luckily, there was an open medical director position up this way so I was able to transfer."

He continued for another ten minutes talking about the various jobs he'd held in his fifteen plus year career. I totally zoned out because I'd heard this same speech about three months ago when he came to talk to my LDI class. I could tell he was a very determined man the first I heard the speech. He mentioned when he interviewed for his current position he spoke with some of his mentors, made up practice interview questions, and even created a portfolio with some of his accomplishments to give to the people who interviewed him. *I have never in my life wanted a job so badly to do that much prep.*

"Part of the program requires you to come up with a solution for a problem you see around the Medical Center. I tend to let the trainee pick his or her own topic, unless I see something that would really improve patient care. I'll have them work on that."

"Ok."

"I want you to get out of the office and visit every department in the hospital. Get to know the chiefs of each department. Make yourself visible because it could help you in the long run." *Great! Here comes the politicking DC is known so well for.*

"I have a project that I want to you get started on today. I'm trying to get a new secretary. Vivian is going to be leaving in about two-and-half weeks. I want someone in place before she leaves so that she can train the person a bit. If you need help, ask George."

"Ok. Just to let you know I don't have computer access."

"Get with George. Tell him, I told you to tell him to get it fixed today. Also, make sure to tell him to get you and Ashley blackberries. I want to make sure you two are always accessible." *Why? This is an internship with the VA not the FBI.*

I nodded my head. "I kind of have an idea of what I would like to do for my project, but I'll wait awhile so I can see what the need is at this Medical Center. Just from the three hours I've been here today the vibe is very different from Baltimore." *I'm going to use the same project I used for LDI.*

"Really? Once you get acclimated I want you to get on my schedule so we can discuss that." *Uh oh, did I just open a can of worms?*

"Sure."

"Let me know if anyone gives you push back on anything you ask for. You are here to learn so people should be accommodating to you. Plus, you work directly for me so they should respect you." *Alrighty then macho man.* "That's all I have for you right now. Go speak with Crissle Jones in HR about getting me a new secretary."

With that, I got up and went straight to George's desk. "Hey George. Mr. Rodriguez told me to tell you that I need to have computer access today. He told me to get the ball rolling on his secretary position."

"He did?" He said as he scrunched up his nose.

"Yes."

"Fine. I'll walk down to the IT department to get your computer access taken care of. Walk with me and I'll introduce you to Crissle," George huffed as he locked his computer screen, grabbed a notepad, and motioned for me to follow him.

The Baltimore VA had a modern urban feel, but I felt like I had been transported back in time as I walked down the hallway at the DC VA. The main hallway had hideous mustard green coloured tile and the walls were either off white or the paint was so old it had started to change colours. At least a dozen ceiling tiles needed to be replaced due to water damage. As we made a left off the main hallway the floor tiles changed from hideous to chaotic. There were three different styles of tile on the floor arranged in a sporadic manner that kind of made your eyes cross, however, the teal walls were nice to look at. *What was the interior designer thinking when they did this?*

"Crissle, this is Carol. She's the HSM trainee."

I shook her hand. When I turned to thank George for the introduction, he was walking away. *Ok. Grouchy much?*

"What can I help you with?" Crissle asked.

"Mr. Rodriguez asked me to get with you to get Vivian's position filled ASAP." Before I could get the statement out, Crissle had sucked her teeth and rolled her eyes. *What is wrong with people here? Everyone has an attitude.*

"He just sent Ashley over here asking for an update."

"I apologize. I didn't know he had so many people working on the same thing." With that, I asked her to walk me through the hiring process for my own knowledge. I figured I'd use the time to get some beneficial information for myself. *Mental note: Check with others when assigned something to make sure I'm not doing double the work and harassing people.*

Each morning at 8:30 am, Mr. Rodriguez held a meeting with all the department chiefs in the hospital. He was briefed on any hot topics or issues that may have arisen from the previous day. To say these meetings were excruciating was an understatement. However, there were days when things would heat up and an argument would break out.

"Susan, what's the status on the patient satisfaction scores?"

"I'm still working on calculating the results. I should have them completed by the end of the week," Susan replied. Susan was the Chief of Patient Advocacy. Mr. Rodriguez tended to pick on her at each meeting. If patient scores weren't high, he would get upset because ultimately it would affect his end of the year bonus.

"I thought I told you I wanted those by the beginning of this week. When I set a deadline it isn't for my health. It's because I have other goals I need to meet. That goes for all of you sitting in this room. Deadlines aren't suggestions!" *Sheesh. I get he needs to have things done by a certain time, but publicly shaming people isn't going to get him what he needs any faster. That tactic would NOT work on me.*

"Sir, I'm still getting surveys in each day. I wanted to make sure I received all the ones that have been mailed out before I gave you a final report." Susan said sheepishly.

"Get me a preliminary report by the end of the day." Susan nodded her head yes as she lowered it in shame. *Damn!* "Moving on -." Mr. Rodriguez managed to berate two more chiefs, and it was at that point he earned the name Diablo from me. I swear I could see a slick evil grin every time he made someone uncomfortable.

I had been at the Medical Center for about four months and had managed to establish relationships with a lot of people. I developed a schedule of how long I wanted to spend in each department based on my interest level. I knocked out most of the ones I was already familiar with first, mainly direct patient care departments. I decided to spend more time in areas like the business and eligibility offices.

"Carol, how are things progressing?" Diablo asked me during our second meeting.

"Things are going fine."

"Is everyone giving you what you need?"

"Yes. All the chiefs have been very accommodating fitting me into their busy schedules." *Even if they weren't, I wouldn't tell you!*

"Good. I know one of the requirements for your program is to participate in a couple of public speaking functions. I have two important events that I would like for you to be the master of ceremonies." *Uh oh! I hate speaking in front of a bunch of people.* "The first one is our Native American Ceremony. We host this every year. A Native American will come and speak to the Vets. The second is the Remembrance of all the Fallen Ceremony."

"What exactly will I be doing?" I questioned. My palms began to sweat.

"The protocol office handles all of these type events. There will be a script that you will follow. Get with Melvin. He will go over all the details with you." I nodded to acknowledge his instructions as I was writing the names of the ceremonies in my notebook.

"I really want you to start speaking up more in meetings. I've noticed that you appear to be very timid." I stopped writing and looked up quickly.

"I'm not timid at all. I just don't feel like something always has to be said. I like to add value to conversations. I don't talk just to hear myself talk." *Unlike all the rest of the people around here who love to run their mouths. Present company included.*

"I always find that my quiet trainees tend to add a lot of value to discussions, but they have to be pushed." *Not me, dude.* "Ashley has no problems speaking up in meetings." *You love Ashley, and she wants to be a lawyer. Lawyers love to talk.*

"I'll get with Melvin about the two programs ASAP. Is there anything else you'd like to discuss with me?" I was trying to end this meeting as quickly as possible. We were supposed to meet on a monthly basis yet every time we had a meeting scheduled something would come up and he'd cancel. Now he was trying to get me to come out of my 'shell.' *Please!*

"Nope. That's all I have for you right now. Do you have any concerns or questions for me?'

"One thing I wanted to go over with you is my project idea. I noticed when I switched my care here from Baltimore there wasn't a briefing or handout on what services are available. In Baltimore, new patients were required to attend a class before an initial appointment could be scheduled. I don't think the class should be a requirement, but information on services should be made available. I would like to devise a handbook, of sorts, to give to new patients." *Guess I'm not going to use my LDI project after all. Look at me being overzealous.*

"Interesting. Did you find it helpful to have that information?"

"Yes, I did. The VA's website is very general. I like to know what is applicable for me, as do most people who are getting out of the service. The briefings we attend prior to separating don't give much information on what each VA has to offer. I think the VA representative who spoke with my group talked about fifteen minutes. All he spoke about was how to file a disability claim and GI bill information."

"That sounds like a good idea. Work with the departments that you feel would provide the best information for newly separated Vets. Let me know if everyone is getting you the information you need. I like the idea and want to stay on the same level, if not surpass, the Baltimore VA." *Really? This isn't a competition.*

"Will do."

"Remember, speak up."

"Ok," I said as I walked out of his office.

****

My dreadful cramps had not let up. In fact, they had started to get worse and more frequent. What really sucked was even though the entire VA system is connected through one record system, I basically had to start from scratch. The doctors seemed to never look at the previous doctor's notes. The one good thing about working for Diablo was people were so afraid of his wrath, they would do pretty much anything Ashley or I asked. I didn't like having that kind of clout based on working for an asshole, but it made my life easier when I needed to schedule an appointment in the women's health clinic.

"Hi Bell," I said. Bell was the Chief of the Women's Health Clinic. "How are you doing today?"

"Hi, Miss Carol. I'm blessed." *Crazy that she calls me Miss Carol. I'm young enough to be her daughter.*

"I was wondering if I could schedule another appointment. I need to change my meds because the ones I'm on now aren't helping at all with the cramps."

"Sure. Let me see what we have available." She opened the scheduling program and started searching for the next available appointment. "I have one this afternoon at two with my new nurse practitioner."

"I'll take it. Thank you so much, Bell." *Sucks that I have to explain my whole medical history, again but at least she'll be able to prescribe new medication.*

"No problem, Miss Carol. I have been where you are, and I know it's no fun. Technology is a lot better now than it was in my day. We will get you some relief." *I sure hope so.*

Two o'clock rolled around, and I headed to the women's clinic. I met with Devina, the nurse practitioner. "Hi, Carol. How are you doing today?"

"Not too great. I have been having a lot of pain, specifically on my left side. It has become increasingly worse over the last year and a half."

"What have you done to help with the pain?"

I rattled off the different medications that I had taken in the past and the different procedures I had done.

"Sounds like you've been going through it. A lot of time people don't realize that pain is relative. What may be super painful for you is nothing for someone else." *Why do I care about how others handle pain? All I care about is relieving mine.*

"I've heard that expression before, usually from a man who has no concept of what women's pain feels like." *I won't be scheduling another appointment with this one.*

"I'm going to change your birth control pills to a different brand, and I want you to take them continuously so you don't have a period. You may have spotting for the first few months which is normal. But by not having a period you should get some relief from the PMS symptoms you are experiencing." *Augh, I've done this before to no avail.*

She went over a few more suggestions on how to relieve the pain. I honestly had tuned her out after the smart comment about pain being relative.

The next morning Bell approached me after the morning meeting. "How'd it go yesterday?"

"Ummm," I stammered.

"What happened?"

"Nothing really. Devina basically changed my pills and told me pain was relative."

"She did what?" *I wasn't trying to snitch, but I still felt some kind of way about that comment.* "That was absolutely inappropriate. I told her my stance on treating patients with respect and dignity. She came from an inner city Planned Parenthood Clinic." *Makes sense now. I'd had several less than stellar encounters with nurses and doctors at Planned Parenthood Clinics when I was in college. Crazy thing, I was only in there once a year for a checkup but got treated like I was a repeat STD offender.*

"I get her attitude now. Working at planned parenthood would make anyone lose compassion, especially when you see the same patients making the same bad choices. I wasn't trying to get her into trouble by any means."

"I know. I will have a talk with her this morning." *Oops!*

٭ ٭ ٭ ٭ ٭ ٭ ٭ ٭ ٭

The Native American ceremony finally arrived. Thankfully, my nerves were under control thanks to Melvin's great coaching. We had done several run throughs of the ceremony over the past few days. I got a chance to practice the script in the auditorium with the mics and everything.

"You're going to do great, Carol. Don't stress it," Melvin reassured me.

The ceremony promptly started at 10:00 am. Diablo shook the hands all the Native American presenters like he was buttering them up before stealing their land. One speaker must have sensed his fakeness and called him out when she spoke.

"Good morning, ladies and gentlemen," I could hear my voice quivering in the mic. *Get it together, Carol!* "It's with great pleasure I will be your emcee today. These types of ceremonies are monumental to -," I continued reading from the script. Thank goodness there was a podium because I couldn't stop shaking my leg. It also prevented everyone from seeing how the script had started to wrinkle in my hands.

I had placed them on the flat on the podium to prevent talking with my hands like a T-Rex.

"At this time, I would like to introduce Spirit Youngblood. She is an elder from the Piscataway tribe located here in Washington, DC." Ms. Youngblood gave me a wink as she took my place behind the podium. I quickly went to my designated seat and began to fan myself. I wanted to cool off before I had to head back up there to introduce the next speaker.

"I have been coming here for the last twelve years to speak during this ceremony. Each time a new director takes over, I take it as a personal challenge to educate him on the special needs Native Americans have. During those twelve years, I have only encountered one or two directors that aren't very receptive to our needs. Considering it was my people who knew this land before it was stolen, I find it very insulting when my ideas are cast aside like rubbish." *Oh snap.*

I could see Diablo's face start to turn a bright red hue. I didn't know all the details, but Melvin had given me a brief synopsis of what had transpired a few days prior to the ceremony. Ms. Youngblood had reached out to Diablo to discuss how long she would have to speak. Diablo told her that she would only have seven minutes because he wanted a few Hispanic people with Native blood to speak about their lives. He basically told her just because she had the floor the majority of the time in the past that she wasn't the end all be all.

"Too many white men think they can do and say whatever they want without there being any consequences," Spirit continued. *OMG! This is going left. She's really upset with Diablo! Crazy thing is he's not white, he's Mexican.*

Melvin gave me a cue to head back up to the podium. I stood next to Ms. Youngblood. She must have sensed her time was up. "I see he has sent this young lady up here to cut me off." She looked Diablo square in the eyes. *Squirm Diablo squirm! Now you see how it feels.*

"Thank you, Ms. Youngblood," I said confidently. Her little rant had loosened my nerves tremendously. After that bit of drama, the rest of the ceremony went off without a hitch. Several of the department chiefs

I'd grown close with came up to me after the ceremony to praise my public speaking skills. *One ceremony down, one more to go.*

****

I had a meeting with Diablo scheduled about six months into my program. I had been feeling a little under the weather and decided to cancel the meeting. The previous two had been less than productive in my eyes, especially compared to the meetings he had with Ashley on a monthly basis. I wasn't in the mood to hear him talk about me needing to speak up more – especially after the last time I spoke up in a meeting.

Two days prior to my meeting with Diablo, Ashley and I were encouraged to sit in on a meeting with a team of executives from VA headquarters and an architectural firm about building a domiciliary care facility on the campus.

"We have brought mock ups of how the facility will look," stated one of the members of the architectural firm.

Everyone was looking at the physical building and commenting how the outside looked. I zoomed in on the interior. "Excuse me," I said. "The inside looks very institutionalized, like an old insane asylum or prison. Most of the Vets that would be using this service will be African American males. I don't think it the would be advantageous to these men to live in a building with cinder block walls that are painted white. The new editions -"

"Why are you speaking in my meeting?" Diablo cut me off. *WTF? After all that noise he made about me not speaking up in meetings, and now he's trying to shame me!*

"I think that's a valid point, Hector. DC has the highest percentage of homeless African American Vets in the nation. We need to be the flagship of what a great dom should look like," said Ruth Haskell, the National Director for Mental Health Residential Rehabilitation and Treatment Programs. *Thank you, Ruth!*

"I agree, Ruth. I want the DC VA to be the model other VAs strive to be like." *Kiss ass! I guess it would be expecting too much for him to*

85

acknowledge his smart comment was unprofessional. I won't hold my breath for an apology.

"Carol, that is something we will revisit. Thank you for that input. That is why I love having young people sit in on these types of meetings. They usually bring a fresh set of eyes to the issues." Ruth said. The other men and women in the room nodded in agreement. All but Diablo. If looks could kill, I would have been sitting there with Xs on my eyes.

After another twenty minutes of discussing the mock up the meeting ended. *Thank God! I couldn't get out of there fast enough.*

The morning after I canceled my meeting with Diablo, I dreaded going in. I had been having true stomach issues for the last couple of weeks. I'm sure it was stress-related because things were starting to get out of control in the director's suite.

"Are there any issues I need to be made aware of this morning?" Diablo asked.

No one said anything. Most people just shook their heads no. Diablo proceeded to go around the room and ask a few people questions. All of their reports were basically the same each day. He took a brief second from reaming Craig, the Business Office Chief, and turned to me, "Carol, don't ever cancel a meeting with me again!" *No he did not just say that to me in front of everyone!*

All eyes shifted from Craig to me, and I swear everyone decided to hold their breaths at the same time because the room was silent. My stomach literally flipped over, and I felt a way of nausea. I refused to succumb to his childish bully tactics. I looked up from my Blackberry, gave him a thumbs up, and continued playing Brick Breaker. *I really wanted to give him another finger.* I heard several people exhale then snicker. When Diablo saw that I wasn't going to fall into his shenanigans, he focused his attention back onto Craig.

"I don't know how much more of this man I can handle," I called Adam on the verge of tears.

"Babe, you only have a few more months to deal with that him. You can get through it."

"I know. I have to make sure I find a job on my own because I don't trust him to put me in an area I like. Knowing him I'll be stuck with someone just as bad as him. Diablo is enough. I don't want to work for Lucifer too. I can't imagine working with anyone worse than him, though." *That statement bit me in the butt six years later.*

"You'll find a job. You are beyond qualified to do anything you put your mind to. Don't let him beat you down." *God truly blessed me when He sat me and Adam next to each other on that flight. He has been extremely supportive over the last couple of months.*

"Thank you. I'm grateful that you stay positive despite all this madness. Let me get off this phone. I'll see you tonight, right?"

"Yeah. You can come over around six-thirty."

"Great. I can't wait to see what you whip up." *Handsome, nice personality, and he can cook!*

The rest of the day was uneventful. Thank goodness. I wasn't in the mood for any more drama. Neither my stomach nor my mind could handle anything else. I found out about an hour after the morning meeting that I was going to have to have an endoscopic procedure due to my recent stomach issues. I hadn't been able to keep down any food for the last three weeks, and when I was able to keep it down my stomach always felt like it was on fire.

Several weeks prior to the scheduling of my endoscopic procedure, the national headlines were ablaze with Veterans coming forward after being diagnosed with HIV or Hepatitis C due to the improper cleaning of scopes in Pennsylvania. News reports were claiming that sterilization procedures had not been followed. Several hospitals claimed that they were using Lysol wipes to clean the instruments that were inserted in nether regions of patients. *Yuck!*

As soon as the news broke, headquarters contacted Diablo and ordered him to present the sterilization records for all endoscopes in-house. He called a meeting to speak with the department chiefs involved in endoscopic procedures.

"We better have everything in order," Diablo started the meeting. "I want to see all the sterilization records for the last two years."

"Hhhhere they are, Mr. Rodriguez," Gregory LaSalle, the Chief of Environmental Management stammered.

Diablo snatched the binders from Gregory's hand. *Rude*. He then asked the Chief of Patient Safety if any formal complaints had occurred. Luckily, there had been none. The Chief of Surgery noted that he had ran a search to see how many Veterans had received any type of scope over the time frame the infections occurred. Only twenty procedures had been performed.

Diablo turned to Susan, the Chief of Patient Advocacy, and said, "I want you to contact these patients and see how they are doing. Don't say anything that would make them believe that we haven't done what we were supposed to because we have. I just want them to feel reassured that their procedures were done correctly and safely. If they have any questions or concerns, they can come in and speak to their primary care doctors."

"Ok. I'll reach out to them today," Susan said.

Diablo barked a couple more orders and ended the meeting. I caught Susan as she was walking out of the conference room. "Do you think I could sit in while you make the calls?"

"That's a great idea. I'm going to start the calls in about an hour. Just come to my office, ok?"

"Sounds good. See you in an hour." I wanted to see if I could see some of the sterilization records that had been passed around the conference room for my own peace of mind. Susan surprised me and had sterilization records available for me to peruse while she was on the phone. Everything appeared to be in order. When I told her that I was having a procedure done the following week she walked me to the surgical suites so I could watch the sterilization process. The tension that had built in my shoulders and neck upon hearing the news was starting to lessen.

Procedure day came and went. The only complaint I had afterwards was a sore throat. The results came back immediately and there were no polyps or signs of cancer. This really let me to know all the issues I was having were stressed related. I made sure to take full advantage of having the remainder of the day off, as well as, the next.

"How are you feeling?" Adam asked as he sat on the edge of my bed.

"My throat is a little raw but other than that I'm good."

"You should try to eat something. You haven't eaten anything since last night. I got some wonton soup while you were sleeping." *This guy is amazing!*

"Thank you. I'll have a little bit."

After I ate, I passed out. When I woke up it was a little after 1:00 am. There was a note on the nightstand.

> Hope you slept well. There is some food in the fridge. Call me, no matter what time, if you need anything. Love you. --A

I took it easy the day after the procedure. I had to mentally prepare myself to return to the work the following day. I had been working on my new patient brochure for the last couple of weeks and was due to present it to top management when I returned. I wasn't one for doing a lot of practicing. That usually made me more nervous. I prepared a couple of talking points, but for the most part, the brochure was self-explanatory.

I arrived to work a little earlier than normal so that I could get my thoughts together for my presentation.

"Good morning," Ashley greeted me when I opened the office door.

"Hey. What are you doing here already?"

"I came in early to study a little bit." Ashley had planned on taking the LSAT in a few months.

"I swear this place is your second home."

Ashley giggled. "Yeah, I can't wait to be done with this test. What are you doing here so early?"

"I came in to prepare my thoughts for this presentation." I started putting my stuff down on my desk.

"Oh Carol!" Ashley gasped.

"What?!" I turned around quickly. I thought she had dropped her coffee in her lap.

"Javier did your presentation yesterday."

Javier was the ultimate kiss ass. Anything out of Diablo's mouth was gold. He had gone through the same program as Ashley two years previously at the Atlanta VA. *I wonder whose ass he kissed in Atlanta to get into the director's office here as the associate director's administrative assistant?* He constantly had his eye on George's job, but George wasn't going anywhere anytime soon.

"You've got to be fucking kidding me?"

"No. He passed the entire idea off as his own. Mr. Rodriguez didn't attend the presentation because he had to go to the regional office for an emergency meeting but all the other big wigs were there."

"Sorry for dropping the f-bomb." I was shaking I was so pissed off. "Where is my green notebook?" This notebook contained everything I'd done over the last nine months.

"I haven't seen it," Ashley said. "Did you take it home with you before your procedure?"

"No. I always leave it here on the corner of my desk." *I bet that little snake took it.*

"I'm sorry, Carol. I wish people wouldn't be so conniving here."

"It's not your fault. Thank you for telling me. I'm going to see if I can find my notebook." I headed straight to baby Diablo's office. He didn't normally get in until right before the start of the morning meeting. He shared an office with Melvin.

"Hey Melvin," I said at the threshold of the office door. He had his head bowed and eyes closed.

"Morning Carol. I was getting my morning prayer on." Looks like I wasn't the only one. Praying before I went into the building cleared my mind of negative thoughts. It was very easy to get caught up in hating to go in every day. I had pretty much exhausted all of my sick days because I felt like I would explode at any minute.

"Oh I'm sorry. I didn't mean to interrupt. That's important! I can come back."

"No you're fine. What do you need?"

"I was wondering if you happened to see the green notebook that I always carry around. It was on my desk when I left for the day two days ago. I was out of the office yesterday."

"Yeah I know which notebook you're talking about." His eyes went to Javier's desk. *Snake!*

"Humph. That's a damn shame," I said as I got my notebook.

"That's why I lock everything up. What you may think is only important to you can be very valuable to someone who has it out for you." *Why would Javier have it out for me? I have no desire to work for Diablo or in the director's office period!*

"Javier's got the wrong person. I have no desire to continue to work in the front office."

"I don't know if you remember a few weeks ago when you were talking about your project to Ursula - how he was eying you."

"Yea, I remember." Ursula worked at VA headquarters and was liked by all who ever crossed her path. Rumor had it if she liked you, she could get you any job you desired. I wasn't thinking about her hooking me up with a job after this program while we talked. I liked her outfit and asked her where she got it. She was a cool lady. To be completely honest, I had been applying for jobs outside of the VA. I needed a break from health care and the VA for a little bit.

"He was ear hustling and heard how much she liked the idea. He came back here and got on the phone with someone talking about how he was going to have to spin the idea like it was his own. When he found out that you were going to be out, he somehow was able to get all the higher-ups to meet with him to pitch the idea." *You've got to be kidding me? He is such a little -!*

"Don't worry," he continued. "Everyone knows the new patient brochure was your idea. I overheard a few people say that it was nice of you to allow Javier to do the presentation. You may think he's got Mr. Rodriguez's ear, but Mr. Rodriguez is only loyal to himself. They are both very political." *Political isn't the word that I would use to describe either one of them.*

"Thanks! That's a bit of a relief to hear that people know it wasn't his idea. I've been working hard on this for the last couple of weeks."

"I know. When he sees people getting ahead without having to kiss butt, it intimidates him. He doesn't have an honest bone in his body. DC is the right city for him. I have friends that worked with him in Atlanta, and they said he burned so many bridges for his antics down there."

"Looks like the VA is the same as the military...eff up and move up."

"Exactly! He has no business working in this office. But you know how that old saying goes, birds of a feather flock together." *I know that's right.*

"Thanks again for letting me know the deal."

"No problem. I can spot the good people because they are far and few between here." *Sheesh! DC is way too cutthroat for me.*

I headed back to my office. "Look at what I found," I said as I held up my notebook.

"Where was it?" Ashley asked.

"You know where. Javier's desk. He didn't even have enough sense to at least put it in one of his desk drawers. He's so blatantly disrespectful. We are going to have a little talk when he gets in." *More like I'm going to talk. He's going to listen.*

"Be careful."

"What do you mean?"

"He tends to run back and tell Mr. Rodriguez everything." *I doubt he'll run and tell him he stole something off my desk, but knowing him he'd say I rifled through his belongings.*

"Thanks. I'll be a little more diplomatic than I want to be. Augh. I'm so over this place."

"Have you talked to Mr. Rodriguez about where you would like to work once the program is over?" Ashley inquired.

"Not really. I have mentioned that I'm interested in working with returning Operation Enduring Freedom and Operation Iraqi Freedom (OEF/OIF) Vets. I haven't met with him half as many times as you, so I'm pretty sure he doesn't remember."

"When do you meet with him again?" Ashley asked.

"Today. I dread it." I plopped down in my chair. I was mentally exhausted and my day hadn't officially started yet.

"You should go in there and tell him your interest in that position. They have created positions in the past for trainees."

"I'm sure he'd create a position for you. I'm not really that interested in staying here. I've been applying for jobs outside of the VA. I really would like to get back in a lab. Not clinical. I've exhausted that area."

"I know you have a plan, but remember it's his responsibility as a preceptor to find you a job. Don't let him get off so easily." *It was also his job to meet with me more than three times in nine months.*

"Yeah I agree, but at this point, I'm over him and this place. I'll bring up the OEF/OIF stuff, but I'm not going to hold my breath."

"Good luck." Ashley smiled and turned back to her study guide. *I hope the morning meeting flies by cuz I can't wait to lay into Javier.*

The morning meeting went by in record time. We were done by 9:00 am.

"Javier, I need to talk to you really quick," I said as he was buttering up someone for information about something that didn't concern him. He told the lady he was talking to he'd call her and came toward me.

"What's up, Carol?" He asked as he looked me up and down. *Whoever told this guy he was a man lied. He's more feminine than me!*

"Let's go to my office. I have to ask you something that doesn't need to be discussed in front of others." *Actually, having others around might be a good thing considering how he loves to twist truths.*

"Ok. Sounds serious," he mocked as he smacked his lips.

We walked into the office and I shut the door. "What would possess you to try to present the new patient brochure as your own idea?" I coolly sat down in my chair.

"What are you talking about?"

"Really? You are going to stand here and try to play stupid. It's not a good look. Spill it." My leg started to shake, but I maintained a straight face.

"I thought I was doing you a favor."

"How so?"

"I knew that you were having a procedure and -."

"Wait, how did you find that out because that wasn't common knowledge?" I felt my temperature rising, and my hands were starting to sweat. *I bet he looked at George's Outlook calendar and saw that I was going to be out.*

"I just so happened to be looking for George last week and saw it on his calendar." *Nosy snake.*

"So, basically, you were snooping around his desk since his calendar isn't out in the open." I crossed my leg to prevent it from shaking.

"I wasn't snooping."

"I'm going to cut you off right there because I know you like to snoop around other people's belongings." I stood up to get on the same level. "I found my notebook on your desk this morning. In the future, don't mess with anything that's on my desk. Don't try to take my ideas and claim them as your own. I know that you have Rodriguez's ear and snitch about what everyone is doing, but keep my name and business out of your mouth!"

Javier stood there with his mouth open and his hand on his hip. "Who are you talking to like that?"

I looked around the tiny office and then dead in his eyes. "Guess?"

"I don't know what you're talking about."

"Of course you don't. That's why I'm making everything crystal clear for you. Don't mess with my stuff or me. Everyone walks around on eggshells because they're scared you're going to run back to him. You can tell Rodriguez whatever you want, but I'm telling you right now if he says something to me about this little conversation, I'm going to open up a can of worms."

"Are you threatening me?" He asked as he rolled his neck.

"Boy, please. I don't have time to play games with you." Little did he know, I was just bluffing. I didn't have anything on him because I didn't want to be associated with him. Whenever he entered a room, I would I steer clear of anything he was involved with.

"What could you possibly know about me?"

"Just think about all the shady things you do when you don't think anyone is watching." At this point, I could see a hint of fear in his eyes. "I've said what I needed to say. You have a good day."

I opened the office door. He stood shocked at my dismissal of him.

"Carol, I did not take your notebook or your stupid brochure idea." *Ignore. He sure does sound shaky and scared.* I didn't acknowledge his lies, I simply logged on to my computer and started checking my emails. He huffed and stormed out of the office.

"Come in, Carol," Diablo waved me into his office for our meeting. "How's the brochure coming along?"

"It's done." I slid a copy of the finished product across his desk. *He better have at least one positive thing to say considering I paid to have this printed at Kinko's with my own money.*

"Wow! This looks really professional. Did you have the media office print this for you?" *Dang, I forgot about them. I could have had it done for free.*

"No. I went to Kinko's during my lunch break."

He flipped through the brochure. "This a lot of information. I think we should condense it down." *I knew he was going to say that so I came prepared.*

"I anticipated you would say that." I slid a shorter version across the desk. His eyes lit up with shock. "I feel the shorter version will only lead to more phone calls from Vets requesting more information. Maybe the short version could be handed out at out-processing briefings to active duty personnel. The VA rep could stick around after his or her briefing to answer any pertinent questions."

"Sounds like you gave this some serious thought." *Duh, I've spent weeks on this thing!*

"Yes I have. I just remember the thoughts that were going through my mind after the VA rep gave his briefing. I felt like he didn't really provide a lot of guidance."

"This looks great to me. I want you to get it down to the media department and have them start printing copies. Let's start with fifty for now. Then drop them off at the eligibility office. Tell them I want this implemented by the beginning of the next month." I nodded. *Poor eligibility. Next month is a week and a half away.*

"It looks like you're done with the hard work. Now to get you into your permanent position." *I wasn't expecting him to actually bring this up.* "Before I tell you where you'll be going, I'd like to talk about something you brought up during our first meeting. You said that the vibe was different here compared to Baltimore. Now that you've been here almost a year can you expound on that?" *Man. I don't feel like talking about that!*

"The biggest difference is the majority of the people that work here aren't from here. Nepotism is prevalent and not hidden at all in Baltimore. With that being said it was hard for outsiders to get the same respect as the people who are from Baltimore. Baltimore wasn't as politically charged as it is here."

"Well, if people didn't make you feel welcomed that sounds like it could be political."

"When I say political I mean you can't really say what you want here because it could be taken out of context and used against you later. You always have to be on your toes."

"That's true. But this is the place to be if you want to move up quickly." *Yeah, that's why you have a bunch of twenty-year-olds running around the front office acting like idiots because they moved up so quickly and aren't mentally prepared to handle the responsibility the job entails.*

"I feel like I'm exactly where I need to be. In due time I'll be in higher positions, but I don't want to rush into that. Higher positions require more commitment and responsibility. I like the work/life balance I currently have."

"That's a good way to think of it, but don't let once in a lifetime opportunities pass you by because you feel that you're too young." *Ok so now he's trying to offer me professional mentoring. Too late! Should have done that month one not month eleven.*

"Any opportunity that I'm meant to have, I will get."

"That sounds like something a person that believes in higher powers would say."

"I don't believe in higher powers," I stressed the word powers. "I believe in God and know He's always got my best interest in mind."

"I believe that we are responsible for our own destiny." *Did I ask what your belief system was? Nope. Funny that he didn't say God. His tongue probably would have caught on fire.*

"I'm sure you have a jammed packed schedule today. Can we get back to where I'll be placed?"

"I've never met anyone quite like you." *What is that supposed to mean? Better question is do I care? NOPE!*

"I'm going to take that as a compliment."

He chuckled. "I want you to be Alice Pierce's administrative assistant. The Medical Center has a plethora of building projects in the pipeline." *WTF? Facilities management. I don't want to work there!* "Alice and I worked together in Biloxi. She was displaced thanks to Katrina. She was in Miami for a little while, but I stole her from them and put her in her current position." *Great. Now I'm going to be working with 'Diabla.' Alice and I never really hit it off when I asked to shadow her for a week.*

"When would you like me to start down there?" I could feel a bead of sweat roll down my back. *Why do I sweat like a hog so much?*

"As soon as you get all of the brochures printed and the people in eligibility up to speed. I told her that you probably would start about a month and a half from now." I nodded. *Let me really get on my grind and start applying for jobs!* "That's all I have for you. You can go now." *No he didn't just dismiss me like I was the help. Jesus take the wheel!*

I got my copy of both brochures back and left. *I'm going to have to get this new patient brochure ball rolling today. I can't stand to be in the same office as this man.*

I walked down to the basement to hand off the flash drive containing the brochure for the media department to print. I asked Marcus, the media tech, for fifty copies by the beginning of the month. He raised his left eyebrow.

"Yea I know. Sorry for the short notice. You know how he is." I pointed in the direction of Diablo's office and laughed.

"I'll hook you up, Carol."

I thanked him and headed upstairs to my office. When I crossed the threshold, Ashley looked like she was going to explode with joy. "What's going on Ashley?"

"During one of my meetings with Mr. Rodriguez I mentioned in passing that wanted to go to Harvard. He just told me that he spoke with the director at the Massachusetts VA and that I am interested in becoming an ethics lawyer. He got me a job as the administrative assistant for the EEO Chief." Ashley was clapping her hands.

"Congratulations. That's amazing!" I walked over and gave her a huge hug.

"It is. I'm so excited. The only bad thing is that he wants me to start in three weeks."

"Oh no. What am I going to do without you here?" I fell into my chair and crossed my arms like a spoiled two-year old.

"I know. I'm going to miss our daily gab sessions."

"I'm so proud of you. I can't wait to say I remember when she and I shared a tiny office where we named a squirrel, that was always outside our window, Steve. Now she's the leading ethics attorney in the nation!" I gushed like a proud parent.

She laughed, "I don't know about all that, but it would be nice."

My eyes started to well up a little. I turned my back towards Ashley pretending to get something out of one of my desk drawers.

She helped me get the eligibility office staff up to speed on the new patient brochure. A few days later she helped me move all my belongings down to my new office in facilities management. The day after that I helped her moved everything out to her car. We gave each other a heartfelt hug and promised to keep in touch. Ashley had been the best thing about working at the DC VA.

****

"Welcome ladies and gentleman to the 2009 Remembrance of the Fallen Ceremony. I'd like to introduce Mr. Hector Rodriguez, Medical Center director –," I started the program off saying. This was my last front office commitment before I solely worked in my permanent position in facilities management.

This ceremony was very emotional for all involved. I found myself getting choked up when family members would speak about their loved ones that had passed away. I even had to clear my throat a few times to gain my composure. All seemed affected in some manner, expect for Diablo. When family members were pouring out their hearts, he was busy emailing on his Blackberry.

When the ceremony came to an end, a fallen soldier's wife who was around twenty-one years old approached me, and asked if she could give me a hug. I was taken aback but said ok. As she embraced me, I felt her shoulders begin to shake.

"Are you ok?" I asked softly.

"I noticed when you were reading the Veteran's names that your voice started to quiver as the list got longer. I just wanted to give you a hug to comfort you." I stepped back and looked her in the eyes, and instead of seeing tears of pain, she had tears of compassion streaming down her face.

"Ma'am, I should be comforting you. I haven't lost anyone."

"The fact that you didn't hide your emotion showed the people who have lost a loved one you truly care about what you are doing here. I appreciate people like you." I couldn't hold back the tears. I pulled the young lady to me. We held each other for about a minute until her toddler made it known he was ready to go.

"Thank you for your sacrifice," I said as I wiped my eyes. Her warm green eyes glowed as she mouthed you're welcome and walked to the exit.

****

"Come this way, Carol," Alice said as she showed me to my new office. "I'm sorry about all the blueprints in here. I'll have them moved out by the end of the week. Once you get settled come by my office so we can talk about what your responsibilities will be."

"Alrighty." I didn't have much so it took a whole twenty minutes for me to get settled.

"I'm ready whenever you are," I said, standing in her office doorway.

"Come in. Come in. I don't know if coming down here was your idea or Hector's, but I'm glad and very appreciative that you're here."

"Honestly, this wasn't my first choice, but it's a job so I'm not going to complain."

"Ha. You must not have worked for the government for long because true government employees can always find something to complain about." There was a slight pause before we cracked up like a pair of girlfriends who hadn't seen each other in years. "Before we get into the reason I called you in here can I ask you a question?"

"Sure."

"Did he say why he put you down here with me?"

"He just said there were a lot of projects in the pipeline and that you needed help. He also said that you guys worked together in Biloxi."

"That's what I figured he told you. He was really cool back then. He has done a complete one-eighty since being here. Back in the day, he never would have people call him Mr. Rodriguez." She made air quotes when she said his last name.

"It's crazy how people change when they get a little authority."

"Girl, yes. I don't know how much longer I'll be able to stay here if he is the director. Because he used to work in facilities, he thinks he can still have his hand in the mix down here. I hope you didn't think you got away from him cuz you didn't." *She must have been reading my mind.*

Contrary to what I thought, Alice was cool. She even apologized for being short with me when I requested time to shadow her. We talked for an hour before she got down to business. She assigned a couple of computer based trainings she wanted me to complete over the next few weeks. She also mentioned that I would be keeping track of each engineers' daily activities to ensure they hit deadlines she established for them.

A month and a half later ...

The day had finally come. I had to let Alice know that I'd accepted a research lab position.

"Carol, I just spoke with HR. They are having some issues getting the position description finalized. I don't know what the problem is, all they have to do is -."

"I'm sorry to cut you off Alice, but I have some news." I scrunched my face up a little.

"Please don't tell me that you found a job elsewhere?" I just looked at her and shrugged a little. "No! I finally got someone who actually works and you're leaving me." She shook her head in disbelief.

"I'm sorry. I asked Adam last night how to break the news to you. He told me to just come out and say it. But you have a very strange way of being able to read my mind. I figured I wouldn't have to say much. You proved me right."

"I'm happy for you. Where are you going?" She sat down in a chair in front of my desk.

"FDA. It's a research lab job."

"I know you said you would like to get back in the lab one day. I was just hoping one day was a few years from now."

"I'm going to miss working for you. You are a tough lady, but you have been a great boss!" I walked around the desk as she stood up and we hugged.

"Stop! Because if you make me cry and ruin my makeup, I'm going to be really mad. Is this your official two-week notice?" She said as she pulled away. Her makeup was still flawless.

I said, "Yes."

"Ok. Technically you are still part of the director's office staff because I haven't gotten the position description finalized yet. With that being said you're going to have to out-process with Hector." *Dammit!* "Let me show you where you can print off the checklist on the shared drive." She walked around the desk and clicked away with the mouse.

I started working on the checklist the following week. I made my rounds to all of the departments and spoke with each chief. Some were genuinely sad to see me leave, and I thanked those for all the time they'd taken to teach me what they do on a daily basis. The rest turned on their political faces and shook my hand like 'great having you here now get out of my office."

My last stop was to the devil's den. "So you're leaving the VA?" Diablo asked as he was signing my paperwork.

"Yes." *I literally didn't want to say more than two words to this man.*

"Where are you going?"

"FDA."

"Oh you'll be right down the street in Silver Spring, right?"

"No. Laurel."

"I didn't know they had offices out there." *Imagine that? You don't know everything!* "It's a shame you didn't stay with the VA. Upper management isn't for everyone." *Was that a dig, like I couldn't be in upper management?*

"I agree. If this program has taught me anything it's that everyone isn't cut out to be in a leadership position. Leaders are born, not taught. Thanks for the signature." His eyebrows raised when I made that comment. *Guess who didn't care? This girl!*

Bye bye VA. Hello FDA!

Cheaters

In the fall of 2009, I accepted a position at the Food and Drug Administration (FDA). This had to be by far the easiest, most laid back position I ever had. There was a lot of turnover in management, three division directors in the four years I was there, but I had little to no issues with any of them. Up to this point in my career, I didn't think it was possible to work for someone who had any kind of common sense, but this place changed my thoughts on that. Management was cool; my coworkers, however, were in a league of their own. Sometimes I felt like this office could have had its own reality show. Some of the events were so drama-filled, Hollywood's finest writers couldn't have come up with this stuff!

Despite the handful of not so tightly screwed coworkers, I built some great friendships and learned a lot about myself. The best memory I have at this job was the engagement party my coworkers threw for me. *And the $300 cash Adam and I received.*

The following two stories were major events that happened to two very interesting ladies I worked with – an over-sharer and a co-dependent barnacle.

Beth's story

"My vagina finally feels like it's back to normal." Those were the first words my co-worker/trainer muttered when we went into the lab. I had been on the job less than two hours, and Beth was already sharing way too much information. Even if I had known her longer, I thought the statement was way too personal. Little did I know that was nothing compared to what she would share in the near future.

****

At this point in my career, I was at my third federal agency. The differences between the VA and FDA were astonishing. After my on-boarding experience at the DC VA hospital, I had no faith in the hiring process. I figured a change to a different agency would be more convoluted than a simple hospital-to-hospital transfer. I was pleasantly surprised how quickly the process went. I must say the interview for this position was a bit intimidating. I had to answer the same sort of "tell me about a time when XYZ happened, how you handled the problem, what was the outcome, etc." type questions, but this time I had to do it in front of a fourteen-person panel. Everyone in the division I would be working in was part of the interview process.

Beth happened to be one of panel members that left a lasting impression on me. When she walked into the conference room the first thing that caught my attention was how tall she was. She had to have been at least 6'2, and she was extremely curvy. She also had a very intense stare; the type of stare that makes you uncomfortable because you feel like the person should either say something or look away. She also took a lot of notes on my responses, more than the division director, who was going to be my supervisor. Fourteen intense performance based questions later and some "tell us a little more about yourself" questions, I was lead to the second floor by Mona, a principal investigator, who had scheduled all the details for the interview. She was an upbeat young thirty something, who was very outspoken. She walked me around the different labs and explained what projects were hot at the time. She went over her own studies, and how she was able to get the Center to buy outrageously expensive equipment for her studies.

"Do you have any questions for me?" Mona asked.

"How soon do you think a decision will be made?" *Why would I want to know anything else unless you're going to hire me?*

"We have three vacancies that we need to fill. We have one more person to interview tomorrow. We will discuss all the candidates and make a decision by the end of the week."

"Great. You guys have a lot of interesting studies going on. I would love to be a part of some of them. I look forward to hearing from you soon," I said as Mona escorted me to the front door of the building.

"Carol, I have to say this. I don't think you'd like this job very much. It's slow pace. You seem to like to be in high paced environments. This type of lab work is nothing like hospital work. I think you'd be very bored." *Damn, this girl is bold. I wonder if she doesn't think I would fit into the group dynamic.*

"Hospital lab work can be slow-paced depending on where you work. I have worked in pretty much all areas of a clinical lab. I'd love to give research a spin. Believe me when I say, I won't be bored. I know how to keep myself busy."

"Ok. I just wanted to warn you so you won't be disappointed when, I mean if, you get the position." *Did she mean to let 'when' slip to see how I would react?*

"I just want to say thank you again. I really do look forward to hearing from you soon." I shook Mona's hand and walked to my car.

As soon as I got in the car I called Adam and asked him what he thought of Mona's Freudian slip.

"You got the job," Adam responded.

"From your lips to God's ears because I'm tired of commuting to DC every day. This place is closer to my house and there's potential for me to get a grade increase."

Two weeks later I got a call from HR offering me the position with a grade increase. After the panel interview, I briefly met with division director. He stated that I would probably stay in my current grade and get a few step increases. *I always found it funny when supervisors talked about salaries. They rarely got it right. Thankfully this guy was wrong. Bored or not, I could definitely live with making $73,000+ a year.*

The first two days consisted of orientation. Same ole same ole. When I arrived at the lab the third day Beth was waiting for me in the lobby.

"Hi Carol. I'm glad you're here. My mother's name was Carol and ever since the interview, I have been hoping you'd accept the job." *Wow, what a greeting!*

"Good morning, -," I was trying to think of her name but I couldn't remember.

"Beth. Beth Smith."

"Yes, I remember now. Beth. How are you doing today?" I asked as we walked towards the stairs to the second floor. She didn't look the same as she had during the interview. She'd gotten her shoulder length hair cut into a pixie cut. She also wasn't wearing glasses today. Her green eyes were piercing a hole through me.

"I'm good. I'm going to be your mentor, as well as the person who handles most of your initial training. We are also going to share an office with another lady named Chanda. She doesn't normally get in until nine."

"Ok."

Beth punched in a code on the office door. "We each have a code to get into the office. I'll let the facilities supervisor know that we need to get you one today. I'm one of the few early birds in the office. I'm normally here a little bit before seven. If you forget your code, I can always let you in." I nodded and walked into the office.

Beth pointed to my desk and showed me how to log on to the network and then Windows. "Read these SOPs and we will head to the lab in about an hour and a half, ok? You may have some emails once you log on. Let me know if you need anything." *Computer access the first day? Oh my!*

As soon as I got settled in my chair I heard Beth on the phone, "Hey honey. It's me. I just wanted to say good morning. Have a great day. I love you." *Ah that's sweet.*

Beth and I entered the lab around nine o'clock. Before she started showing me where materials were located, Beth went into great detail about numerous doctor visits she'd gone to for a recurring yeast infection she always got after her and her husband had sex. *I won't gross you out with the details!*

After I picked my jaw up off the table, Beth got into the meat of the training. I guess my deer in headlights stare gave her a clue I was uncomfortable. She was an extremely thorough and patient trainer. Luckily, I had worked with one of the analyzers used to identify bacteria before. I was able to breeze through that explanation. The other analyzer had a similar setup which allowed me to pick up on it quickly as well. Within three weeks of her training me, I was able to work independently.

Turns out Beth wasn't as early of a bird she made herself out to be. My first week I was settled in and sipping on my second cup of coffee before she made it into the office. Thankfully, I had my code to get into the office because the next few weeks things started to go downhill quickly.

Every day Beth made it a point to call her husband, Peanut, when she arrived to work and wish him a good day. *I hope 'Peanut' isn't on his birth certificate.* Those calls didn't stop, but in the past he must have not answered the phone so she'd leave a message. Now he would answer, and they'd get into the most uncomfortable arguments you can imagine.

"Peanut, you need to find a job. I can't believe it's taking you so long to find one," Beth nagged. "I don't know how much longer I'm going to be able to carry this family. You've gotten so lazy since you were laid off. Being laid off isn't the same as being fired, and your unemployment checks are about to run out."

I could hear Peanut on the other line hollering back at Beth, all the while her voice remained steady and calm. This same conversation happened every single morning. One day after a thirty-minute conversation Beth slammed the phone down and started crying.

"You ok?" I asked. *Boy oh boy did I open a can of worms!*

"No, I'm not. I don't know how much more I can handle. Peanut has been acting like such a jerk, and his drinking has gotten out of control. When I bring it up he gets so angry. I don't know what to do," said Beth. Tears started to fall. *Oh no, I'm not ready for this. Why do people always feel like they can cry and vent to me? I'm not a shrink!*

I took a deep breath, said a little prayer, and said, "Maybe you guys should go to counseling, or maybe he needs to go to AA."

"He'd never go to AA. He doesn't think he has a problem. He just can't seem to hold a job longer than six months. I thought he was going to actually hold on to this one longer."

The way our office was set up we could talk to each other without actually seeing the other person. I had to push about two feet away from my desk to see Beth. Chanda and I's desks were back to back so the only way we could see each other was to physically get up and walk around to the other side. Chanda sat right across from Beth which allowed them to see each other without having to get up. Whenever Beth got into these heavy conversations Chanda would make it a point go to the lab. Chanda very seldom was in the office. She basically came in the morning, dropped her purse down, headed into the lab, and only came back into the office to eat her lunch and pick up her belongings to go home. I should have followed suit, but I didn't have as much work as she did.

Beth continued, "He has this dream of becoming a comedian." *Are you kidding me? This guy has to be at least forty. It's kinda too late to try to break into that industry and really ... we're in Maryland.*

"How old is he if you don't mind me asking?"

"He's forty-six." *Bingo! Too old!*

"What was he doing prior to getting laid off?" I questioned.

"He was a forklift driver at a manufacturing company. He went to work and got into an argument with his boss and then a week later he was laid off." *That doesn't even make sense. Who gets in an argument with their boss and isn't 'fired?' Oh wait – a government employee.*

"He should be able to get something if he's a trade worker, right?"

"Well, Peanut has had some issues with the law." *Go figure!* "Nothing serious. Mainly just not paying child support." *That's not serious?*

"I'm assuming he's aggressively looking for a job so that he doesn't go back to jail for not paying child support."

"He's been looking, but I wouldn't say aggressively. I've been paying child support for two of his kids, Annette and Brandon," Beth proudly replied. *WHAT? How many freaking kids does he have?*

"How many kids does he have if you don't mind me asking?" *Honestly, I didn't care if she minded or not. She was telling me all her business, might as well get the entire scoop!*

"I don't mind. Including our child, Amina, he has five. No, I mean six. I just found out a few months ago he has an older boy who's almost 18. He and that mother can't stand each other. He avoids talking to her at all costs."

"That mother? How many baby mamas does he have?" *Oh yea, I'm getting all in her business!*

"Including me – five." *WTF?! I've seen the pictures of Peanut on her desk, and he is far from anything spectacular to look at. I guess his personality is on point to have all these baby mamas.*

"Wow! You are a great wife to support all of his kids and carry your own family's financial burdens. Not too many women would do that." *This one especially!*

"I know Peanut loves me. When we met I had just gotten out of a very chaotic relationship. Being thirty-five and divorced twice doesn't make me too appealing to a lot of men."

"That's not necessarily true." I could feel my underarms getting damp. This conversation was getting way too personal.

"My first husband had a gambling problem. We had to file bankruptcy, and we were in our early twenties. My second husband cheated on me with my cousin." *How do you offer someone you've only known for a few months encouragement on stuff like this? I really wish Scotty could beam me up right now!*

"How long were you married to each of them?" I asked. *I know I shouldn't be asking more questions since I don't feel comfortable but this seems unreal.*

"I was married to Alex for four years. We got married right out of undergrad. After we divorced I wanted to work on myself so I didn't date for about three months, then I met Jose. He swept me off my feet and we got married six weeks later." The cup of coffee I had resting on my lap fell to the floor. Thank goodness I was almost done and the coffee was cold at this point.

I grabbed a couple of paper towels I had stashed in one of my desk drawers and started cleaning up the mess. My mishap didn't stop her from continuing. "Jose is the reason I moved from Wisconsin to Maryland. When I caught him with my cousin he said some of the most hateful things to me." Beth's eyes began to well up with tears.

"We can talk about something else." *Please let's talk about something else.* "I can tell this subject is really upsetting you."

"It's ok. You're the first person I've talked to about this." *Oh lawd! Why me? I'm not a counselor or Jesus. That's who she really needs to talk to! Jesus take the wheel, please!* "I feel like we have this amazing connection. You are so easy to talk to." I turned on a small fan I had on my desk. I was beyond uncomfortable.

"I'm sure you could share this with a sibling. They could tell you some really useful advice. Better advice than I can give you considering we have only known each other for a few months."

"I'm the only child. When my mother was alive I used to share everything with her even though she treated me like trash. I remember I would go to school all day, then to a part-time job for six hours. I'd come home and she'd expect me to clean all the dirty dishes she and my stepdad had left. To top it all off, they never left any food for me to eat." *OMG....issues!*

"That sucks."

"Yea it really did. You remind me a lot of my mom. Did I tell you her name was Carol?"

"Yes, you told me her name was Carol. I don't know if that's a compliment since you said she treated you so poorly."

Beth laughed, which by the way, was the first time I had ever seen her laugh since I started working there. "No, I mean she was sweet when she wanted to be and you always listen to me when I'm going through things. There have been several people who have sat where you're sitting but moved to a different office as soon as a spot became available." *I wonder why?*

Beth decided to get back on the subject of Peanut, "Peanut said that he was going to take this time off and find himself. He's been going to open mic nights in DC and Baltimore performing his comedy. He gets a few chuckles from the Baltimore crowds, but the DC crowds tend to be brutal. When he comes home from those gigs he's usually in a really bad mood. His coping mechanism is drinking."

"You do know that drinking isn't really coping. He's just trying to mask his true feelings." *Look at me! That sounds like something a therapist would say!*

"I've told him that many times. That only makes him madder. He tells me that I should be supporting his efforts and not nagging. He said he supported me when I told him I wanted to have a child." *How does he figure he's being supportive? He's not taking care of the kid, considering he doesn't have a job.*

"What do you mean he supported you when you said you wanted to have a child?" I asked. I had pit stains the size of tea cup saucers at this point.

"Peanut told me when we first got married that he didn't want to have any more children. He said that he had enough already." *True.* "I was very adamant about having a baby. I wanted someone to love me no matter what. Just in case we didn't work out I wanted someone around that would never leave me." *Really?! That sounds like something straight out of a Lifetime movie. Don't women know that kids grow up and eventually leave!?*

"Ok. Does he help you with Amina? How old is she anyway?"

"Yes. He gets her ready for daycare every morning." *Daycare? Why is she in daycare and he's not working? That's a bill they could eliminate real quick!* "He has way more patience to do her hair than I do."

"Humph," was all I could muster up. "I'm about to go in the lab to take care of a couple of isolates. I know you're going through a lot but just pray about it. God will help you and Peanut get through all of this stuff. You just have to rely totally and completely on Him. It's hard but He's bigger than our problems." I tripped over the door stop we had in place to keep the office door ajar. I was trying to get out of there as fast as possible.

"Thanks Carol. I really needed to hear that."

By the time I came back in the office Beth's computer and desk lamp were off. That was a sign she had already left for the day. Chanda poked her head in, "Is she gone?"

"Yep."

"Great. I'm going to have a very peaceful afternoon." Chanda smiled from ear to ear.

I giggled to myself because I had thought the same thing. The next hour and a half was the most peaceful our office had been in weeks.

The next day Beth's desk lamp and computer were still off around ten o'clock. She had started coming in to work later than her normal time but never this late. As soon as the thought of where is she crossed my mind I saw an email from our division director pop up on my computer screen.

All,

This email is to inform the division that Beth will be out of the office for the next couple of weeks due to some unfortunate personal circumstances. I ask that Carol and Chris help cover Beth's work while she is out. Just a friendly reminder all teams need to have all susceptibility testing complete by 30 Sept. Thank you in advance.

Eric

What? That was the vaguest email ever.

Beth's life might have been a little chaotic but her desk surely wasn't. I was able to look on her desk and figure out exactly what isolates she had processed last. As I was going over her work, I noticed that she was way behind schedule. She had signed up to use certain pieces of equipment every other day for the last couple of weeks, but by the look of things she hadn't done any work. *Great! Now I have to make up for all the time she sat in the office yapping on the phone with Peanut.*

Chris, Beth's teammate, and I decided to come up with a plan to catch up on the work and get ahead. Since Eric's email didn't say exactly how long Beth would be out, we planned to finish all the work before the 30th, which was in five weeks.

The next three weeks flew by. Chris and I were on top of everything that Beth had let slip through the cracks. One day I happened to look out the window of the lab door and saw Beth walking past towards our office. I quickly took off my lab coat, washed my hands, and walked to the office.

"Hey!" I exclaimed. I noticed she had on dark shades and a scarf. The shades weren't shocking because it was a sunny day, but the scarf was odd because it was the middle of May.

"Hi," she said barely above a whisper. "I'm just here to get my computer."

115

"How are you doing? Eric sent the entire division an email saying that you have some personal issues going on. Is everything ok?"

Beth took off her glasses and I gasped. Her eyes were rimmed by a sickly green hue, remnants of black eyes. Her left eye, which was slightly still red, had a large gash above it with butterfly stitches.

"What happened?!" I stepped closer to give her a hug. When I did her entire body tensed as if my touch was hurting her.

Beth began to cry. "I called his phone several times before I left early the last day I was here. He wasn't answering so I decided to go look for him. When I passed one of his baby mamas house's I saw his car parked outside. I figured I'd wait to see how long he was going to stay. Three hours passed and he finally came outside." *She really waited in the car for three hours? Couldn't have been me. I would have knocked on the door and been like what's up?* "When the front door opened, she was standing there in a thong, and they were kissing."

"What!"

"Yes! I drove home as fast as I could. I'm surprised I didn't get in an accident. I ran a lot of red lights. When I got home I called his cell phone and he finally answered. I asked him when he was coming home. He said that he had been looking for jobs all day. He was going to stop by his friend Omar's house and have a couple of drinks before coming home." *This fool gave a detailed lie.*

"You didn't call him out on his lie?"

"No. I figured we'd talk about it once he got home. I didn't want to upset him while he was out."

"Wait. You just saw him cheating with your own eyes but you didn't want HIM to be upset? Were you upset?"

"Yes of course. I was more upset that he lied to me versus him cheating. I always had a feeling he was still messing with his youngest son's mother, but I didn't think he would say he was looking for a job and actually wasn't. I'd seen several job applications he'd half filled out on the kitchen table for days now. He knows that money is tight. I'm so stressed out." *She's stressed because he lied about looking for a job while he was probably in that house making another baby she's going to have to support. Last time I checked an application has to be filled out entirely and turned in for you to be considered for a job.*

"What happened when he got home?"

"He didn't get home until almost midnight. I'm glad my neighbor was able to take Amina for the night. When he stumbled in the door I knew it was going to be a long night. I asked him where he had been, and why it took him so long to get home. Out of nowhere he slapped me. He slapped me so hard I literally saw stars. He had never hit me that hard before."

"He's hit you before?" I asked even though I already knew the answer. She often used having lupus for her constant aches and pains, but I knew something else was up.

Beth lowered her head and put her glasses back on. She shook her head yes and continued with the story. "He told me to never question him about anything ever again. He said that he was the man of the house, that he could do whatever he wanted to. I was merely there to support him."

All I could do was shake my head as she was telling the story. I found it so hard to believe that someone I knew was going through this type of abuse and honestly seemed ok with it. *I'm going to need a heavy dose of Botox after this story. My facial muscles are getting a workout; I have shown shock, fear, disgust, and anger, all in the matter of twenty minutes.*

"Once I got up, I backed away from him slowly. He started to charge at me so I took off running to the bathroom. I figured I could climb out the window and get to my neighbor's house easier versus trying to run out the front door." *Climbing out a window is easier than running out the front door? I guess people really don't think clearly when they're put in dangerous situations. Beth wasn't the smallest woman so I found it strange that climbing out a window was even an option for her.* "He must have been reading my mind because he blocked me from running in that direction. I was so scared when I looked in his eyes. He didn't look like his normal self. He looked possessed by the devil."

"Oh my goodness," was all I could muster up to say.

"When he charged at me, I froze. I couldn't move. I felt like I had been taken over by a spirit. He tackled me. I landed so hard on my back I thought I was paralyzed. I knew I wasn't because I could feel that I had peed on myself." *Ack. No she didn't just tell me that she peed on herself. I'd never tell anyone that happened.*

"I was just about to scratch his face but he pinned my arms to the ground. He had his knees on my shoulders and kept slapping my face. I started kneeing him in the back. I was hoping that I would hit him hard enough to make him snap out of the trance he appeared to be in. This only made him more enraged. He grabbed my throat and squeezed." Beth took the scarf from around her neck. I could vaguely make out what look liked finger marks around her throat.

"Oh my goodness." I didn't know what else to say. I placed my face in my hands as I shook my head back and forth. *This is unreal!*

"Once he had both hands around my neck, I got a strength I didn't even know I had. I could just imagine Amina walking in and seeing me. I didn't want her to be without a mother because I knew damn well he couldn't take care of her. She'd probably end up in foster care. With all of my strength, I punched him in his left ear. When he went to grab the side of his head, I jabbed him in the eye."

"Damn!"

"He was still sitting on my chest so I had to figure out a way to get him off me so that I could run for help. Once he got over the shock of what I had done, he went into an even deeper rage. He slapped my face, and his ring sliced open my cheek. I guess seeing my own blood drip off his hand sent me into a rage. I bucked so hard I was able to get him off my chest. When he stumbled back, I punched him in his right ear. When he grabbed his head I wiggled a few feet away. I was trying to catch my breath, but I saw a look of pure hatred in his eyes."

While Beth was telling me the story she remained pretty composed. A few tears had fallen, but she never completely broke down. I was shocked because Beth tended to be very emotional. I guess having been through so much had toughened her up. I, on the other hand, was wet with perspiration. I could feel beads of sweat running down my back, and my palms were clammy.

She continued, pale faced. "With all the strength I had in me, I pulled myself up using the coffee table as a crutch and threw everything that was on it towards him. He managed to dodge everything until I threw the plotted plant my mother had given me right before she passed. The pot struck him on the right side of his face. I guess he was still a little dazed since I had just punched him because he fell back and was out. My mother literally saved my life from the afterlife."

"Then what did you do? I hope you ran like hell out of the house to get help."

"I stumbled over towards him because I thought that maybe I had killed him." *If you did, it was self-defense!*

"He looked so defenseless and like his old self. I felt bad for hurting him." *You've got to be effing kidding me. This guy literally just whooped your ass and you feel sorry for him? Couldn't have been me. Adam would have gotten kicked and punched some more had he done that to me.*

"I checked his pulse, and he still had one. I noticed that he was breathing so I got up to run out, but before I was out of arm's reach he grabbed my leg and I fell. When I fell I hit the edge of the coffee table. I heard a loud crack, and I thought I had broken my arm or wrist. Peanut started crawling towards me. I didn't look back and just kicked. I hit him in the same spot the pot had. He was out cold. This time I didn't turn around. I got up and ran outside. I yelled at the top of my lungs for someone to help me. Meghan, my neighbor who was watching Amina, came outside, as well as two other people in the cul-de-sac. The older lady who lives next door came out and called 911."

"Thank God you have neighbors who aren't afraid to get involved," I said. *I know if this would have happened in my neighborhood no one would have called the cops.*

"I know. I have a pretty good relationship with all my neighbors. Meghan stayed outside with me until the police came. I didn't go in her house because I didn't want to take a chance that Amina would wake up and see me in the shape I was in. I guess my adrenaline had worn off because I was starting to feel every hit Peanut had landed on me."

"I bet. How long did it take for the police to get there?" I asked

"Maybe five minutes. I wasn't outside long. The first officer who arrived saw the condition I was in and called for back-up. He asked me who did this and where was the person at? I told him my husband was in the living room, passed out. He pulled out his Taser and walked cautiously into the house. He hadn't been in the house a minute when his backup arrived. Then I heard Peanut scream. I guess he came to and tried to charge the officer. It took four officers to get Peanut under control after he'd been tasered twice. When they brought him outside, he was handcuffed and had bruises all over his face. He looked at me and said 'I should have killed you, bitch.'"

"Why didn't the cops put you in a car or the EMTs put you in an ambulance? They should have protected you from him!"

"When the EMTs arrived, I told them I was ok." *Really? You got choked out, slapped, punched, and you heard your arm crack, but you're ok. If that's the case, why didn't you come to work the next day? Just saying!*

"I wanted to see Peanut. I wanted to make sure he was ok."

"Are you serious?" I hope my disbelief and disgust echoed in my voice. "This guy nearly killed you, but you were concerned about HIM?" I had watched enough episodes of *Law & Order: Special Victims Unit* to know that victims sometimes act strangely after attacks, but this was out of control.

"It's hard to explain. He's my husband. You're not married so you don't understand. I never would have thought in a thousand years he would have ever done anything like this. He's the father of my child. I told you he wasn't himself. The look in his eyes was pure evil, like he had been possessed by the devil." *Yea, if the devil's name was Jim Beam.*

"Did you end up going to the hospital to get all of your injuries looked at? Did he break your arm?" I had to ask questions about her because she was starting to go into a direction I wasn't feeling. *How was she so concerned for a dude who obviously doesn't give a rat's ass about her?*

"My arm wasn't broken, but I have a really bad sprain. As you can see I have a lot of bruises on my face and neck. They look a lot better than they looked a few days after the incident. Turns out I have four ribs that are bruised." As Beth finished pointing out the many bruises she had she stood up. I thought she was getting ready to pack up her computer, but before I knew she had pulled her pants down and was showing me the bruises she had on her legs. *Ok! I really didn't need to see granny panties and bruises. I have a very vivid imagination so I could have pictured what they looked like.*

Quick, say something! "Thank God it wasn't more serious. Granted the whole situation is horrible but it could have ended a lot worse. God was truly watching over you that night."

"I know He was."

"What's the deal with Peanut? Are you pressing charges?" I asked.

As Beth pulled up her pants she said, "I wasn't going to, but the district attorney told me it's not up to me. He was booked and charged with second-degree assault. He called me to bail him out, but something told me not to do it." *Yea, common sense!* "Meghan told me I better not bail him out. Matter of fact, she told me that I should get a restraining order against him. I went to the courthouse the week after the incident and filed one. He's not allowed to be within a hundred yards of me or Amina. He also can't call either of us."

"Good. Whatever you do please don't go back to him. I'm sure he has probably reached out to you, said how sorry he is, and that it will never happen again. Beth, be honest, how many times has this happened before?"

Beth looked at her hands and shook her head no, as if she was trying to erase the memories. "This was the first time it ever got this out of control. He never does this to me when he's sober. When the police ran his blood alcohol level it was zero point sixteen, double the legal limit, and he had traces of cocaine in his system."

"Did you know he did heavy drugs?"

"We've smoked a couple of joints here and there, but he never did heavy stuff that I knew of."

"Please tell me that you are done with this man. You know you can do so much better, even if so much better means being ALONE! There is nothing wrong with being single. There are so many single moms in the world that live very productive and happy lives. Their children are able to see that mom can do it on her own and still be there for them. Look at Shauna, she's a single mom, and her daughter has everything her little heart desires." Shauna was a lady who worked in our division who used to share an office with Beth. She changed offices shortly before I arrived. *I wonder why?*

"I think I'm done." *That didn't sound at all convincing. All I know is I'm done with this. She can vent to me, but she'll just get a head nod here and a whhhaaattt there.*

"I spoke to my father last week about this, and he said that I should give Peanut another chance. He said everyone makes mistakes. He just found the Lord so he said the Christian thing to do would be to forgive him and make it work."

Ok, I know I just said that I wasn't going to say anything else but I couldn't sit here and let this one slide. "The Christian thing to do would be to forgive him and not hold a grudge. There is nothing in the Bible that says that a woman should put herself in a situation to get beat over and over again. If you think about it, you have given him a second and probably a third chance, since you said this wasn't the first time he's laid hands on you. It's not just you anymore. If you want to take ass whoopings on a regular and you didn't have Amina I wouldn't say anything, but you have her to think about. Do you want her to grow up and think these types of relationships are ok or healthy? You don't have to tell me how your mom and dad's relationship was, but if it was like you and Peanut's you need to break the cycle so Amina can have a chance at having healthy relationships."

"I still love him. He's not bad when he's sober." *She didn't hear a damn thing I just said. Augh! I wish I could take Amina and raise her. She has said many times how the girl gets on her nerves. She even called her a bitch. How can a four-year-old be a bitch?*

"Beth you are going to do what you want to do. Hopefully, next time he doesn't kill you or Amina because, guess what, there will be a next time."

I could tell that last statement had rubbed Beth the wrong way. She finished packing up her computer and printouts to take home. She had been cleared to work from home for the next two weeks. How she had convinced Eric to let her work from home that long was beyond me. I had entered ninety percent of the data into an excel sheet for her, and Chris had reviewed my work to ensure I had entered everything in correctly. I guess she planned on reading emails for the next two weeks because that's the only 'work' she had.

"Thank you, Carol, for listening to everything. I'll keep you posted on the court hearings. I have several to go to over the next two weeks." *Bingo! That's what she'll be doing. By saying she's working from home she won't have to use any of her vacation days. And people wonder why the government is so inefficient. Here she is handling personal business while 'on the clock.'*

"You're welcome. I wish you a speedy recovery. Take care of that precious little girl of yours. You are her first example of how a woman should be!"

Beth stood up and walked over to my side of the office. I figured she was coming to hug me so I stood up. She extended her arms out when she was still two feet away from me. When she did reach me she pulled me into her chest slowly as she kissed me on the cheek. *Personal space please!*

The next two weeks were interesting, to say the least. As promised, Beth kept me informed on the status of Peanut's court hearings. He ended up being charged with second-degree assault in Beth's case.

While he was out on bail for that case, he met a woman named Paula. They quickly started a 'relationship.' I guess Peanut decided to be upfront with this woman and told her all about him and Beth's incident. Like so many women who think abuse equals love, Paula thought Beth had antagonized Peanut to the point where he finally snapped. It wasn't until Peanut did the same exact thing to her that she could relate to Beth.

Paula had gotten Beth's number from Peanut's phone while he was sleeping one afternoon. Paula called Beth frantic saying she was afraid Peanut was going to kill her. Paula said she saw a look in his eyes like she had never seen before. *That's hard to imagine considering they'd only known each other a few weeks. Had she really seen all of Peanut's 'looks' to know this one was out of character?* When Peanut found out that Paula called Beth he was livid! He called Beth and told her never to interfere with his life again. He thought that Beth had ruined his life by putting him in jail.

This must have been Beth's 'ah ha' moment. "I can't believe he had the gall to blame his arrest on me," Beth said. All her physical scars had healed and she was finally back at work full time. "When he called and told me not to get into his business with Paula I could have gone through the phone -." The rest of what she said got ignored. I was sitting at my desk typing an email to Ann about all the drama that was about to ensue that day. Beth talked a good game about 'what she was going to do' but never followed through with anything. I had her on disregard until I heard, "That's why I called my case worker and reported his ass. He violated the restraining order. He'll probably be back in jail by the close of business today." *Had I worn pearls I would have clutched them. I can't believe she did that.*

"Good for you! I'm glad you aren't letting him bully you. I know that took a lot for you to do but it's for the best."

"Thanks. I needed to hear someone say that I did the right thing."

About two months later, Beth came into the office later than normal. I knew she was going to be late because she had to go to court to testify.

"Good morning. How'd your testimony go?" I asked.

"Hi. It went amazing!" Beth exclaimed. It had been a long time since I'd seen her in such a good mood. "Peanut got sentenced to ninety days in jail for second-degree assault on Paula."

"Wow. That's good. I guess your testimony really helped the judge see this is a pattern of behavior for him."

"Yes. He looked miserable. He's gained so much weight. I don't know what I ever saw in him." I didn't either. The first time I met him was at Amina's baptism, and instantly I thought he was a creep. He was talking about how great God was all the while staring at my chest. He was the type of guy who had been told his entire life that he had such pretty eyes (they were hazel) and that had gone to his head.

"Guess what?" Beth said.

"What."

"Paula is pregnant." *OH LAWD. This man needs to have a vasectomy because he obviously doesn't know what a condom is, let alone how to use one.*

"Oh no! I hope she's mentally prepared to raise this child on her own."

"She seems a lot weaker than me," Beth stated. "She cried so hard when they took him away in handcuffs. I have a feeling she's going to stay with him through all of this."

"I don't understand. She called you to testify against him so she knew that he was going to probably do time. Why would she still want to be with him." *Why did I ask that question?*

Beth went off on this long explanation about how women who have been in abusive relationships tend to seek out more unhealthy relationships. She had been attending a support group for victims of domestic abuse and was getting individual counseling from a psychiatrist. She had become very active in the support group and even volunteered her house as a 'safe haven' for women who needed temporary housing.

The next year and a half Beth saw more lows than highs. She did a huge purge of her house and got rid of all of Peanut's belongs. While doing so, she discovered a sex tape of him and one of her friends. She noticed that the tape was filmed around the same time she was having her 'vagina issues.' Peanut had given her a STD, luckily she had gone to the doctor when she did.

Beth was a bit of a food hoarder due to her childhood experiences with food. While cleaning out the freezer she noticed a Tupperware container of Hamburger Helper Peanut had cooked. As soon as she saw the container she got a flashback of eating it. She had vowed never to eat Hamburger Helper again because she had gotten violently ill. She decided to bring the container to a friend she'd acquired through her domestic violence support group who did toxicology analysis on food. She found out that Peanut had added amanita mushrooms (which are highly toxic in small amounts) to the Hamburger Helper. Luckily, she picked most of the mushrooms out because of the weird flavor, otherwise, she could have died within days.

Eventually, the two divorced, and she won sole custody of Amina. She started dating *(way to soon in my opinion)* and was duped several times. One guy had her buying him extravagant gifts. Another guy had her doing things sexually she didn't feel comfortable doing. *And things I wasn't comfortable hearing about!*

As many before me did, I decided to switch offices. The last straw for me was when she tried to discredit my work in a meeting with Eric. She passive aggressively made smart comments in the meeting, and rather than tell Eric how she falsified her timesheets every two weeks, I took the high road a made a quiet exit. Trust me when I say, I spoke up for myself during that meeting and made sure to let Eric know that Beth was being ornery.

Shauna gave me a pat on the back one afternoon and said "I don't know how you lasted that long in that office. The stuff she went through when I was in there was enough to drive Mother Teresa to drink."

I chuckled and said, "All the stuff she went through would make Jesus Christ turn every single pitcher of water he touched into wine and chug it. I'm shocked I lasted as long as I did." *Lucky for her I was building a stronger relationship with the Lord.*

Once I moved out of the office, Beth and I only said hi and bye to one another in the hallway. Despite all her personal drama, she was good at her job, when she showed up. I pray Beth has gotten some enlightenment through her experiences and changed her outlook on dating, parenting, and working with others.

****

In the midst of all of Beth's drama, all my relationships were better than ever. Adam and I were in the healthiest relationship I had ever been in. Ann and John, her husband, lived forty-five minutes away. That was the closest Ann and I had ever lived since she left home for college in the early 90s.

"Hey babe. What weekend do you think Ann and John will be available to come over for dinner?" Adam randomly asked me one afternoon.

"I don't know. I'll text her and find out."

Two weekends later, the four of us decided to have dinner at a swanky new restaurant that turned into an after-hours club in Fells Point, a Baltimore neighborhood. When we walked into the restaurant I was pleasantly surprised to see red rose petals scattered around our table which had a reserved tent delicately placed on it. Our table was located under a white canopy of white silk sheets draped elaborately over four pillars. Each place setting had a contemporary silver pearl charger, a slight off-white dinner plate, with an opaque salad plate.

"This restaurant really goes all out of their customers," I said as the hostess left us to decide on what drinks we wanted.

"They really do," Ann piggybacked. We were both in awe of all of the tea candles that had been placed around the perimeter of the room. There had to be at least two hundred. I even noticed a photographer snapping pictures, I assumed for the restaurant's website. When Adam told me where we were going I looked it up online. I hadn't expected the place to be so decadent because the website was extremely basic.

Shortly after we ordered our first round of drinks, Adam raised his glass for a toast. Ann and I had been so enthralled in our own little world that I had forgotten we were a foursome. "Carol, we have been dating a little over a year and a half now." *He better not be doing what I think he's going to do.*

"What are you doing, Adam?" My cheeks started to flush, and I could feel the sweat beading up on my top lip.

"I can't imagine not having you in my life. You have opened my heart up to a level I never thought possible." He reached in his sport coat pocket. *OMG, he is doing this!*

I'm sure the rest of what he said was beautiful, but I couldn't tell you what it was for a million dollars. All I saw was a gleaming four-and-a-half carat solitaire diamond. The way the candles reflected off the ring illuminated and made it sparkle like nothing I'd ever seen before.

"Carol. Carol?" Adam said.

I snapped out of it and threw my arms around his neck. "Of course I'll marry you." As Ann and John congratulated us, the photographer I thought who had been taken pictures for the restaurant's website came from around the corner and started snapping pictures of me and Adam. He had hired her to capture the moment. The rest of the night was a blur. I couldn't help but stare at my ring. *I was going to be someone's wife!*

We both knew we wanted a small, intimate wedding. Over the next year, I single-handedly planned everything down to the smallest detail. We were married on April 2, 2011, with fifty of our closest friends and family. Looking back, the day was a whirlwind. My fondest memory was when our pastor told us we were officially husband and wife, and rather than kiss we did a chest bump. *That was my idea of course.*

Jessica's Story

SMACK! Jessica could taste blood in her mouth. She had never been hit so hard in her life.

"I'm sorry. I'm so sorry!" Jessica repeated after each blow landed on her face.

As Cate gained momentum Jessica lost her balance and landed on the kitchen floor with a loud thud. To protect her face and chest she curled up into a ball to block the blows that were more vicious by the second.

"You will NEVER do this to me or any other woman again," Cate screamed.

"Please. Stop!" Jessica pleaded. She was starting to feel woozy and didn't think she would be able to take much more. "I'm sorry. Stop!"

Stop was the last thing Jessica remembered saying before her world went completely black.

Two years earlier

"Congratulations ladies. You two are officially homeowners," Brad beamed.

"Thank you," Jessica and Cate replied in unison.

"Here is a bottle of Mumm Napa DVX sparkling wine to celebrate. I hope you two enjoy the house. It has been a pleasure working with you two," Brad said. "Whenever you two decide to sell this house keep me in mind."

"Thank you, Brad," Cate said. "We know that it has been an interesting journey finding us the perfect house, but you did it. We really appreciate all of your hard work."

Brad handed the house keys to Cate as Jessica signed the last page of the mortgage documents. The women had just purchased a five-hundred-thousand-dollar townhouse in a trendy suburb of Baltimore, Maryland. A five-hundred-thousand-dollar house may be expensive for most, and even more expensive for two girls right out of college, but these two had decent paying government jobs in the DMV (DC, Maryland, and Virginia area). Cate was an electrical engineer, while Jessica was a research chemist.

The two met in middle school and instantly formed a bond. Cate had moved to the US from India when she was twelve years old. Jessica's parents were immigrants from India. Though Jessica had been born in the US, she didn't know any English when she started elementary school. There weren't many teachers who were patient enough to spend extra time with Jessica for her to really grasp English, which lead her to struggle socially throughout her formative learning years. When Cate arrived at Booker T. Johnson Middle School in the spring of 1992, Jessica was elated to finally have another girl she could speak to in her native tongue.

They were inseparable throughout middle and high school. As many teenagers, both girls went through an awkward stage. However, once the pair ventured off to college in southern Maine, Cate blossomed into a beautiful woman. Her long dark hair was to her waist, which she normally kept in a braid. She was fair skinned and had piercing blue eyes. Jessica on the other hand never quite felt comfortable in her own skin due to years of constant reticule about her weight. She was lucky enough to not gain the 'freshman fifteen.' In fact, she lost all of her childhood weight while attending college, but never wore clothes that showed off her new shape. She always felt inferior to Cate because she had a caramel coloured complexion, dark eyes, and wavy hair.

After college the two were able to find jobs in Maryland, and as the old saying goes the rest was history.

"Can you believe we did it? That we actually bought a house together," Jessica squealed.

"Well," Cate started off, "yes I can! We planned, researched, and saved a lot to buy this house. I'm so happy we did this together." She reached over and gave Jessica a hug.

Cate was the outgoing one of the two. Whenever they went to parties it was usually due to an invite Cate had received, and she would automatically take Jessica as her plus one. Most people they encountered thought they were lesbians. Both ladies refused to let men distract them from their goals. They rarely went out, even once they graduated, but when they did they would flirt and party like any other twenty-something.

Though quite timid and shy, Jessica always managed the courage to go out with Cate. Cate tended to attract the guys with her fun loving personality. She made it a point to talk to men who had at least one single friend so that Jessica wouldn't feel like the third wheel.

"When do you think we should have a house warming party?" Cate brought up one afternoon after the two had completely moved in all their furniture.

"I don't care when we have it. It just can't be within the next two weeks because I have a lot going on at work," Jessica replied.

"Yea I've been extremely busy at work as well lately. Jeff and I have been working on this one project that has both of us going out of our minds."

Jessica internally cringed when Cate brought up the name Jeff. Jeff was one of Cate's coworkers who she had recently started dating. He wasn't like any other guy that Cate had dated. He was the loner type. Everyone at Cate's job thought Jeff was the type of guy who'd come in one day and shoot everyone because he had reached his breaking point. Jessica couldn't believe how much Cate talked about him, 'Jeff said this today or Jeff was wearing that.'

Recently, Cate and Jeff were going out on dates at least four days out of the week after work. Rarely did they go out alone because Jessica made it a point to somehow weasel her way into their plans. To Jeff's frustration, Cate never protested. In some sort of strange way, Cate felt it was necessary to include Jessica in all her personal activities.

You may be thinking did Jessica have any friends other than Cate? She did but a very select few. I happened to be one of the people that she confided in and spoke to truthfully. *So I thought.*

Knock. Knock.

"Come in," Jessica answered.

I walked into Jessica's office that she shared with a sweet older chemist by the name of Tamika. "Good morning, ladies."

"Hi, Carol," Tamika smiled.

"Hi," Jessica said. Her mouth looked like she had just eaten a handful of sour patch kids and the sourness hadn't turned to sweetness yet.

"I'm going to head into the lab," Tamika stated. "Please try to cheer her up. She has been in a bad mood since she walked in the door this morning."

I looked over to Jessica. She avoided my gaze. "Girl, what's wrong with you?" I asked in a playful tone. "It's way too early to be this depressed." As soon as I said that tears poured down her face. *Oh Lord, not another one!*

"Carol, I feel like my world is coming to an end."

"Ok, it's way too early to be this dramatic," I said as I nudged her playfully.

"No really. I have the worst news." *Oh no.* All I could think was Cate asked her to move out. She had told me about six months ago that Jeff had moved into their house because the lease on his apartment was up. Since him and Cate were getting serious it only made sense for him to move in.

"What? You are starting to freak me out. What's going on?" Jessica was bawling at this point. I rubbed her back to try to calm her down. She finally got her tears under control and said, "Jeff asked Cate to marry him last night while we were eating dinner."

"That's good news, right?" I pulled Tamika's chair closer to Jessica's desk.

"No!" *This girl is really upset that her best friend is getting married!*

"Why isn't it good news? Aren't you happy for your friend?" My brow was furrowed with confusion.

The tears started to pour down Jessica's face. *She's really crying hard and it's starting to make me feel a little uncomfortable. Plus, the walls in these offices are so thin I'm sure her boss, who's right next door, can hear this entire conversation. I've got to get this girl to stop crying ASAP!*

"Jessica, take a deep breath," I instructed. "I need you to just breathe. I know things may seem crazy right now, but everything is going to be ok." I rubbed her back again.

Jessica took a couple of deep breaths and started to calm herself down. I just noticed how puffy her eyes were. She must have been crying all night.

"Did you get any sleep last night?"

She shook her head. "No. I couldn't sleep at all. All I could think about is how things are going to change. How Cate has already changed since Jeff has been in the picture." *Did she really think that things were going to stay the same from when they were in college? I know she's naive, but she can't be that naive!*

"Jessica, don't you remember we had a conversation about this before Jeff was even in the picture? Remember I asked you what would happen if one of you found a guy, fell in love, and decided to get married?" Jessica shook her head yes. "You said that the guy was just going to have to be cool with living with the two of you."

"I know. I remember that conversation, but I honestly didn't think that Cate and I would have to be dealing with this so soon. When Jeff moved in I looked at him as a roommate. He stays in the basement for goodness sake. Cate and him don't even sleep in the same bed." *Ok, I knew that Cate was a religious girl and that Jeff was a preacher's kid but whoa. He really was living like a roommate. I'll never forget the time Jessica told me they made him pay $1800 a month for rent. He could have had his own place, a nice place, for that price.*

"Didn't you say that Cate planned on saving herself for marriage? If so, that makes sense that they wouldn't sleep in the same bed. It's kinda wrong for you guys to have him sleeping in the basement and he pays so much for rent."

Jessica snickered, "He's not in the basement anymore. He sleeps in Cate's bed. It's too cold in the basement for him to sleep down there." Jessica told me once that they didn't turn the heat or AC on unless the temperature remained at either thirty-two degrees and below or eighty-five degrees and higher for so many consecutive days. *If you have ever lived on the east coast, you can only imagine how miserable living in that house must have been. Brutally cold winters and super humid summers are no fun!*

"Wait. You just said that they don't sleep in the same bed."

"Cate and I sleep in my bed together." *Ummm, did I just hear that correctly? Is this girl in love with Cate?! How can I ask that without seeming heartless?*

"Did you just say that the two of you sleep in the same bed?" My mouth was wide open.

"Yes, but it's not what you think. I don't like women. I like men." *Right!* My left eyebrow raised. "Really. I have a crush on a guy, but he doesn't even know I exist." I guess she saw the doubt in my face.

"Does this guy's name happen to be Jeff?" I blurted out. The thought had crossed my mind several times before, but it just seemed absolutely clear now. Plenty of times in the past Jessica had mentioned how mad Jeff made her because he didn't compliment something she had cooked for dinner or a new outfit that she had on. She even came to work in tears one day because Jeff had told her she would be an attractive woman if she got LASIK. *Her glasses were pretty thick, but who was he to say what she needed to have LASIK. Better yet why did she care what he had to say considering he wasn't her man.*

With hesitation, she shook her head no. *Not convinced.*

"Carol, I have to tell you something, and you have to promise you won't tell anyone," Jessica's voice was trembling, "Last night I looked in my medicine cabinet and saw all the medication I used to take for the pain associated with my rheumatoid arthritis, and I thought about ending it all."

No, this girl isn't thinking about committing suicide over her best friend's engagement. "You were going to kill yourself on your best friend's happiest moment? That's kinda selfish don't you think?" I crossed my arms as I leaned back in the chair waiting on her response.

Jessica sat at her desk in shock. After a few moments, she nodded her head in agreement. She said, "I don't think I can live without Cate in my life."

"Did she asked you move out?"

"No, but I know that she and I won't have the same type of relationship that we've had over the years." The tears started to fall again. I truly felt sorry for this girl. She had a few neighbors that she hung out with every now and then, but no one could compare to Cate in her eyes. Cate was her God! I hate to use that comparison, but Jessica truly worshiped the ground Cate walked on. Jessica had told me she didn't believe in God but would go to church with Cate just so she didn't have to be at home alone.

"Things are going to be different because Cate's priorities are going to change," I stated. "She isn't going to be able to focus all her attention on you because her husband is going to be her top priority and that's something you need to come to grips with." *And quick, because if you don't, you're going to lose your mind.* "Before you really start to freak out, they just got engaged. They haven't set a date yet so you still have time to come to grips with this. Whatever you do, don't act like a sour puss around her because you don't want to steal her joy. If you really care for her like I know you do, you will be happy and supportive. Let me ask you something." I leaned forward a little in my chair.

"I know I need to be supportive," Jessica said. "Sure. Ask."

"Are you in love with Jeff, and you're jealous he's marrying Cate?"

Silence!

"Well," I insisted.

"No. I don't love him. I barely like him." *Right! That wasn't convincing at all.*

"Ok. Tell me how he proposed."

Jessica took a deep breath and gave me all the details. Once she finished I asked her to describe the ring.

"He hasn't bought a ring yet. All three of us are going to go to Costco this weekend to pick one out." *I swear my hearing is bad because I could have sworn she just said Costco.* "Cate and I got online and were looking at rings after he proposed and she found one she loved. It costs about eight thousand dollars." *WOW, nice, but Costco, really?*

"Why are you going with them to get the ring?"

"Jeff doesn't have a credit card that has a limit that high so we are going to put it on mine. Plus, I'll get airline miles for such a large purchase." *Ok, where are the cameras? I'm getting* Punked. *This girl is buying her best friend's engagement ring.* "Jeff is going to write a check to pay the bill, and send it into the credit card company."

After another thirty minutes of me reassuring her that things were going to be ok she finally gave me a smile, and I went on with my day. *Yes, I did manage to get work done even though I played Dr. Phil several times a week.*

Week of the wedding

"Carol, I am so stressed out," Jessica approached me in the lab the Thursday before the wedding. *Why is she stressed? She's not getting married.*

"Why are you so stressed? You've been planning everything for the last eight months. Just remember something will go wrong on the wedding day. Your main responsibility the day of is to make sure Cate doesn't know what's going on behind the scenes. Keep her calm and keep a glass of wine ready for her at all times." *If you're thinking that's great advice...I know. I didn't want to know what was going on behind the scenes at my own wedding, and that half of bottle of Riesling made walking down the aisle that much easier!*

"I just want everything to be perfect. I worked extremely hard on this, and it has to be perfect." Jessica's cheeks started to flush.

"Girl, calm down! You and I both know there's no such thing as perfect." Jessica took a deep breath and exhaled. *Me telling her to breathe so much finally sunk in.* "You have put a lot effort into this wedding. What are they getting you for all of your hard work?" I asked.

Jessica's face lit up. "Jeff's buying me the latest iPad." *These two suckered her. An iPad is expensive but nowhere near how much a wedding planner would cost.*

"Are you coming to work tomorrow?" I asked.

"No. I have some last minute things I need to finish up. Besides it's going to be the last time I get to spend time in the house with her as a single woman." *Humm, ok. Strange thought for another woman to have but this whole situation is suspect, so why am I trying to make sense of things now?*

Jessica continued to rattle off more of the details she needed to finalize and before I knew it was almost time to go home for the day.

"Well, I look forward to seeing pictures on Monday of the bridal party."

"Don't worry, I'll take plenty of pictures."

I gave her quick hug and reminded her not to get overwhelmed on Saturday.

The week after the wedding was extremely difficult for Jessica. She had been staying at her parents' house because she wasn't comfortable staying at home alone. She had bags under her eyes and was extremely grouchy due to lack of sleep. She said she tossed and turned every night and couldn't wait for them to return from Hawaii. *Are you kidding me? She can't sleep in her own place? A place where she's paying the mortgage? I bet their electric bill would be incredibly low this month considering everything is off and probably unplugged.*

Once Jeff and Cate arrived home, Jessica's mood and attitude improved tremendously. There were a few days every now and then that she would come in pissed off and wouldn't want to talk, but I just chucked it up as PMS and living with a married couple. She made a deal with the lovebirds shortly after their return to spend weekends at her parents' house so they could have a little alone time. Mondays tended to be the days she was in rare form.

"How's life treating you?" I asked Jessica about nine months after the wedding.

Teary eyed she said, "Jessica is pregnant." *Oh Lord, they are about to give this girl the boot or she's about to have two jobs, this one and nannying at night.*

"Jessica, you knew this day was coming. Cate told you she wanted to start a family relatively quickly."

"I know, but I was hoping she'd wait at least a year before they started trying." *Best friends or not she needs to get out of that girl's uterus.*

"Let's have a big girl conversation. What are your plans after this baby is born? Your house is just a two bedroom. They're not going to want to have the baby's crib in their room."

The tears began, "I know. Cate and I had a conversation the day she told me she was pregnant. She said that she and Jeff want to sell the house and get their own."

I put my arm around her shoulder and said, "This isn't a bad thing you know. You can get your own apartment and see how it feels to live on your own. It's amazing."

"I don't want to live on my own. I don't think I can do it."

"You are a thirty-two-year-old woman. I guarantee you can do it. You have a good job and no debt other than your LASIK payments." *Yes! She spent $4000 on LASIK!*

"I can't do it. I'll probably just end up going to back to my parents' house."

"I know you've never lived on your own, but it's nice. You can come home, veg out in front of the TV, eat what you want, you don't have to share anything, you can walk around the house naked," I tried to convince her.

"I don't want to do any of those things. I love being around Cate. I want to be around Cate!"

At that point, I didn't have anything left in me to try to convince this girl that things were going to be ok; that she was more than capable of living on her own. She cried for ten minutes straight. I told her I had some work to take care of and that we could go out for dinner to get her mind off things. She gladly accepted the invitation. *Uh oh, what did I just do? Did I open a dam where this barnacle would spill over into the sea I call life?*

Unfortunately, two weeks later Jessica came to work and told me that Cate had a miscarriage. She said Cate wasn't handling it too well and was very depressed. I could sense a small sense of happiness in Jessica's tone when she told me the news. I felt bad for Cate but knew she would be ok because she had a very strong sense of faith.

Just as quickly as Cate had miscarried, Jessica came to work about a month and a half later and told me that she was pregnant again. *They truly weren't playing around when it came to making a baby.* This time, Jessica didn't seem as upset, matter of fact she seemed excited.

"How's Cate doing?" I asked one afternoon while Jessica and I were in the lab working on separate projects.

"She's doing great. She's being super cautious and strictly following the doctor's orders. He told her that she needs to cut down working so many hours and she's actually doing it. I never thought I'd see the day when she would pick me up at four." These two literally did everything together. They carpooled to work. They took turns each month on who'd drive. Crazy thing is they had the same exact make and model cars but different years. They figured they could save money on gas and maintenance if they rode to work together. Cate usually would work ten hour days which would leave Jessica sitting around the office until six surfing the web.

"That's great. I'm glad she's listening to her doctor."

Adam had been applying for jobs across the country and finally accepted a position as a production manager in Phoenix, Arizona. This was one place I had always wanted to live and was uber excited. He headed out there a month before me. I wanted to have a job in place before I moved, plus someone had to deal with selling our house.

I made it a point to give my contact info to those I wanted to truly keep in contact with and bid all the other people adios. About eight months after moving, I got a text from Jessica. We hadn't texted each other in a while, but we kept in contact mainly through Facebook. I figured she was texting me to let me know Cate had the baby.

Jessica: carol how r u? i'm not doing good. pls call me asap!

Oh no! I hope nothing bad happened to Cate's baby. I'd seen pictures on Facebook of Jessica, Cate and Jeff on a regular. Cate looked healthy, but you never know what's really going on with people on Facebook. *Everyone looks happy on Facebook right?*

Me: I'm driving home from my volunteering gig right now. I'll call you in about 10 mins.

Jessica: thxs. pls call me.

"Hey girl," I said. Jessica picked up the phone on the first ring.
Before I could ask what was going on Jessica began to cry. "Cate lost the baby."

"Oh no! What happened? I thought everything was going great. From what I saw on Facebook everyone looked happy and healthy."

"Things have been bad here. Really bad," Jessica mumbled.

"Start from the beginning and speak up. I can barely hear you."

There was a long pause, and I mean a long pause. At one point I thought the call had dropped. "Cate lost the baby a few weeks after you and Adam left for Arizona."

"Wait, what? Why didn't you text or call me?" *Now I understand why all the pictures Cate on Facebook were from the chest up or she was hiding behind someone or something. I thought she just didn't want people to see her gaining weight but now that I think about it, she did look thinner than normal.*

"Cate was in denial for a long time. She thought that she was doing something wrong, and that's why she kept miscarrying. She didn't want to tell anyone that she had miscarried again. She was hoping that she and Jeff could get pregnant again right away and that no one would ever find out." *What? So she thought people would think she was pregnant for over a year and that would be normal? OK.*

Jessica continued, "Well she got pregnant quickly after the second miscarriage. Unfortunately, she miscarried again."

"WOW! Maybe she should give her body a break. This can't be good for her, physically or mentally." My heart truly went out to her because I could only imagine how painful it would be to get pregnant and lose not one but three babies.

"Well, that's not the bad part." *Ummm what could be worse than losing three babies within a year time frame?*

"What could be worse? Did she find out that she can't have kids at all?" I asked.

"No. The doctor said she can have kids. She's going to have to take a break for a while so that her body can recoup. He also told her because she's so thin she's going to have to gain weight. You know she's always had body image issues so gaining weight has been an issue for her. She feels so bad that these issues have caused her to lose three kids. She is overwhelmed with guilt." *You truly never know what's going on with people! I knew she worked out A LOT, and that Jessica said she was a picky eater, but wow!*

"I'll be praying for her to get that demon off her back. I know she wants to have kids so she's going to have to get those issues in order before thinking about bringing life into this world."

The line went quiet. "Hello? Are you there Jessica?" I pulled the phone away from my ear to see if the call had dropped.

"I'm here," Jessica replied. I could hear her sobbing.

"You said there was something worse? What's going on?"

Jessica was bawling at this point. I had to take a deep breath because she was being real dramatic. I turned on the TV because I figured she was going to drag this crying thing out for the next five minutes.

"Cate kicked me out!" I dropped the remote.

"She kicked you out of where?" I asked as I scrambled to collect my thoughts. *I know she didn't kick her out of the house because her name was on the mortgage, legally it was her house just as much as Cate's.*

"The house." *Whoops, I was dead wrong.* "She is so angry at me. I've never seen her this upset about anything."

"I'm lost. She kicked you out of the house because she's angry. Angry at what? What did you do?"

"Jeff...affair...guilty...confess," Jessica rambled. Those were the only words I could decipher between her wailing. *Please don't tell me Jeff and her had an affair!*

"Jessica, I need you to take a deep breath and exhale slowly. I can't understand what you are saying."

I could hear Jessica attempting to take breaths, but it sounded like she was starting to hyperventilate. "Jessica, take slow breaths!" I said loudly into the phone. Slowly her breathing started to come back to normal. She had stopped crying, and I could hear that she had set the phone down and was blowing her nose. Once she got back on the line, her voice was shaky, and she sounded out of it.

"Jeff came to me last night and told me he was going to tell Cate that he and I had been sleeping together." *WHAT THE F*CK!* "He said this last miscarriage was the last straw. He said that he had been praying and God told him he needed to come clean. He said that he felt that our wrong doings have been the reason Cate can't carry a baby to term. That God is punishing him."

"Wait! You and Jeff have been sleeping together? For how long?" My body was heating up. I could feel the sweat starting to bead up on my top lip.

"Since he moved in," Jessica replied barely above a whisper.

"Please tell me you haven't been sleeping with him since he and Cate got married!" I was pacing as I waited for a response.

Silence.

"Jessica, what would possess you to sleep with your best friend's man? I asked you several times if you liked him or had feelings for him and you always told me no. Why'd you feel the need to lie to me?" *No wonder she would get so mad when he would complement Cate and not her. She must have thought he was somehow her man too.*

"I saw how he looked at her. He loves her so much. She would always tease him and say they weren't going to have sex until they got married. She would come to my room after they'd been in their room doing God knows what and laugh. She'd say 'he'll do whatever I want him to do. I've got him wrapped around my little finger.' The next morning, he would come downstairs and look miserable like he went to sleep with blue balls." *I know I didn't just hear her say blue balls. This man is over forty years old. He knows how to relieve that problem. Besides that's his problem, not hers.*

"What does that have to do with you? I'm sure they had a discussion about sex when he moved in and he knew where Cate stood on the issue right?"

"Yea they had a discussion. It just made me mad that Cate would play with him in that way."

"I'm totally confused because I don't get how that's any of your business. I know that you two tell each other everything, but she was probably just telling you to tell you, not for you to help solve a problem." *I know this girl isn't trying to be dude's saving grace. I knew I didn't like him when I met him. He seemed creepy, and just as I suspected, he's a creep!*

"Carol, when we were alone together he made me feel so special." *Made you feel special, he told you your glasses were so thick they looked like coke bottles. And how can a man that's not available make*

143

you feel any kind of way other than disgust when he's coming on to you?! "No guy has ever paid any attention to me the way Jeff did."

"Ok Jessica, I know that you're telling me this because you are hurting and upset. What I'm about to say is coming from a place of love because we are friends. You were wrong for doing this! You are lucky that Cate didn't kick your ass, literally. Jeff told you what he knew you wanted to hear so that he could get what he wanted."

"She was very upset with me and hit me several times. Do you really think that he just told me those things to get me to have sex with him?" *She better be glad we've been friends for some time because if not she would be hearing the dial tone right about now.*

"Ummm yes! Who did he marry?" I'm fanning myself at this point.

Jessica dropped the phone, and I could hear her crying hysterically.

"Jessica! Jessica! Pick up the phone!" I yelled.

"I GAVE HIM MY VIRGINITY," Jessica screamed. This time I dropped my phone. *Oh shit and the plot thickens!*

"You're kidding me!" I scrambled to pick it up. I decided to lay down on the cool tile floor to help me cool off. It came out so quickly I didn't even think about how she would react to my brutal honesty.

"No. He was my first." At this point, I'm rubbing my temples because this can't be for real. We are grown ass women in our thirties, and he's in his forties. This sounds like it could be an after school special about why it's smart to know your self-worth.

"Please tell me this happened maybe three or four times." *Not that it would make the situation better but everyone knows that sex is horrible the first time. Maybe she did it two more times to see if she really liked it or not. I'm grasping at straws here trying to make sense of this whole debacle.*

"No. We had sex on a weekly basis before they got married and maybe every other week once they got married."

"WHAT THE .... You .. have .. been .. having .. sex .. with .. your .. best .. friend's .. husband .. while .. she's .. been .. dealing .. with .. trying .. to .. get .. and .. stay .. pregnant?!" I managed to stammer out. I literally felt my blood boiling.

"Yes," Jessica replied sheepishly.

I dropped my phone again. I heard her saying my name over and over. I managed to pick my mouth and phone up off the ground to ask her a very important question, "Did you two use protection?"

"No." *This is a dream. I need to pinch myself so I can wake up because I feel like I'm about to pop a gasket.*

"Okay, you were inexperienced, not a very valid excuse because you are thirty-two years old, but it is what it is. Did it ever occur to you how you were going to explain getting pregnant? You aren't dating anyone!"

"I didn't think I could get pregnant because of all the medications I've been on. All my doctors told me it would be highly unlikely that I would ever have kids."

"They told you it was highly unlikely, not impossible, but wouldn't you want to protect yourself from getting a disease? Jeff wasn't a virgin. He could have had something and given it to you AND Cate. How would you explain getting a STD and you're not seeing anyone?"

"I never thought about those things. Plus, he told me he was clean." *OMG this girl – I really mean girl – is so naive. All guys say they're clean. What guy is going to say yeah, I have an STD, but you're still going to let me get some right?*

"The first thing you need to do tomorrow is call your GYN and schedule an appointment to get every STD test that's out there ran on yourself."

"I know, but I'm embarrassed." *I can't. This conversation CAN'T be happening. She's embarrassed about getting a girly exam and some blood work drawn, but she's not embarrassed about telling me that she's been sleeping with her best friend's HUSBAND for the last two and half years.*

"Jessica, I'm assuming you called me for support, right?"

"Yes. And advice about how I can fix this. I can't imagine not having Cate in my life."

"Ok. I am going to be brutally honest with you. I'm not trying to hurt your feelings...remember that. Cate is probably never going to talk to you again. The best thing you can do right now is move out, get the mortgage situation settled, meaning have them buy you out or sell the house, and move on with your life."

"Do you honestly think Cate will never talk to me again?" *Girl, for real?*

"As possessive as you are, would you talk to Cate if she did the same thing to you?"

"I think in time I would be her friend again, but not right away."

"Ok, so if you feel that way you need to back off. Give Cate her space and let her and Jeff work things out, if that's even an option."

"Yeah, they're going to try to work things out. Jeff always said he knew Cate would never divorce him no matter what he did. He said that she took her vows seriously." *Well, at least one person in that marriage knew what the vows meant because he surely didn't. He went into the marriage knowing he was going to continue doing what he was doing.* "I can't believe all of this is happening to me. Where am I going to go? How am I going to live without Cate?"

"Did you think about those questions when you were having sex with Jeff?" *Oops, that just came out.*

"I can't believe you just asked me that. I never intended to hurt Cate. I just really loved the attention that Jeff gave me. I honestly didn't really even like having sex. He just made me feel wanted. No one had ever made me feel that way." *OMG, I have never in my life encountered someone so thirsty. I thought those type of women only went after pro-ball players not regular everyday guys.*

"I'm sorry. I didn't say that to hurt your feelings or to be mean. I knew you had feelings for Jeff because it didn't make sense that you would get so worked up over some of the dumb things he said to you. I just never thought that you would stoop so low as to sleep with your best friend's husband."

"Are you disappointed in me?" Jessica asked barely above a whisper.

"I'm disappointed in your actions. I just hope that you learned a lesson and won't do anything like this to anyone else." *Cheating struck a serious negative chord with me. I had been cheated on in the past. Anyone who condoned cheating rarely got a second chance with me.*

Jessica started to cry again and this time I was done. I couldn't take any more surprises. She must have sensed that I was over it because she ended the call by saying she would keep me updated on her living situation. She had planned on getting all her stuff out of the house over the weekend and moving back home to her parents' house.

Jessica emailed me several times over the next eight months giving me updates on her life. She and Cate put the house on the market but because it was a two-bedroom townhouse they weren't getting any offers. They decided to take the house off the market and try again in a few months. The second time, the house sold within a month and a half of the listing date.

Jessica and Cate have not talked since the day Jeff decided to come clean. Jessica started seeing a psychiatrist about her co-dependency issues and feelings of wanting to be wanted. She has even started to date with the help of eHarmony and Tinder.

Recently, I texted her to see how life has been treating her. She said she's met a great guy and they've been dating exclusively for two months. She sent me a picture and told me a little about him. He told her that he was in the Army reserves and had been called back to active duty. He said he'd be deploying to Korea for three months. *I didn't know that Korea was a deployment option but hey I wasn't in the army so what do I know?* I did a little investigative work and come to find out he's not who he claims to be. Based on the name and picture she sent me he appears to be in a relationship with someone … in Korea. *How convenient that he's deploying there for three months!*

Have I told her what I found? Nope. She genuinely seems happy, and who am I to get in the middle of true love? Besides, we all know what karma is!

Dirty Jobs

"This was a great idea coming up here," I said as Adam and I crossed into Flagstaff city limits.

"It'll be a nice break from the heat. The temperature is only going to be in the seventies." This was our first trip since I arrived in Phoenix a month ago.

We continued driving until we arrived at a quaint bed and breakfast located near the outskirts on the north side of town. As we pulled into the driveway both our eyes were astonished by a beautiful two-story white stucco house that looked like it had been transported straight out of the Mediterranean. The lawn was perfectly manicured with the greenest grass I had seen in over a month. *It's amazing how you take greenery for granted when you're around it all the time. Phoenix was beautiful, in a brown, tannish type of way.*

We walked through the heavy wooden front door and were greeted by the owner. The inside was just as beautiful as the picturesque outside.

"Good afternoon."

"Hello," Adam said.

"Welcome to Sunnyvale Bed and Breakfast. How was the drive from Phoenix?"

"It was nice. Very scenic once we got out of Phoenix," I said.

We continued with small talk for another five minutes before the owner showed us to our room. Adam had reserved the biggest room at the property, which happened to have a Tuscan theme.

"This room is nice," I exclaimed when I excitedly walked into the room. I walked over to the French doors that overlooked a man-made pond located on the property.

"I had to get a room that was almost as beautiful as you," Adam said as he embraced me from behind.

"Take a look at this," he said as he let go of my waist.

I looked to the left and there were half a dozen chocolate covered strawberries with a note that said:

> To the love of my life -- You are such an amazing woman. I look forward to the new adventures we'll have in Arizona. I love you with my whole being. -Adam

"I can't wait to see what Arizona has in store for us too. I love you," I said right before I kissed Adam.

As we munched on the delicious strawberries, we decided to explore the room. The French doors led out to a private balcony that overlooked a man-made pond where two large white swans glided smoothly over the still water. Adjacent to the French doors was a large California king bed draped with a brown mink blanket and half a dozen throw pillows. As I looked behind the bed, instead of a headboard hung a sixteenth-century tapestry that displayed a medieval battlefield scene. As lovely as the fireplace was, we were glad we didn't need to use it. Just when I thought I might have a sensory overload from all the different paintings on the wall, we went into the second room which housed a jacuzzi tub that could hold at least four people comfortably. I couldn't wait to relax in it. Right behind the tub was a large window that had a stunning view of Red Mountain.

I was mesmerized by the view when a knock on the door brought me back to reality.

"I forgot to tell you two breakfast is between eight and ten o'clock," the owner told Adam.

"Great. We'll make sure not to miss it."

As I came around the corner back into the bedroom, I noticed my cell phone was blinking, indicating I had a voicemail.

"Hi, Carol. My name is Lucy Conrad. I am the laboratory's evening shift supervisor at the Phoenix VA. I'm calling to schedule a telephone interview for Monday at ten o'clock. If this time doesn't work for you, please call me back at 610-555-1600 to reschedule. Otherwise, I'll talk to you Monday. Have a great fourth of July weekend." *Wow, looks like I have an interview on Monday.*

I found it kind of strange that the interview was going to be over the phone. I had two phone interviews from the seventy-five jobs I had applied for prior to moving to Phoenix. I figured since I lived in the area the interview would be face to face. *Oh well, I prefer phone interviews. No fretting about what to wear, no sweaty palms or pits, no traffic.*

We enjoyed the rest of our weekend at the bed and breakfast. We only left the room to partake in Flagstaff's fourth of July fireworks, which had to be the most disappointing firework show I'd ever seen. *Living near Washington, D.C. had spoiled me.*

Monday came, and I must say looking back, this had to be the least stressful interview I ever had.

"Hi Carol. How are you?" Lucy started off the interview with.

"I'm good. Thanks. How are you?"

"Good. I'm actually on vacation."

151

"What in the world are you doing working on vacation? You should be relaxing," I said.

"I really need this position filled, and this was the only time I could do the interviews without being interrupted. I have a few questions I would like to ask you. Are you ready?"

"Sure. Fire away," I replied.

"What test is used normally used to diagnose a heart attack?" Lucy questioned. *Wait what?! She's asking me lab related questions, not 'tell me about a time when you had to' questions. I haven't worked in a hospital setting in YEARS. Please don't let me say the wrong thing!*

"Troponin is the most commonly ordered cardiac marker. Some doctors usually order a CK and CK-MB as well," I replied.

"Great. If a patient were to have a TRALI how would you perform the work-up?" was her next question. *I know she's not talking about a trolley you ride in.*

"Can you tell me what the acronym stands for?" *I guess the first question was fluke that I knew the answer off the top of my head.*

"It stands for transfusion related acute lung injury. It's a term used in blood bank," Lucy replied. *Uh oh, I haven't done much blood banking since I left Del Rio.* "Do you have any experience working in a blood bank?"

"Oh it's a transfusion reaction. I would work-up the reaction according to the lab's protocol," I replied. *Honestly, I wouldn't know where to begin.* "I have some experience working in blood bank. At my first job out of college I worked as a generalist. I was trained on the gel method, but to be honest with you that was well over ten years ago so I'm sure technology has changed."

"I'm sure the technology has changed since then, but you have experience working with gel which a lot of people don't. That's wonderful. I have one more question for you. Are you comfortable working with minimal supervision?" *For real? Did she just ask me this? Who in their right mind would say 'No, I need someone watching over me at all times?'*

Lucy continued, "I ask because this is a night position. The hours are midnight to eight in the morning. I supervise both evening and night shift personnel, however, I work evening shift hours which are three thirty to midnight."

I happily replied, "I work fine with minimal supervision. If you were to ask any of my previous supervisors, they would tell you that once given a task to complete you can consider it done. I am a fast learner and willing to take on tasks most people would shy away from. I'd like to have the opportunity to give back to our Veterans. Having been treated at several VA hospitals, I've noticed some VA employees see serving America's heroes as a chore and not a privilege." *Yea I was laying it on kind of thick. I had been on leave without pay status for about thirty days and only had two more weeks left before I'd be forced to resign. I wanted to make sure I didn't have a gap in service.*

"That's a great attitude to have. I don't have any more questions for you. Do you have any for me?"

"I have one question. How soon do you think you'll make a decision on who you're going to hire?"

"I'm interviewing two more people today. I plan on making a decision by Wednesday at the latest. You have been with the government long enough to know once it's out of my hands and into HR's it takes forever," Lucy replied with a slight giggle.

"Oh yeah, I totally understand. I want to thank you for the interview. I look forward to hearing something positive from HR soon," I said with a lot of confidence.

Lucy responded, "Like I said earlier I plan on making a decision quickly. Currently, we are having to have other shifts cover the night shift because of staffing issues." *Staffing issues? Does that mean a lot of people retired at once or was there a huge exodus due to drama?* "Thank you for making yourself available for the interview on such short notice. It was a pleasure talking to you."

"Thank you. Try to enjoy the rest of your vacation," I replied bubbly.

"Oh thank you. I'll try. Bye."

"Bye."

I received a phone call two weeks later from HR offering me a job. *Hallelujah! I can come off leave without pay status.* The position was only a GS-9, however, with the night differential and coming on as a step 10 I was pretty close to my old salary. I had worked nights before but never while being married. I couldn't help but think how this was going to take a toll my body, as well as my marriage. If anything, I was going to use it as a stepping stone just to get into the Phoenix VA system. I'd work a few months and start applying for jobs at a higher grade that were on day shift.

New hire orientation was the second week of August. I expected to hear all of the same ole boring things I'd heard in the past. About halfway through the orientation, we were blessed with the presence of the Medical Center Director, Susan Stegers.

"It's with great pleasure I welcome all of you to the Phoenix VA, to be a proud part of the best healthcare system in the world. I know all of you possess a lot of knowledge our Veterans will benefit from," Susan began. "By a show of hands, how many Veterans do we have in this class?"

A few people raised their hands. She continued, "That's amazing! I want to personally thank you for your service. It's by the grace of God you've come back after serving our country. Since you were willing to take a bullet for us, for our freedom, it is now my duty to give you the best care possible." *Wow, that sounded really, really rehearsed. Too bad she couldn't open up more appointments for all these fabulous Veterans she's praising. I called to schedule an appointment when I first got here and two months later I'm still waiting to be seen by my primary care doctor.*

"Let me tell you a little bit about myself." *Really? Why do directors love to talk about themselves? We know how to read, and your bio is online.* "I'm a mother of five and a wife to a disabled Veteran. My kids range in age from five to seventeen years old. In my spare time, which is limited, I like to run marathons." *I would've never guessed she liked to run. Her suit was so tight I could see what she had for breakfast.*

The next forty minutes I swear I only heard, "Wah wa, wah wa, wah wa, wah wa, wah wa, wah wa, wah wa, wah wa, wah wa, wah wa, wah wa." *She should try out as a voiceover actor for the next Charlie Brown movie.*

She ended with, "The Veterans are why we are here. I live and breathe the VA's mission. The Veterans are always my focus. Welcome to the Phoenix VA!" *Geesh! Forty-five minutes of my life I'll never get back.*

The orientation lasted two days so I officially started training Wednesday. Thankfully, the training was during day shift. Only problem with that was traffic and drama (day shift had more people than nights, which meant more clashing personalities), but at least Adam and I would be working the same schedule for a few more weeks.

Training consisted of working in each department of the lab for a couple of weeks. I was given a time frame on how long I would be in each department, but if I picked up the information quicker I was allowed to move on to the next department. Luckily, I had worked on several of the chemistry analyzers so I breezed through that department.

After two weeks, I was happy to bid everyone in chemistry adieu and start in microbiology. I had only been designated to be in that department for a week.

"Good morning, Carol," Jack, the micro supervisor, explained. "I'm going to introduce you to everyone in the department. Then you'll sit down with Lei. She is the person who sets up all the samples that come through this area. Since that's pretty much all night shifters do you'll be working strictly with her."

"Sounds good."

"How much you know about setting up micro samples?" Lei questioned in a thick Taiwanese accent after Jack had properly introduced us. *Great, I'm going to have to pay close attention.*

"I worked at the FDA as a food microbiologist. I'm familiar with micro setup techniques and media. I haven't worked with clinical micro samples in years so you can train me like I don't know anything," I replied.

She laughed and responded, "Ok. That make things easy for me. No bad habits to break."

Considering I was only going to be setting up cultures and running flu DNA analysis I figured three days would be plenty of time for me to pick everything up. I had some leave and money, so I booked a flight back east to visit Ann at the end of the week. Spending time with Ann would break up the monotony of training. I also couldn't wait to see my niece.

Lei's workstation was situated right across the hall from Jack's office. The first day I noticed Britney, a young blonde phlebotomist, making at least two trips to his office an hour. I thought it was strange but didn't pay it much attention until the second day. From the short time I had been working, I picked up that Britney was fairly new. She came over to several of the senior lab technicians and repeatedly asked the same questions. *Maybe she should invest in a notebook and write some of the answers down.*

"Jack, why didn't you call me last night?" I overheard Britney say.

"Close the door, Britney," Jack responded in an annoyed tone.

"No. I want everyone to hear this." My ears perked up. I had noticed Jack's wedding ring the day he introduced me to everyone in the department and from the sound of this conversation it was clear Britney wasn't his wife. Jack was a stout middle-aged fairly chubby man – picture George Constanza from *Seinfeld*.

"Close the door now!" Jack's frustrated was at an all-time high. Britney slammed the door. *Unprofessional much? Hasn't he ever heard don't shit where you eat?*

Even though the door was closed everyone in the department could make out the muffles.

"Lover quarrel," Lei said as she came back from getting samples from the front of the lab.

"Can I assume Britney isn't his wife?"

"She not. Jack has thing for young girl. Whenever new phlebotomist start he pounce on them like lion." *Ha! Her accent made this drama even funnier.* "He a dirty man. I hope she tell on him."

"Tell on him to who? It's not like they're hiding anything. She comes over here at least seven times a day."

"Molly."

"Who's Molly?" I asked.

"She lab manager. She turn her head all the time. Maybe Britney be first to snitch on Jack about him cheating." *No she didn't just say snitch, hilarious!*

"I met Molly my first day in chemistry. She seems very laid back."

"She too laid back. This lab horrible since she took over." Funny thing was, Lei wasn't the first person to tell me that.

"Looks like Britney may not need to 'snitch.'" Lei turned around as Molly approached where we were working.

"Good morning, ladies," Molly said to us. "Is Jack in yet? I called his office, and he didn't answer."

The muffled moans we heard earlier coming from Jack's office had stopped a few minutes earlier. "He in there," Lei pointed using her head. She looked at me and winked. *Ohh, Lei! Messy boots.*

Molly knocked once and then knocked again. Jack opened the door and his face was beet red. Britney's scrub bottoms were way more wrinkled now than they were when she entered his office a few minutes ago. She quickly said hi to Molly as she scurried back to the drawing room.

157

"Um good morning, Jack. I've been calling you all morning. Are you busy?" Molly asked. *Not anymore!*

"No. What's up? What can I help you with?" Jack stammered as he tried to smooth out his shirt. One of his buttons had thrown off the entire alignment of his shirt. He looked like a teenager who had been caught red-handed with the farmer's daughter.

"I was calling you because I need you to give a presentation about the Applied Biosystems DNA Analyzer to a few of the new residents that started their rotations in the ER."

"Oh sure." *I swear I saw beads of sweat pop up on his forehead.* "When do you need me to do the presentation?"

Molly paused for an awkwardly long time before saying, "I have a feeling that something inappropriate was going on in your office." *Oh man. I have never seen a supervisor get busted before. This has to go down in history.* Molly had a very stern look on her face. "I need you to meet me in my office in ten minutes." *OMG! It's about to go down!*

Jack didn't come back that afternoon. Matter of fact, he hadn't returned by the time my training rotation in micro was up.

Upon my return from the east coast, my training continued in my least favorite part of the lab, hematology. (The hematology department was comprised of hematology, urinalysis, and coagulation. Rather than say all those names, it was commonly referred to just as hematology.) Because hematology was composed of so many sections I had been designated to be in the department for four weeks. I prayed the next four weeks flew by.

Aneka was the team lead for this department and had as much personality as a doorknob. She was one of the most condescending people I had ever met, and she thought by beginning or ending her sentences with sweetie or baby it would soften the blow of her tone.

"I'm going to have you read more slides," Aneka said close to the end of my time in hematology. *I hate looking at slides.*

"For an entire day?" I asked.

"Yes, sweetie. You picked up the instrumentation part fairly quickly, but I feel like you need more practice identifying cells under the microscope. I also want you to go through the slide boxes to make sure they're all in numerical order, kiddo." *Cut the sarcasm, I'm not a child.*

"Before this gets out of hand, I don't appreciate your little terms of endearment, nor are they appropriate. I'm not a kid or your sweetie. Please stop speaking to me in that tone. I appreciate your thoroughness but looking through hundreds of slides to make sure they're in numerical order isn't a good use of my training time." I said with a smile.

She rolled her eyes and pointed out which slides she wanted me to focus on. *She's got some nerve. Get out of here with that!*

I wrapped up everything in hematology and headed to blood banking for my last month of training. To ensure I felt completely comfortable, since I hadn't worked in blood banking since my first job after graduating college, I planned on taking the full month.

"Hey Carol, do you think you'd be ready to start nights on Monday?" Lucy asked me about three weeks into my training. *I must be doing a good job because technically, I still have a week left of training.*

I looked at Julio who was sitting next to me reviewing one of the documents I had just filled out for accuracy. Julio was the tech with the most blood bank experience and responsible for training all new employees. "I guess I'm ready."

"You have been ready," Julio said with a big smile.

"Ok, you'll start nights on Monday," Lucy said.

"Sounds good."

At that point, I finished for the day and decided to take off early to make a surprise dinner for Adam. Our days on the same shift were numbered. I was going to take full advantage of the next three days.

"What is all of this?" Adam questioned when he walked in the front door. There was a path of red rose petals from the front of the house that lead to the door. When he opened the front door the rose petals led to the kitchen where I had prepared a home cooked dinner.

"Hey babe. I wanted to surprise you with a special night in," I greeted him with a hug and kiss.

"Whatever you are cooking smells great. The petals are a nice touch."

"I fixed all your favorites."

"Rosemary chicken, roasted potatoes, and steamed carrots?"

"You know it. Guess what's for dessert?"

"Peach cobbler?"

"That and something else," I said with a wink.

During dinner, Adam and I talked about how different things were going to be in a couple of days once I started nights. I didn't want to dwell on the inevitable so after we finished dinner I told him to follow the rest of the rose petals.

The next day at work Lucy pulled me into her office right before I was leaving for the day. "Hey Carol. There is one more place I would like you to spend some time in."

"All of the department supervisors have said that I've done a great job. Which one do I need to get a refresher on?" *I bet Jack wants me to go back to micro since I was only there for three days.*

"I want you to spend the rest of your time in the drawing room." *When did we get a children's play area because I know she's not expecting me to draw patient's blood?* "Sometimes the night shifters have to draw blood during morning rounds if a phlebotomist calls out." *That sounds like something the phlebotomist supervisor should have a contingency plan for. I will NOT be drawing blood even if everyone calls out. I didn't go to college to be a phlebotomist.*

"Drawing blood has never been something I've been particularly good at."

"That's why I'm having you practice. Besides, it's very rare that you'd have to do it." *Ok, if I just told you I'm not good at it, and you said it's very rare that I'll be doing it, why am I wasting time 'practicing?' Breathe it's going to be ok. It's going to be ok!*

I must admit the time I spent in the drawing room was fun. I spent more time gabbing with the Vets than drawing blood. Drawing blood was technically in my job description so rather than flat out say I wasn't going to do it, I pulled a typical government employee move – I did as little as possible to get by. I drew maybe three patients over the three days I was in the drawing room. That way I could honestly say I drew a couple of patients.

On my last day in the drawing room, I was sitting at the front desk when an older man approached me. "Hi young lady. My name is Edwin Smalls, last four three six one zero. I'm here for my Urology appointment."

"Sir, this is the lab. Do you need to have lab work done before your appointment?" I asked. It was very common for the older Vets to get turned around in the hospital. For some reason, they always ended up in the lab.

"I don't think so. I was just next door, and the fruitcake at desk told me to come over here." *Fruitcake? What is he talking about?*

"Hold on a second, sir. I'm going to find out where the Urology clinic is. I haven't been working here long."

"Go back next door," Trina, the lead phlebotomist said from her office. The way her office was situated, she could hear everything that happened at the front desk. Trina was a frail older lady who always looked pissed off. She would have had a sour puss face even if someone gave her a million dollars, no strings attached.

"I'll walk with you," I said to Mr. Smalls.

"You don't need to walk him over there. I just told him where the Urology clinic is," Trina said still from her office. She hadn't even gotten up to acknowledge me or Mr. Smalls.

I mouthed to Mr. Smalls "I'll walk over with you."

He smiled as I locked my computer terminal to ensure no one could do any work under my login. There was a phlebotomist who was known for trying to stir up drama amongst people she didn't like by sending emails out under someone else's account. If you left your computer unlocked, you could probably bet money she would try to set you up.

"Thank you, young lady. There aren't very many people left like you at this hospital. It seems like ever since that wench took over care has gone to shit." I giggled. I always found it funny how older Vets said whatever was on their mind. "I can't miss this appointment. I scheduled it over three months ago."

"No problem! If it wasn't for you I wouldn't have a job. Plus, I hope when I get to your age people will help me out."

We walked into the Urology clinic, which was actually two doors down from the lab. "'Sup," the clerk said to me as he popped his gum. *Ok, now I know who the fruitcake is.*

"Mr. Smalls has an appointment today. He said when he came over here he was sent away."

"Last name, last four"

Mr. Smalls replied slowly, "Smalls, three six one zero."

"Your appointment isn't until one, it's only twelve fifteen. I told you that when you came over here a few minutes ago. I said you could have a seat or go walk around."

"Thank you," I bent down to look at his nametag, "Scooter." *He actually had the name Scooter printed on his nametag. For real?*

I escorted Mr. Smalls to the waiting area where he took a seat. I told him he was checked in. Then I went back up to the desk.

"Scooter, it's obvious this gentleman didn't understand you. Maybe next time you can think of him like your grandfather or father, and treat him with respect. If it wasn't for him, you wouldn't have anyone to get an unnecessary attitude with."

"Girl, bye. You ain't my supervisor." *Really? This pop tart is getting an attitude with the wrong one!*

"You are very right." As I looked past him I noticed his supervisor's name on a plaque. As soon as I got back to the lab I emailed her and told what had transpired.

When I returned to work Monday at midnight I had an email from Lucy.

> Carol,
> It was brought to my attention by Sally, the Urology Manager, that you went above and beyond to help a Veteran out Friday. She said that her staff had blown the guy off but you physically walked him to his appointment to make sure he didn't miss it. She wanted me to tell you she made it a point to talk to Mr. Smalls after his appointment. He couldn't stop talking about how he wished there were more people like you that worked at the hospital.
>
> Good job! Keep it the good work.
>
> Lucy

That's nice! Crazy that I get a pat on the back for something that was normal practice at every other VA I'd worked at.

My first week on nights was straightforward but hell on my internal clock. I was late a couple of times because I called myself trying to catch a 'quick' nap at 10:00 pm knowing I would be cutting it close because I had to shower, get dressed, and drive forty minutes to make it by midnight.

"One week down," Adam said as I walked into the house Saturday morning.

"I know. I'm exhausted." I sat down on the sofa. Adam took my shoes off and started massaging my feet. "Thank you. That feels amazing."

163

"I know working nights isn't fun but something better will open up soon. This is just a stepping stone."

"I hope so. This is only the first week, and I'm already over it. I'm going to take a quick shower."

As I walked to the bathroom I could feel my stress level slowly rising. *Why am I freaking myself out? Nothing bad has happened.*

I turned on the shower to let the water heat up. The combination of steam and calming lavender scent engulfed my senses. I instantly could feel my nerves and the tension in my shoulders melt away.

"Hey babe, are you almost done?" Adam asked as he peeked his head in the shower.

"I'll be out in a minute. Thank you for putting the lavender pellet in the shower for me."

"You're welcome."

I forced myself to get out of the shower a few seconds after Adam left. As soon as I opened the shower door I could smell bacon. I dried off quickly and threw on a comfy pair of yoga pants and a tank top.

"Wow! You really outdid yourself this morning. What did I do to deserve this?" The kitchen table had a smorgasbord of food beautifully laid out. Golden Belgian waffles, pancakes, thick cut bacon, scrambled eggs, and mango punch were staring at me.

"I wanted you to get a good breakfast in your belly before you lay down."

I walked over to the sink where he was rinsing out a skillet before putting it in the dishwasher and hugged him from behind. He dried his hands and turned around. He placed a delicate kiss on my forehead as he led me by the hand to the table.

I placed a Belgian waffle along with some scrambled eggs and a few slices of bacon on my plate and dug it. Adam poured us two glasses of mango punch before he sat down and started eating.

"Thank you so much. This was absolutely delicious. I love you so much."

"You're welcome. I love you too. I'll clean all this stuff up. Why don't you head to bed?" Adam started clearing the table.

"I can help clean the kitchen, then I'll head to bed."

Thirty minutes later, I was fast asleep in our pitch black bedroom.

****

About two months in, I was working in hematology when a nurse from the ICU came down to get a unit of blood for a patient.

She rang the bell that was clearly marked to ring only if no one was in the lab. "I'm right here," I said slightly annoyed. This nurse had the tendency to make everything a big deal. Her name was Betty, and us night shifters nicknamed her BB for Bothersome Betty. Considering this was my tenth consecutive night at work, I wasn't in the mood to deal with BB's attitude. The faster I could get her in and out the better.

"I saw you with your head down and assumed you were asleep." *Really? That's her first assumption.*

I chose to ignore her stupid comment, "Who are you here to pick up blood for?"

"Mr. Williamson." Before I could get to the fridge she was already opening it looking for Mr. Williamson's unit of blood.

"Betty, everyone down here has told you that you can't go into the fridge. Can you please wait?" I rolled my eyes. *I wonder how much trouble I'd get in if I rolled this piece of paper up and hit her while saying no repeatedly. She's worse than an untrained puppy.*

I walked over to the fridge and pulled out the unit of blood. Then I started getting all the paperwork organized so that we could check name, social security number and other pertinent information together to ensure she was picking up the right unit for the right patient. As I was getting everything ready, I noticed out the corner of my eye that

Betty had already started checking stuff off. If it wasn't a FDA regulation that two people had to check off the information, I would have let her do her thing, but since I had to do it I was annoyed she couldn't wait ten seconds for me to get organized.

"I'm responsible for making sure Mr. Williamson gets his blood in a timely fashion," Betty said.

"I understand. If I didn't have to explain this procedure to you every time you came down here, you'd get the blood a lot faster. Patience is a virtue." *If she didn't have it, she'd learn by the time I was done with her.*

"Humph, I miss Michael," she said under her breath. Michael was the tech who I had replaced. He had been with the VA thirty plus years and to say he didn't give an eff about work was putting it lightly. There were plenty of times he issued the wrong blood product for the wrong patient or didn't call a critical result to a doctor. After three years of mess-ups, Lucy finally had enough ammunition to get rid of him. Though Michael should have been fired, he was allowed to retire because lazy Lucy didn't want to fill out all of the termination paperwork.

"I'm sure Michael misses you too. Are you ready to go over the forms?" I asked.

As we finished up, I had BB sign in the designated area showing she had picked up the unit of blood, and I signed under her signature.

"Your signature isn't legible," she said abrasively. "Hospital policy says it must be legible." *Me not spelling my entire last name is against hospital 'policy' but her trying to take the blood without going through the proper checks established by FDA is ok? Breathe!*

"If I'm able to cash checks with this signature I'm sure it's fine here."

"Humph."

"Have a good night Betty," I said as she walked out the lab.

As I was pulling into the garage once I got off, it dawned on me the next day was Thanksgiving. I didn't have anything to prepare a dinner for me and Adam. I threw my car in reverse to head to the grocery store.

"Hey Carol," Jules, our next door neighbor, said as she was waving to get my attention. "Do you and Adam have plans for Thanksgiving?"

"Actually we don't. I just got off a ten-day stretch. I'm heading to the store now."

"You guys are welcome to cover over tomorrow. We plan on having dinner around five o'clock. Since the weather is going to be so nice we are going to set up tables out back." *Thank you Jesus!*

"Thank you for the invite! What can we bring?"

"Your appetites." *I can do that.*

"We can't come over and eat all your food without bringing anything. We'll bring some adult beverages."

"Great. See you guys tomorrow."

I pulled back into the garage and texted Adam to pick up a case of beer on his way home before laying down.

****

Adam and I decided to take a trip to Las Vegas at the end of December to meet up with his cousin who was going to be in town for a college basketball tournament. Halfway through the trip, I started experiencing very intense cramps. When we returned I called to schedule an appointment at the VA. I was told there was no availability for three months, and that I would be put on an appointment waiting list. If someone were to cancel between now and my appointment date they would give me a call. *Three months? That's a long time.*

Each week I started to feel progressively worse. I kept calling the appointment line hoping someone had cancelled or that more appointment times had opened. To no avail, that didn't happen.

I drudged through the next couple of months. Adam and I's interactions were growing less and less. There were times where we would cross paths for about two hours before he would lay down for the night, and I would head off to work.

The ten-day stretches were starting to take a toll on my physical well-being. It seemed like if I didn't have a cold, I had some other kind of ailment. I had only had the flu one other time in life, but managed to get the flu twice while working here. The first time lasted a week, and the second time it lasted a week and a half. My cramping issues started to get to the point where I would call out sick or leave work in the middle of my shift because I could barely stand up straight.

After eight months of working night shift, I couldn't take it any longer. Between the ten day stretches, numerous vacation requests being denied, and working opposite Adam's schedule I felt like if one more thing were added to the equation I was going to breakdown.

"One of my evening shift workers is going to be gone for a month to Thailand. And a couple of the other people are going to be out for a day or two for surgery or personal reasons," Lucy explained after we had gone over my mid-year performance evaluation.

"I'm just asking for two days, yet Mayling can have an entire month off?"

"Well, she does it every year so I know when to expect it."

"Ok. Still seems like a lot of favoritism is going on."

"I don't want you to think I'm playing favorites because I want everyone to have time off." *I don't have to 'think' anything, it's obvious.* "Since I have you in the office I wanted to let you know that I'm going to need you to go upstairs to draw some patients' blood within the next couple of days. Phlebotomy is short staffed because several of them are out with the flu." *You've got to be kidding me?! You deny my leave request and now you expect me to draw patients' blood. Umm NO!*

"I don't think that's a good idea. I'm still not a hundred percent over the flu myself. I know I did a brief 'training' session in the outpatient lab before I started nights, but I've heard horror stories about the patients' veins upstairs. Even some of the most skilled phlebotomists have come down and said they had to stick a patient several times to get blood."

"Yea I know it seems daunting, but it would be maybe a day or two and you'd probably have to do six or seven patients max." *Seem daunting? That is daunting for someone who can't draw blood. This is the last straw!*

"Ok." *I'm not drawing one damn patient.*

Two days later, Lucy told me as she was leaving for the night that I would have to go up and draw nine patients in ICU during morning rounds. *NINE patients in ICU! Those are the sickest of the sick. I guess she didn't hear a thing I said the last few times we talked.*

Six am rolls around, the time phlebotomists head upstairs to draw patients. Lucy had obviously emailed the head phlebotomist to let her know I was going to be joining them.

"Carol, we are heading upstairs to draw. Are you ready?" Trina, the lead phlebotomist, asked.

"I'm not drawing any patients. I'm still not over the flu," I responded.

"Then why did Lucy email me saying you were going to help?"

"Good question. You should ask her because I told her I was still sick."

Trina and the rest of the phlebotomists left grumbling curse words under their breaths because that meant they'd have to draw more patients. *Oh well! I'm not going to get Vets who are already sick, sicker because management doesn't know how to call a temp agency to get phlebotomists in here!*

A few days later, I caught Lucy before she left for the night. "Lucy, I want to let you know that April fourth will be my last day."

"What! Why?" Lucy exclaimed in utter shock.

"This job has just taken a toll on my physically. I don't think I can continue to work this shift and the long stretches."

169

"Night shift is fully staffed now so you guys haven't had to work ten-day stretches in over a month."

"I have to take care of my health. I've never been sick this often in eight months. I've had the flu two times in three months."

"I really appreciate you giving me a month's notice, but between you and me, I hired you with the hopes you'd fill my position when I retire next year. That's why I gave you such a great review on your performance report." *People will say anything to keep an employee.*

I chuckled because there's no way I'd take her position. Her bratty evening shifters would hate me. No more two-hour lunches as a 'group.' No more favoritism. All that would be shut down! "That's nice you have confidence in me to take over your duties, but I need to take care of me."

"What are you going to do for money?" *Nosy much!*

"Trust me when I say, I've thought this through."

"Ok. I'm sad that you're leaving. You have been an extremely hard worker. I know your fellow night shifters are going to be upset when you tell them."

"I'm going to miss them, but like I said I need to get healthy. I'll send my official resignation to you via email for your records."

"Ok. Man, I'm really going to miss you," Lucy said as she started to gather her things to leave for the night.

That night I told my fellow night shifters that I was leaving. They took it as well as expected.

The next few weeks flew by; I guess because I could see the light at the end of the tunnel. The week before my last day, there were VA police cars blocking off a large area of the parking lot. I drove around the blockade and made my way to my normal parking spot. As I was getting out of my car a police officer approached me.

"Ma'am, you can't park here."

"I work the night shift. My car will be gone by the time patients start coming in the morning," I responded. I knew that I where I parked was designated as patient parking, but there were no outpatient clinics open at midnight so I knew I was fine parking there.

"I need you to park on the north side of the hospital tonight. We haven't finished our investigation."

"Investigation?"

"There was an incident this afternoon, and we are still investigating." *I hope they bring in real cops because these idiots don't know what they're doing half the time.*

"Fine." I drove my car to the north side of the hospital and found a spot. *Now I'm going to have to come down here around 6:00 am to move my car. Augh!*

When I got upstairs I started doing the daily maintenance on one of the analyzers. About ten minutes later Peter, my partner for the night, came in and asked me where I parked.

"I parked on the north side. Did Barney Fife make you park there too?"

"Yea. Did he tell you want happened?"

"No and I didn't ask. Didn't want to slow down their 'investigation.'" *I knew Peter asked. If he saw something going on he was quick to ask what the deal was.*

"You know I asked." *Knew it!* "Turns out a Vet shot himself in the head in his car this afternoon. Barney said the guy left a note and it said something like maybe now you'll take Vets seriously when they say they need to see someone in mental health."

I dropped the bottle of reagent I was holding and it bounced off the analyzer I was standing next to, "What the f--? I know the wait times are long, but that's crazy."

"Yea. He said the note mentioned her highness, Susan."

"Damn. He called people out in his suicide note. I can't believe this. It seems like a scene out of a movie."

The news shook me. It was the first time since I had started that I made several mistakes throughout the night. After Peter finished telling me what else Barney had said, I started to clean up the sticky reagent that had run down the front side of the analyzer and formed a pool of yellow liquid. Just as I finished cleaning up that mess, the phone rang and as I turned to answer it managed to knock over four patient urine samples. I ran from the lab and headed straight to the restroom. *Take a deep breath, Carol.*

Breathing did absolutely nothing. I found myself consumed with the same bundle of nerves and anxiety I had experienced after my first week on nights. All I could do to release the tension was cry. I sat in the restroom for twenty minutes balling my eyes out for a Veteran I had never met. My heart hurt for this man who's only immediate need was to talk to someone. I collected myself and splashed cold water on my face. I vowed to myself to continue to serve the Veterans who had blood work to the best of my ability.

My last physical day in the lab was April 4th, but due to the fact my leave had been denied so often, I had two weeks' worth of time-off. Rather than get a lump sum payment, I wanted to use it. About half way through my last paid week of vacation, the Phoenix VA was all over the news. What started off as a local daily story quickly turned into a national media frenzy. Forty Vets died while waiting for care on a 'fake' waiting list. *Fake' waiting list? I'd been told I had been placed on a waiting list. Granted I never got a call, but why are they calling it fake?*

For a week and a half, I was glued to the TV. Upper management had been dimed out by a former VA employee who was tired of seeing Veterans die at the hands of unscrupulous people. This employee had been terminated because she was running too many tests on Veterans that came in through the ER. She figured she'd help them out since they couldn't get a regular primary care appointment.

Susan Stegers was put on paid administrative leave for seven months before she was officially fired. Her second in charge locked himself in his home threatening to kill himself after being terminated from his position. After the police broke down his front door and sprayed him with pepper spray, he came to his senses and realized how cowardly that would have been. Two additional men on Susan's management team were placed on paid administrative leave for nearly two years. As of December 2015, they have been reinstated into their old positions. *Thank God I abandoned that ship before it went down.*

Once I left the Phoenix VA, I had a completely different outlook about the entire VA system. I had worked with my fair share of dirty people before when I was in DC, but never on this level. It's hard for me to grasp that people in the VA healthcare system were so caught up in meeting performance measures, that are set by men and women far removed from patient care, that they were willing to compromise lives and morals to achieve these metrics. If it weren't for the men and women who sacrificed legs, arms, sanity, and time with their families the VA wouldn't exist and these dirty, corrupt managers wouldn't have jobs.

I was beyond ecstatic when I said bye bye crooks!

The Biggest Loser

While I enjoyed my paid time off, I fully intended on taking advantage of every second of free time. One of the first things I did was book a ticket to go see Ann and her family back east. Her and her husband recently welcomed their second child into the world, and I was excited to meet him. God truly was looking out for our family's finances because I was able to find a plane ticket for $285. *To this day, I've never been able to find a ticket that cheap!* Between kissing on my nephew's chubby sweet cheeks and playing with my niece who was growing like a weed, the week I spent there flew by.

Upon my return to Arizona, I decided to start volunteering at a Meals on Wheels nonprofit and a food bank a few times a week. My stress level had dramatically gone down, my sleep pattern had returned to normal, and I really felt like I was contributing something of value to society. Most importantly, Adam and I were spending more quality time together without me being a hazy fog of sleep deprivation.

About a month and a half into my 'lady of leisure' lifestyle, I received a call about an interview for a Consumer Safety Officer (CSO) position I had applied for prior to quitting the VA. *Did I really want to go back to work? We weren't struggling financially like I initially thought we would.*

"Hey babe," I said as Adam walked in the front door from work. "How was your day? Guess what?"

"Long. I'm beat. What?" He replied as he kissed me on the forehead and sat down on the sofa next to me.

"I got a call today about an interview. It would be working for FDA. What do you think?"

"I told you that you wouldn't be out of work long. You are an amazing worker. Anyone would be foolish not to swoop you up. What's the job?"

"Consumer safety officer. Funny thing is, I don't even remember applying for it. When I went back on usajobs.com and read the description it doesn't even sound remotely interesting. I think I just applied for it because it would get me back to the salary I was making in Maryland."

"What would you be doing?"

"That's a good question. I couldn't really get a good grasp on what I would be doing based on the description. We'll see when I go to the interview, which is next Tuesday."

"You'll do great. Since you don't know much about the job maybe you can do a little research to prepare yourself."

As we talked more about the interview, we moved to the kitchen where I prepared a quick dinner of spaghetti and meat sauce, a small side salad, and homemade garlic bread. Bellies full and kitchen cleaned, we moved back to the living room to watch *The Real Housewives of Atlanta* as we snuggled on the sofa.

The next day I followed Adam's advice and searched for information about the job on FDA's website. I texted one of my friends in Maryland and told her that I had an interview for a CSO position. At one point in her career, she worked in the area of FDA that my interview was in,

Office of Regulatory Affairs (ORA). She also was really close friends with a director of one of the divisions in ORA. I asked my friend if she could ask her friend what kinds of questions the hiring manager may ask. She reported back to me, and I made sure to write everything down so I wouldn't forget.

Interview day came. I was as prepared as I was going to be. The office was only twelve miles from our house and approximately two blocks from Arizona State University. There were kids on skateboards, bikes and walking everywhere despite the dark sky. The sky looked like at any point it was going to open up. *It never rains in Phoenix. What is going on? Is this a sign I don't need to go back to work?*

Unlike most federal offices, this one was located in an office building that housed an array of different businesses. Luckily, there was a parking garage attached to the building because as soon as I parked my car, thunder and lightning commenced, and the sky unleashed a torrential downpour. I rode the swanky elevator to the second floor and rang the doorbell located outside of the office. I was able to see a tall African American woman approach the door through the glass windows. She escorted me through two locked doors, introduced herself as Donna Simpleton, the office supervisor, and told me to sign in on the visitor's log sheet. *This is the FDA not the CIA, what's up with the two locked doors and sign in sheet?* Four steps later, I was in the conference room where Monique Maxim, the Director of the Investigations Branch for the Los Angeles district, was waiting.

Introductions were made, but before the true interview questions started, Monique told me a little about what the job would entail. If hired, I would be performing inspections at manufacturing companies that were regulated by FDA. *I applied for this? Doesn't seem like something I'd be remotely interested in, but it's a job. Plus, I'll get back to my old salary.*

Monique said, "The job requires a lot of travel, stateside and internationally, and at times the candidate would work odd hours." *A lot of travel is cool when you're twenty-something. I'm in my mid-thirties and very comfortable going to work from seven to three thirty and calling it a day.*

176

Monique asked, "Are you ok working on Sundays?" *Wasn't this a federal job? I just left a job where I had to work weekends. My senses were increasingly moving towards thanks but no thanks.* "By working, I mean traveling. Most travel days are Sundays. That way you can start an inspection or training first thing Monday morning."

"Sure, not a problem." *Whew. I wasn't feeling a true work day on a Sunday.*

Monique proceeded to read the job description to me. *Pay attention, pay attention!* She then asked me to repeat what I'd heard and understood. That little mantra kind of worked. I say kind of because once I finished what I felt was a good summary of the eight-minute job description she read she kept prompting me with "And?"

Approximately twenty minutes in, we finally got to the real interview questions. "What does FDA regulate?" Monique started off with. *For real, that's the first question?*

I raised my eyebrows as I responded, "Food, drugs and cosmetics."

"Can you be more specific?" Donna questioned as she sucked her teeth with annoyance. *Y'all did read my resume and see I worked at FDA in the past for four years right?*

"Human and animal drugs and pretty much all food with the exception of meat, unless it's 'exotic' meat." I guess that was a better answer because they moved on to the next question.

"Tell us about a time when –," type questions went on for a couple of minutes. Then rather abruptly Donna asked, "Why have you had so many jobs in the last couple of years?" *Really? I haven't had 'so' many jobs, but ok.*

"I enlisted for three years in the Air Force. Once I separated from the military, I moved to Houston where I accepted a job at M.D. Anderson Cancer Center. I left that position for a GS eleven position at the Baltimore VA hospital, which I didn't have to interview for. The VA has a year-long program that allows current VA employees to see how a hospital is run from the top down. I applied for it and was accepted. After the year was up, the VA would either place a person in a position or he/she could find their own job. I decided to find my own job, which is when I started at the FDA in Laurel, MD. I left that position because my husband's position brought us out here."

Monique asked, "Why did you leave the Phoenix VA hospital?"

"Have you been watching the news?" I said matter-of-factly. Both women gave each other a look that screamed 'No she didn't just say that to us.' Monique's face said it all but she asked for more clarification.

"It was a night position. The supervisor showed favoritism to her evening shift staff. She would let them take off whenever they wanted but would deny night shift staff's requests on a regular. Plus, it wasn't a healthy place to work." I could tell both women weren't too happy with my initial response. *Oh well.*

I noticed Donna's posture became tense when she asked, "Does your husband's job move him a lot?" *What kind of question is that? Even if the answer was yes, they move us every year on the dot, did they really think I was going to say that?*

I knew we'd be in Arizona two years max, but I replied, "We will be here awhile."

"We don't have any more questions," Donna said. "Do you have any questions or concerns for us?" *Not really because I really don't think I'd be a good fit for this job, but since I prepared for this interviewed I better ask a couple.*

I asked a few questions about how training was conducted since Donna had previously mentioned the candidate is on probation for a year and must pass an audit before being kept on permanently. *A year? What are we doing, learning how to start a manufacturing company ourselves?*

After I asked all my questions Donna began to talk about salary. "Are you ok coming on as a GS nine?" *Not really. I just left a GS-9 position.*

"I'd prefer to come on as close as possible to the grade I was in Maryland, which was a twelve."

Donna exhaled loudly and replied, "Because this position has different phases the highest we could bring you on would be a GS eleven." *That's not true. Yet another ignorant supervisor talking about salary issues but doesn't know the facts.*

"Eleven it is," I said.

Throughout the entire interview, I was never able to gauge how well I was doing. Donna had perfected resting bitch face, and when she did show any kind of emotion it was pure annoyance. I even caught her staring at my hair a few times while Monique was asking me questions. She was definitely sizing me up.

Walking out of there I was about 99% sure I didn't get the job. Crazy thing was, I wasn't even upset like I had been on several other interviews I'd had since quitting the VA. I was really enjoying my time volunteering and spending quality time with Adam. The only reason I would accept this job if it was offered to me was for the money. Inspecting manufacturers wasn't something I was remotely interested in, but I did like the thought of a steady paycheck. I was so sure I didn't get the job I called Adam and said, "I'm going to book our tickets to San Diego for Labor Day weekend."

Two weeks later

"Hello."

"May I speak to Carol?"

"This is she."

"Hi. My name is Maria Walters. I'm calling from the Los Angeles FDA regional office. You have been selected for the CSO position you interviewed for a few weeks ago at the Tempe resident post."

"Ok," I replied with absolutely no enthusiasm. *Humph, I got the job.*

"Are you still interested in the position?" Maria questioned.

"Sure," I aloofly responded.

Maria confirmed my email and mailing addresses. She also informed me I would need to get fingerprinted and have a background investigation ran. I figured the process would be quick since I had just had a background check and fingerprints done at the VA a few months ago. If they couldn't get that information from the VA, my fingerprints were on file at FDA headquarters back in Maryland.

"Great. When would you like your start date to be?" Maria asked.

"July 28." *That gives me a month to get my mind right about working again.*

When I received my tentative offer letter I was pleasantly surprised to see that I was being offered the highest grade the job had been advertised at. *I was back to my old salary in Maryland. Strike one for Donna. She didn't know what she was talking about.*

Once my background investigation and fingerprints cleared, I was formally offered the job two weeks later. *I had to have both redone AND pay for it out of my own pocket.* I received an email from Maria congratulating and instructing me on how to complete the mandatory computer security training. I had to complete this training prior to starting on the 28th, otherwise, I wouldn't be able to log on to the network. After I completed the training, which literally took me seven minutes, I made sure to advantage of the next four weeks of free time.

****

The day had arrived. I really had no idea what to expect when I arrived at the office. The only instruction I received was to be there at 8:00 am. This was the first time I had ever lived within twenty minutes from work. *This was going to be amazing!*

I arrived a little early and rang the doorbell. "Good morning," I said when Donna opened the door. She was wearing a pants suit that was a little too snug. When I had interviewed she had braids, but now she was rocking an asymmetrical bob, very 1987 Salt 'n Pepa.

"Hi," she mumbled. *Ok someone isn't a morning person. Mental note made.* "This is Lori Musselman. Today is her first day also. You two are the first of my new hires. I hired two more people and one will be starting in two weeks. The other at the end of August."

The office had enough space to seat twenty-two employees. At the time Lori and I started, there were only nine people in the office. Three of which were rarely around, as their positions required them to travel out of the country at least three weeks a month. The Tempe resident post had seen a recent turnover of employees who had either quit, transferred to another agency or were harassed to the point they decided to retire.

After the brief introductions, Donna showed Lori and I to the conference room where we watched the new employee orientation via live broadcast from Silver Spring, MD. The orientation was a few hours each morning for two days. Our first afternoon consisted of setting up our cubicles the way we wanted and getting to know each other. I learned Lori was from South Dakota and had done ten years in the Marine Corps. She was a petite red-head whose hair was always in place, makeup flawless, outfit flattering with heels to match. She consistently showed the utmost respect to people in authority, and rarely if ever, did she question Donna's instruction. She was truly the opposite of me, but we clicked instantly.

Mary Bachelors was the office's consumer safety technician (CST), basically a glorified secretary. She handled all administrative duties for the office. Her most important role was office timekeeper. About half way through my third week, I overheard Mary talking on the phone. I had perfected the art of blocking out other people's conversations while sharing an office with Beth, but when I heard my name my ears perked up.

"Carol may not get paid next week." *WHAT?!*

"The people working in payroll are having some issues with your account. You may not get paid next Friday," she said as she walked past my cubicle towards the copy room.

I jumped up and headed to the copy room. "Who do I need to call to get this straightened out?" I asked.

"I just spoke to the person who handles this office's payroll issues. She isn't sure what the problem is. I hope you have some money saved up." She said with a giggle. *No she's not laughing.*

"Ok," I said. Rather than show my fiery side, I decided to walk away. I went to Donna and asked her who I needed to speak to resolve this problem as quickly as possible.

"Mary is the timekeeper. She can help you." She didn't look away from her computer screen.

"Mary wasn't very much help. She just told me she hoped I had some money saved."

She stopped typing. "She said that?"

"Yes."

She rose from her desk and replied, "I'll take care of it." Before I could get settled back at my desk, I heard Donna march into the copy room and demand an explanation as to why I wasn't going to get paid. *Little did I know that I just added fuel to an already intense fire.*

The rest of the day Mary gave me the cold shoulder. I never intended on getting her in trouble but that paycheck was the only reason I came in every morning. This position was far from my dream job. The only reason I accepted the position was to feel like I was contributing to Adam and I's family. We weren't hurting for money, but I didn't get married with the intentions of being a 'kept' woman.

The two new employees Donna had mentioned to Lori and I started approximately a month after us. They were Public Health Service (PHS) officers. PHS officers are people who usually have a medical or science background. The program is set up similar to the military except they don't deploy overseas nor do they carry weapons. They usually deploy to areas in the US where a natural disaster has occurred. Plus, their training is way less intense than any military boot camp (even COT). They can be recognized by the Navy uniform they wear. Jacob Paul was a radiologist by training and had worked on a reservation in southern New Mexico. Melissa Jones was a pharmacist by training and also worked on a reservation in Oklahoma for ten years. Lori and I made sure to help them out with anything we could to make their onboarding experience a lot easier than ours had been. The four of us quickly become extremely close.

Several weeks into the job, Donna and I had a meeting to go over my performance management appraisal requirements. "As you can see the elements you are required to meet are self-explanatory. Once you pass your level one audit, I'll hold you accountable for the items on this list. For right now, I want you to concentrate on getting all the training modules done. When you are completely trained I expect your accomplishment hours for completing a task to decrease. For example, if something takes you twenty hours to do now, it should take you less time to complete a year from now. Does that make sense?"

"Yes. What are some things I need to do to get the highest rating? At all my previous jobs I have always exceeded expectations and would like to do the same in this position." I replied.

With a slight huff, she leaned back in her chair, crossed her arms, and replied, "It's very hard to get the highest rating. I've been in this position for almost two years and have done a lot. I've managed to get rid of employees who weren't carrying their weight. I have acted for Monique and several other supervisors in their absence. Yet, I have only gotten a meets standards rating. I brought it up to Monique at my last performance meeting, and she wouldn't budge. I had to respect her decision." *I could have sworn I asked what do I have to do, not what did you do.* "When I talked to your references everyone gave you rave reviews. I don't doubt you'll do a good job in this position, but it's unlikely I'll give you the highest rating because there is always room for improvement." *Always room for improvement sounds like a cop out for not praising people they way they deserve.*

She continued, "In order to get that highest rating you would have to do an inspection that lead to the company getting a warning letter or getting shut down."

"How is my performance going to be rated based on someone else's decision? As a CSO, it's my job to collect 'evidence' of wrong-doing. Doesn't compliance handle disciplinary action for companies?" I felt my palms start to sweat.

"I worked as a compliance officer before I took this position and –," I crossed my arms and started out the window behind her. *How is it that she can make everything about her?*

Donna's annoying sucking teeth habit snapped me back into reality, "I am going to need you to type up a little blurb about what Mary said to you about your check. I also need for you to write up something about the two Mary 'incidents.'" *She totally didn't answer my question, and now she wants something from me?*

Mary incident #1: The day one of the guest inspectors left he brought pizza for the office as a token of appreciation for us welcoming him to the office. After he gave a speech and everyone got their pizza, Mary decided to give an 'I hate Donna' monolog. I didn't like the pizza nor did I want to hear Mary's mouth so I decided to exit stage left.

Mary incident #2: I overheard Mary cursing like a sailor on the phone one afternoon. I don't know who she was talking to, but I knew it had something to do with Donna because she had just left Mary's cubicle. Whatever Donna asked or told Mary to do had her in an uproar.

I am a firm believer of 'no snitching.' Even though I wrote a brief memo about the two incidents I didn't feel bad about it because both times she had done stuff in front of multiple people. Little did I know that Donna was trying to get rid of Mary and was using these incidents as ammunition to fire her. I'm all for getting rid of lazy people, but from the short amount of time I had interacted with Mary she had proven to be useful, except for the payroll incident. Had I known at the time Donna's 'request' was against union rules I would have never done it.

****

After years of going to the doctor, taking pill after pill, and having multiple failed procedures I found out that I needed a hysterectomy. I'd been diagnosed with several conditions over the years: ovarian cysts, endometriosis, and menorrhagia. It wasn't until I had a pelvic MRI done that I was diagnosed with adenomyosis, a condition where uterine tissue burrows into the surrounding muscle and acts like it's still in the uterus. The tissue continues to thicken, break down, and bleed, thus causing excruciating pain. The news was devastating to me and Adam.

Here we were only three years into our marriage and hit with the news that we would never have a traditional family.

I had only been at the job for two months and didn't have much sick leave. I was going to be on leave without pay status. With the advance of technology, I would only be out for two weeks. Honestly, I didn't mind being off from work because I wasn't really feeling the job. My one concern was having to tell Donna. *I like to keep my personal issues just that, personal.*

"You need to tell her what kind of surgery you're having," Adam said once we both had come to the realization that this was really happening.

"You know I don't like telling people my business. Especially this woman. I guarantee you she is going to find a way to turn this whole situation around and make it about her."

"You never know she may be sympathetic and let you work from home. That way you don't have to be on leave without pay status." *Yea right. That would make too much sense and require thinking outside of the box. She's not that type of manager.*

I decided to listen to Adam's advice. The next day I went into Donna's office. "Do you have a second?" I asked.

"Sure," she said as she shuffled papers around her messy desk. *How did she find anything in this office?*

"I'm going to be out of the office for two weeks starting on the 23rd. I have to have a hysterectomy." *Ah that was painful. Hate telling my business!!*

She stopped shuffling her papers. "I had a hysterectomy nine months ago in Dallas. I didn't know any doctors out here so I decided to have my gynecologist there do it. I spent the first two weeks of healing in Dallas, then came back here. A couple of days after I got back I was having horrible pain and went to the ER. I was admitted on the spot and spent a week in the hospital. I gained thirty pounds of fluid and had to have an additional surgery." *Ummm, really! I knew she was going to make it about her, but did she really have to tell me this horror story.*

185

When she saw my eyes start to roll she said, "I'm going to need a note from the doctor saying how long you're going to be out of the office." *Strike two. Thanks for the empathy! I just told you how long I was going to be out. Oh yeah, you probably didn't hear me over your own story!*

She emailed me a few minutes later and asked me if I was all right. *Why wouldn't I be?*

I civilly responded with I'm fine. *Too little too late. I'm a one and done type of girl.* From that point on it was a downward spiral.

$$* * * * * * * * * *$$

My recovery was a lot easier than I anticipated. Adam did a great job of taking care of me and things around the house. I actually enjoyed my two weeks off. I was able to get hooked on another reality show – *Naked and Afraid.*

I dreaded returning to the office. Upon my return Donna called a staff meeting. "The Tucson office is closing because the lease on the space is up. I'm going to need two of you to come with me to clean the office out."

"How far is Tucson from here?" I asked.

"It's about an hour and a half," Lori said.

"Lori and Carol, I want to take you two with me tomorrow. This way Jacob and Melissa can catch up with where you two are on computer based training modules." *I'm done with all the modules. And how is one day of Lori and I being gone going to allow them to catch up when we had a month and a half head start? I guess!*

"Ok," Lori and I said unison.

"What time would you two like to leave?" Donna asked

"Any time is fine with me," Lori replied.

"We can leave at seven," I replied.

"I'd like to leave at six am," Donna countered. *Why did you ask what time do we want to leave and then suggest a different time?* Technically, she wasn't allowed to change our work schedule with only a day notice - union rules.

"That's too early for me," I replied. "I can do six-thirty."

She rolled her eyes and with a huff said, "Ok, six-thirty."

The next day I arrived a little bit before 6:30 am. When I walked past Donna's office, her door was locked, and the lights were out. *Great! Doesn't look like we are going to be leaving on time.* Lori arrived a few minutes later.

"Hey girl. She's not even here yet," I said as I rolled my eyes and took a sip of my coffee.

"Go figure. I'll go get the SUV ready. That way by the time she gets here we can get on the road," Lori said.

"Great idea."

Seven o'clock comes and goes. Finally, Donna emailed me and Lori around 7:30 am stating due to personal issues she wouldn't be in that day. *Are you kidding me?*

The second attempt to go to Tucson happened a few weeks later. Once again, we agreed to meet at the office for a 6:30 am departure. We arrived at the Tucson office at 8:00 am. When Donna unlocked the office door I thought I was going to pass out. The office space was approximately 450 square feet and to say it was messy would be an understatement. This office made the people's homes on *Hoarders* look like Martha Stewart's house in the Hamptons. *How in the world did three CSOs work in this chaos?*

"I know this place is a mess, but we need to get rid of everything in here," Donna instructed. "We need to keep everything that's important. Inspectional records are held for ten years." *No one has been in this office for months. Is anything really that important?*

We began to rifle through the stacks of paperwork. A lot of the stuff was so old it was yellow. Thirty minutes into decluttering Donna said, "Oh I forgot to tell you if you see anything union related set that to the side. It doesn't matter how old it is. Don't show it to me because I'm technically not allowed to handle union documents." *For once she got something right!*

Donna had several grievances filed against her so needless to say there was one section of the office that was full of documents with her name on them.

Five more trips were made to Tucson over the course of a few months. I was lucky enough to only go on one of them. Each time Donna took her place in the back seat as if we were driving Miss Daisy. Prior to the last trip, Donna had mentioned she probably should have taken Jacob and Melissa for all of the trips. If the union President found out she had seen union files and wanted to take her to court, Jacob and Melissa wouldn't have to testify because they couldn't be represented by the union. However, Lori and I would have to testify since we could receive union benefits. *Duh, she was such an idiot.*

Bob Gross, the union President, seemed to be a semi-organized person. I started going through his area of the office when we arrived. He had four large filing cabinets labeled accordingly and within each filing cabinet, he had folders that were also labeled. *If it's older than 2010 I don't care what it is it's getting tossed. If he wanted all this crap he would have taken it with him when he left.*

I made sure to keep his investigation paperwork separate from the union files. I was finishing the last drawer in the second filing cabinet when I came across a 1985 *Penthouse* magazine. I pulled the drawer out further and found lube and a crusty towel. *Thank you Lori for bringing gloves today!* Further back in the drawer I found more naughty magazines and what appeared to be old love letters from someone who lived in El Paso, Texas dating back to the 1990s. I showed Donna this and she quickly emailed Monique. Monique told her to pack all of those things up and bring them back to the office in Tempe. *Can Donna make a decision without having to run it past Monique – ever?*

We finally finished going through everything. The only thing left in the office that day was the dingy 1970s furniture. *HOORAY! I would never have to come back to this office again.*

Donna summoned me to her office a few minutes after we had unloaded everything from the SUV. "Monique would like you to take pictures of all the items you found and write up a short memo detailing each item. Once you've done that you can pack everything in a box and mail it to Bob."

"Ok," I said. "As far as taking pictures and saving them, I don't want porn on my computer so I'll save them to a CD."

"It's ok, don't worry about it." Donna tried to say in a reassuring tone. *I'm no fool. I could get fired if that filth was found on my computer.*

"I emailed you the memo, and here's a CD with all the pictures I took," I said a few hours later.

"Why'd you burn a CD? I told you it was ok to keep them on your hard drive."

"Like I said earlier, I don't feel comfortable having that kind of stuff on my computer. I packed a box with all Bob's stuff. It's ready for FedEx to pick up."

"Thanks," Donna said curtly. She went back to the personal call she was on.

I really felt some kind of way about mailing those items back to Bob. This was just another one of Donna's mind games of trying to embarrass someone. She knew if he received a box with those contents, it would start a fight between him and his wife.

A few weeks later a mass email was sent out to the Los Angeles District employees from Bob Gross entitled, "My FDA journey has come to an end." In the email, Bob gave a brief summary of all the positions he held over his thirty plus year career with the FDA. He also announced that he would be retiring effective immediately. This came as a shock to many, even in our office, but the four of us knew he had been harassed to retire by Donna and Monique. Bob said his reason for retiring was due to health issues. He had suffered a major heart attack a few months back and recently his brother-in-law had just passed away from one. He did say he would continue to answer emails regarding union issues. *Interesting.*

****

Donna and I went on my first bioresearch monitoring program (BIMO) inspection in late November 2014. (BIMO inspections were to ensure doctors who participated in clinical trials were following the protocols correctly.) A week before we started the inspection, Donna called the doctor's office to let him know when we wanted to start the inspection. Since this was my first time she had me sit in her office as she made the call.

"Dr. Buress' office, how may I help you?" The receptionist said in a bubbly tone.

"This is Donna Simpleton calling from the Food and Drug Administration. I'm calling to let you know I'll be performing an inspection on the weight loss study Dr. Buress is participating in. I'll arrive this coming Monday."

"Ms. Simpleton, I need to check his schedule to see if Monday works for him. Can I get a phone number to call you back at?"

"There's no need. I'll be there at nine am. I will only need to speak to him briefly when I initially arrive to let him know what the scope of the inspection will be."

"Ms. Simpleton, Mondays are Dr. Buress' busiest day. He's in and out of surgery all morning."

"Like I just said, I only need to speak to him briefly. Please let him know I'll be there Monday at nine." *OMG! She has no clue about surgery times. He can't just leave a patient open on the table and come meet with us.*

"Ok," the receptionist hesitantly said. "I'll let him know."

"Bye." Donna disconnected from speakerphone. "When you schedule with these doctors you have to be stern, otherwise, they'll try to get you to come when it's convenient to them."

"Wouldn't that make more sense considering we need them to provide us with information?" I questioned.

"They have to provide us the information we ask for! It's the law," she snapped. *How many things are we supposed to do because it's the law but don't?*

"Ok." I wanted to say so much more, but figured since this was my first time I'd sit back and learn what *not* to do. Once I was out on my own, I would never speak to someone like she just had to that receptionist.

The doctor's office was in Scottsdale, AZ, which is normally a twenty-minute ride from the office. That day the traffic was horrible, and it ended up taking about forty-five minutes. *Why am I always stuck in a car with this woman?*

"How are you enjoying the job?" Donna asked as she was typing away on her cell phone in the passenger's seat. *Enjoy isn't a word I ever associate with work. She should ask how am I tolerating this job?*

"Fine."

"Thank you for stepping up and helping with some of Mary's responsibilities." She was now applying makeup. *How do chauffeurs deal with pompous people?*

"No problem," I responded.

"Mary is a troublemaker. She likes to stir the pot."

"Humph." I was trying my hardest not to engage in this gossipy behavior.

"She can't stand me," Donna said. *I wonder why?* "She said all the office managers she'd worked for in the past taught her something new. According to her, I haven't taught her anything. She's probably eating those words now after I made her do a sample collection." I could

191

definitely see Mary making that statement. *I know I'm learning what NOT to do from Donna.*

Mary had been out of the office on medical leave before I had gone out for my surgery. There was talk around the office that Mary had been diagnosed with Multiple Sclerosis. It was triggered from doing a sample collection in an extremely hot warehouse. Sample collections were rarely done by people in Mary's position but Donna had highly encouraged her to do it as a way of learning something 'new.'

"She said that to your face?"

"Of course not. Another CSO told me she said that."

"Basically, it's just gossip. You can't always trust people who run to tell you what others are saying about you. What are their motives?" *Unprofessional much?*

As we continued driving she started to talk about some of the other new hires. "Lori is going to be my workhorse. She seems eager to please whoever she works for. I like that." *Lord, come into this car and give me peace. Let me keep my eyes on the road and not get hostile. Amen.*

"What's your opinion of Melissa?" I gripped the steering wheel so tightly my knuckles started to ache.

"What do you mean what's my opinion?"

"What do you think about Melissa? She seems kind of timid, don't you think?" Donna questioned. I turned up the air condition in the car. I could feel my back getting damp.

I replied, "Melissa is not timid. She speaks when she has something valuable to add to a conversation. Plus, she's from the South, she's very lady-like and polite." *Ha, take that! I knew she was fishing for negative feedback.*

"I'm concerned that she's not going to do well in this position. It's a good thing she got promoted before getting this job because I wouldn't promote her." Donna had pulled out a nail file and was working on her nails. *Strike three. What in the world? I'm not your home girl who you can talk smack about others to.*

"Melissa is more than capable of doing this job. Just because she isn't aggressive doesn't mean she won't be a good CSO." I defended Melissa. *Hell, I would I have defended anyone at this point.*

"I don't know. It's just crazy to me that someone starts a new job and asks for a week off two months in," said Donna. *Ah the truth is coming out.*

"Well she did interview for the job back in January, right? She didn't start until August. She's planning a wedding so it's not like she could put her life on hold waiting to hear whether or not she got this job." Donna shifted in her seat.

Finally, we arrive at the doctor's office. I had never been so thankful to walk into a doctor's office until that moment. We were greeted by the study coordinator and QA manager. Dr. Buress joined us a few minutes later, at which time Donna explained the purpose of our visit, what information we planned on reviewing, and approximately how long it would take.

I don't know how Donna got through forty-five years of life speaking the way she did. At one point she said "We was looking through these papers." I stopped reviewing the document in front of me, took a deep breath, and excused myself from the conference room. There was only one word that could describe how I felt the entire time we were at this inspection - embarrassed!

"You need to slow down," Donna said about halfway through the second day.

"Why? These charts are organized and easy to get through." *I'm not splitting atoms over here.*

"I just want you to understand what you are reading." She said as she popped a piece of gum in her mouth.

"Donna, I've caught eight mistakes thus far. I think I have it under control." *We aren't all blockheads like you.*

Three days later we finished the inspection. The entire time we were there, Donna was either busy emailing people on her blackberry or completely clueless as to what she was looking at in the subjects' records. One good thing out of the experience was I felt like I had found my niche.

I couldn't stand one more day or car ride with her. On our way back to the office the last day, she decided to drive and continue our conversation from the first day. "Jacob did a great job during his interview. All of his references gave him rave reviews, but I don't think he's cut out to do this job. What do you think?" Donna asked me.

"What do you mean what do I think?" I asked as I looked out the passenger side window.

"Do you think he's capable of doing this job?" *First off, why would my opinion matter? Secondly, he's already been hired. Too late for the what ifs.*

"I think Jacob, like the rest of us, is very capable of doing this job. Jacob is very detailed oriented which is a great trait to have for this job, right?" I adjusted the radio volume subtly to show I didn't want to have anything to do with this conversation.

"Jacob gets too caught up in the small things. I think he focuses on stuff that's not important." She turned the radio off.

"He might be the type that likes to know the theory behind the mechanics of something." *Mental note - tell Jacob he should try to focus on big picture stuff and not get hung up on small details.*

"I always considered you the wildcard out of the bunch." *That's it! I'm done with this woman!* All I could do was laugh to prevent from going off. "Monique didn't want to hire you, but I felt like you would do a good job." *What am I supposed to do with this tidbit of information?*

I took my sunglasses off and rubbed my eyes and temples with the tips of my fingers. Just as I'm about to put my sunglasses back on and say something smart to Donna, she swerved abruptly.

"Did you see that idiot?" She hollered as she slammed on the gas to catch up with the guy who cut us off. Just when I didn't think I could get any more embarrassed, she rolled down the passenger's side window and roared, "Watch where you're going, stupid?"

I lowered my head into my hands and bent my entire body forward. If I could have morphed into the seat, I would have. The guy in the car flipped Donna off and sped away. Ten minutes later we pulled in the parking garage at the office right at 3:30 pm, the time I normally leave for the day. *Hallelujah.*

"See you tomorrow," I said as I collected all my belongings from the trunk.

"Are you going upstairs?" Donna asked.

"Yes."

"I will not approve any credit time since we finished working at the time you normally get off." *I didn't want my computer and printer sitting in my car overnight because it surely wasn't coming in the house with me.*

I cut my eyes at her and said, "Bye, Donna. "

****

Donna would often request we send her detailed emails outlining what our work week would look like. Every time she would reply back and tell us what she wanted us to do instead. The first time I was like oh well. Second time I was like really? Third time I was like ENOUGH!

I sent her the following email after the third switcheroo:

> Donna,
> In the future, can you provide exact guidance as to what you want done and when you want it done by? It seems like when I come up with a plan, changes are made that better suit your plans. I don't mind doing it your way, it's just frustrating when I have

something already planned out a certain way and it changes several times. Thanks.

Carol

She responded back with:

See me please.

That's the whole reason I sent an email, to avoid a long drawn out conversation.

"Come in and close the door." *Here we go!!!*

"Is there a problem between the two of us?" Donna asked with an attitude.

"No," I reply with just as much attitude.

"This email was very disrespectful."

"How so?" I questioned with a slight smirk on my face.

"You have to understand that things in this job change quickly and that you have to be flexible."

"Donna, I had someone who's opinion means a lot to me read the email prior to sending it to you to make sure it wasn't disrespectful. I'm allowed to be frustrated and to voice my feelings. I have no issues with being flexible, but when asked to come up with a schedule every week and then that schedule is changed, is a waste of my time. Especially if you're going to tell me what to do instead. That's why I said I don't mind doing it your way." I paused for a second to let what I just said sink in. "I get the impression that you feel a good manager is supposed to ask for our opinions on stuff, but honestly, you could care less. That way we can never accuse you of not asking for our input. I was in the military and have no problem doing what I'm told. I do have a problem with being made to feel like my opinion matters when in reality you could care less." I could feel a tension headache starting to mound.

"Everyone's opinions matter, but I am ultimately responsible for what happens in this office. I have to make sure things get done in a timely fashion. When Monique tells me to do something, I don't question what she says, I just do it. You always ask why." Donna's eyes were practically bugging out of her head.

"Considering I'm learning to do a job I've never done before; it only makes sense for me to ask questions for clarification. Your name is not Jesus Christ so please don't think I'm going to blindly follow you."

She folded her arms, "You make it seem like I'm a militant boss."

I felt like John Quinones from *What would you do?* was going to open her office door followed by a camera man and say "We have been documenting you for the last eight months to see how you would handle being managed by this type of supervisor. We're surprised you've last this long. We didn't want to torture you anymore." *Wishful thinking.*

"When I accepted this supervisory job I knew I was coming into an office that needed a huge overhaul. I did a detail for a month prior to applying for the job. I got a chance to see how people in this office came and went as they pleased. You have read some of the reports written by the investigators that were here. You can kinda see what I had to deal with. I moved here wanting to accomplish a goal - add diversity to this office. I feel like I'm doing that. I don't want people to see that we can't get along. What's that going to look like?" *She's all over the place! Can she stick with one thought, we discuss it and then move on?*

"First, let me say that I don't have the power to make you seem like something you are or aren't. Secondly, we don't have to 'like' each other to get the work done. All we have to do is work together to get these inspections done. Just because we are both black women doesn't mean we are automatically supposed to like each other. Race has nothing to do with how I get along with people. I accepted this position to be gainfully employed. I don't understand exactly what else you want from me."

I could start to see that she was getting frustrated and honestly, I had been over this conversation ten minutes ago. *Again, this was the whole reason I sent an email so she could respond with an 'ok' or 'noted.'*

"Your email came off very disrespectful," was her lame response.

"I apologize if that's how you took it because that wasn't my intention. I'm used to planning out my work and having a supervisor trust in my ability to get the work done without having to be told exactly how to do it. I feel like I'm picking everything up relatively quickly." *That was a Real Housewives apology.*

"You do appear to be learning quickly, but I can't help but wonder if you're grasping everything you need to grasp." *Did she really just say that?*

At this point, my head is pounding from talking in circles. I'd been in her office for thirty minutes and didn't see any sort of resolution happening soon.

"What have I not done to make you think I'm not picking up the essentials?" I asked. "Because you've allowed me to have close-out meetings in your absence. You've had me train Jacob and Melissa on several things."

"I can't give you an exact example because I have never gone behind you while we were on an inspection to catch something you may have missed." *Ok! I d.o.n.e.*

She is on something. I will no longer feed into her madness. I stood up, walked towards the door, and went back to my cubicle. If I stayed in her office a second longer I was going to really show her what disrespectful was! She didn't follow me nor did she talk to me the rest of the day. Matter of fact, she started giving me the cold shoulder. *Was I supposed to be upset because she was no longer talking to me? Sorry sista, not happening!* I felt bad for Lori because Donna had latched on to her.

The end of March couldn't come fast enough. Donna was going to India for three weeks. Once it arrived you could literally feel less tension in the office. Everyone had a little more pep in their step. It's truly amazing how one person can have such a negative effect on so many people.

****

The first week Donna was gone Adam and I celebrated our fourth wedding anniversary in Napa Valley. The second week she was gone I decided that I would do a sample collection. These usually require very little brain power, and since I killed thousands of brain cells in Napa, I needed something easy. The next day I got an email from Donna telling me to log on to instant messenger. I logged on and she called me.

> Donna: I noticed you didn't add the ATM surcharge for pulling money out on your voucher for the avocado sample.

> Carol: I must have forgotten. *As she was talking, I calculated the amount it would be – $2.85.*

> Donna: Do you want to redo the voucher?

> Carol: No. It's three dollars. It's more of a hassle to redo the voucher. I'll suck it up and pay it out of my own pocket. In the future, I'll make sure to add that fee.

> Donna: Are you sure you don't want to resubmit the voucher? You are cheating yourself out of money. *Oh no, now I can't get the Prada bag I had my eye on. Get out of here!*

> Carol: I don't think three dollars is going to break me. I'll resubmit it if it's that serious to you.

> Donna: If you don't want to do it, then don't.

> ** Donna Simpleton has disconnected from chat.

No this woman didn't just hang up on me because I didn't resubmit a voucher! Saying I had lost all respect for her doesn't even express the thoughts that were running through my mind.

****

The day Donna returned to the office from India was a sad, sad day. I knew it wasn't right or healthy for me to harbor so much resentment towards this woman, but I couldn't help it. I couldn't stand to hear her voice. Couldn't stand to smell her funky perfume and definitely couldn't stand to see her face. Prior to her leaving for India, our conversations were very limited but now they were non-existent. I spoke to her only if I was spoken to first. If she walked by and didn't say anything, neither did I. Matter of fact, if I could hear her talking to Lori and had a feeling she would stop by my cubicle on her way to the breakroom, I would get up and leave the office for at least five minutes. I figured that was enough time for her to do what she needed to do in the breakroom and head back to her office. I wanted to say as little to her, so much so, that when she would say good morning I'd reply hi. *I wish there had been a greeting that was even shorter than hi.*

A week after she returned from India, she informed Lori and I that we would be going to Long Beach and San Diego, respectively, to do our level one audits the second week in May. I had been assigned a tortilla manufacturing company. I did the normal background preparation for the inspection and emailed Biff, my auditor, my plan of action.

San Diego was just as beautiful as I had remembered it. The only difference was, this time Adam wasn't with me. As soon as I checked into the hotel room, I pulled up the uber app on my phone to get a ride to the beach. It was such a nice reprieve from the Phoenix heat to feel the cool Pacific coastal winds blowing in my face. As soon as the sun began to kiss the horizon, I decided I better head back to the room and mentally prepare for the next day.

I arrived at the San Diego FDA office around 6:45 am. I rang the bell to get in the office. Unlike the Tempe office, I wasn't able to see who would open the door for me. I was greeted by an older Indian gentleman who showed me where I could put my laptop and inspectional equipment. Then he brought me to Biff's office.

"Good morning," I said.

"Morning. I'm working on some emails. Give me ten minutes," was his pleasant reply. He never looked away from his computer screen.

"Do you want me to get the car pulled around so when you're done we can head out?"

"No!" He kept typing. *Oookk! Who's he emailing Obama?*

Once Biff finished his emails we headed down to the parking garage. "I prefer to drive when people come here to do their audits because I am familiar with the freeways."

"Cool. I have never driven in San Diego before. California traffic is nuts."

That was pretty much the extent of our conversation on the way to the company. The entire forty-five-minute ride he had the worst road rage and was constantly twitching. *What's wrong with the guy?*

Once we arrived, I conducted the inspection. I thought it had gone fairly well and planned on closing out with management the next day. On our way back to the office on the second day, I did one of the things Biff hated, I asked him a question. "How long does it take for an auditor to make a decision on whether someone has passed or failed?"

"You seemed to have done ok. As long as your report isn't a case killer, you're fine." I was smiling ear to ear on the inside.

I asked another question, "Do I need to cc Donna on the email I send you that will have my report attached?"

"No, send it to me! She doesn't need to see!" *Ok calm down. I'm not sending you the winning Powerball numbers.*

When I returned to my hotel room that evening I called the company we used to book our travel arrangements and changed my flight to leave first thing Wednesday morning. I couldn't wait to get home and have this audit behind me.

I arrived back at the office on Wednesday around noon. I walked over to Melissa's cubicle to tell her how my audit had gone. "Hey girl. How are you?" I greeted Melissa.

"I'm good. How'd it go?" Melissa asked pleasantly.

"I feel pretty confident. Biff told me as long as my report wasn't a case killer I was good."

"Praise God," she said as she clasped her hands together. *She was always so encouraging.*

"Melissa, do you have that paper I gave you earlier?" Donna interrupted. *This heffa is so damn rude.* I walked off. Whatever she needed to talk to Melissa about had nothing to do with me, plus I was done telling Melissa about my audit.

By Friday, I had completed the report for the inspection and emailed it to Biff.

> Hi Biff, Attached is the EIR for my level one audit. I have not signed off in FACTS because I need to know how many hours you want me to put in for you. I entered my label review in FACTS. Please let me know if you have any questions. Carol

Just to give you a brief description of what the above acronyms mean: EIR stands for establishment inspection report. This report describes everything about the company and any unfavorable observations that were found during the inspection. FACTS is the system used to enter anything related to an inspection or collection report. It's also where we document how many hours it took to accomplish a certain task.

Biff replied:

> It was an audit. I was not an active participant of the inspection. I don't get hours.

My reply:

> The instructions on the new hire website says to record the auditor's time in FACTS under PAC 99R342, Op Code 92. I copied and pasted a link so that he could see first-hand what the instructions say.

True to Biff form he replied:

Enter your time.

The following week the office was cursed with Monique's presence because we had two new hires start. Mark Blunt was going to be a CSO and Antonio Mash had just graduated from grad school in Alabama. Antonio was going to fill Mary's position, as she was still out on medical leave. During the introductions, we went around the room and said a little something about ourselves. *So annoying, are these new guys really going to remember eight different names and bios?*

"We are happy you're both here," Monique said after everyone had given their spiel. "I want to meet with everyone individually. Schedule a thirty-minute meeting on my outlook calendar."

"Are you going to be here all week?" I asked.

"One thing I can't stand is having to repeat myself," Monique replied with a slick grin.

"Had I heard you say you were going to be here all week; I would have never asked the question. It wouldn't be smart for me to assume what your schedule looks like," I replied with just as slick of a grin. *I didn't give a damn! The two new guys looked at each other like WTF!*

Once I left the conference room, I put myself on her calendar for Wednesday morning and kept it moving. Then I sent Donna an email:

> Change of plans. I am not going to do the BIMO. I'm heading out to do an inspection at a coffee manufacturer.

I hit send and left the office. I figured she changed my schedule numerous times in the past, this time I changed my own schedule.

The company was located on the other side of town so it took about forty-five minutes to get there, only to find out it was out of business. I headed over to a second location that had been listed in the company's file. That location was closed as well. When I returned to the office around 3:00 pm I had an email from Donna waiting on me.

What happen to this plan to start BIMO?

203

I responded:

> I'm here four days this week and didn't want to take a chance it went over like the last one I did.

Send. I shut my computer down and left for the day.

Donna decided, probably after speaking to Monique about the situation, to send me the following email: ***This email is the EXACT email, word for word, that she sent me! ***

> This inspection was assigned to you back in March. You put in your leave request around April 24th for May 22nd, 26th and 27th. I approved your leave trusting you in good faith that all your assignments would be handled appropriately. Your inability to complete your assignment because you have schedule leave and now think you won't have enough time to do your work is unacceptable.
>
> Per the assignment memo you only have to review a minimum of 10 subject records and 10 informed consents. In reviewing the protocol for the study, I don't understand why you thought you couldn't look at 10 records in addition to other study related documents in 3-4 days. If needed I could have arranged for someone to go with you to assist. You should have discussed your desires to change your inspectional plans with me in advance.
>
> Going forward I will expect you to consider your workload obligations when planning your personal leave. Most of our assignments are given far enough in advance to were this should not be a problem. Prior to approving your leave in the future you need to send me an email in advance affirming you have no outstanding assignments or reports that conflicts with your request.

Who wants to walk in and the first thing you read is this garbage? I was furious. I took a deep breath and left the office for fifteen minutes to collect my thoughts. When Donna assigned the BIMO to me in March, I expressed I wanted to get it done sooner versus later. I was literally sitting around the office for weeks waiting on her to give me direction on what she wanted me to do next.

Once I composed myself, I decided to respond to the email. I knew she was on the road with Monique heading to Tucson. *Why not give them something to talk about on the ride there and back?* I unlocked my computer and my fingers flew across the keyboard as I explained why I had done what I had done, her confusing management style that changed from day to day, and that I wasn't even technically supposed to be doing those inspections solo. I exhaled loudly right as I clicked send and left the office.

I attempted to find the coffee manufacturer one more time. I found it and thankfully, it was a very small place. It took me two hours to inspect. When I returned to the office, I started writing my report and before I knew it was time for me to leave for the day. I was thankful the day had passed without me having to see 'frick and frack.'

The next day, as anticipated, I had an email waiting for me from Donna. She basically said we needed to talk. *Augh, not another one of those long drawn out conversations where she says the complete opposite of what she said last week.* I wasn't in the mood because on top of meeting with her, I was meeting with Monique later that morning.

She walked past my cubicle and said, "I need to see you now."

"Give me about five minutes. I'm in the middle of writing an email." I didn't even look in her direction. She huffed and stomped away.

I finished what I was doing in less than five minutes and went to her office. I stood in the doorway. "I'm in the middle of something. I'll have to meet up with you later." *Really? You were able to get that involved in something that now we can't meet?*

"Ok," I replied and turned on my heels and walked back to my desk.

When I got back to my desk I opened my Bible and read Proverbs 29:11, 'A fool gives full vent to his anger, but a wise man keeps himself under control.' I had started reading scripture every day because I felt like she was one of Satan's many helpers trying to taunt me into doing something bad.

She literally came to my cubicle two minutes later. "Now I'm ready. Let's meet in the conference room." *Control freak!* "I don't understand what the problem is. I don't know where we went wrong," She started the conversation with. *Were we dating, and I didn't know about it?*

"I do. It was when you hung up on me while you were in India." My defenses were up, and I knew this was going to be a challenging day.

"What are you talking about? I didn't hang up on you!" She slammed her hand on the conference room table.
"I was about to say something and you hung up before I had a chance. I can tolerate a lot of things but being blatantly disrespected is not one of them."

"I didn't know that you were going to say anything else. I assumed the conversation was over. I didn't hang up on you. If I did I'm sorry. I would never do anything like that. That's unprofessional. I would hang up on my husband but never someone I worked with," she babbled. Her mouth was saying one thing but her stiff, rigid body language spoke volumes. *If you'd hang up on your husband, you'd sure as hell hung up on someone you work with. Supposedly you love your husband, you don't even really know me.*

She continued, "If you weren't finished talking why didn't you call me back? That's what I did when Lori hung up on me." *First, you said you didn't hang up on me. Then you said if you did hang up you were sorry. Now you're trying to deflect. All within two minutes. Can someone please bring her some lithium?*

"I wasn't going to call you back to get into an argument over something I felt wasn't important. Whether I paid the three dollars out of my own pocket or not wasn't something I felt warranted you getting upset about. You clearly were so I figured I'd let you work that out on your own." I folded my arms across my chest.

She stared at me for a while, maybe taken aback by my last statement, but it was true. If she wanted to be pissy about something that really didn't have any bearing on her personal finances or the government's she should have let it roll off her back. The same way I let those $3 roll off mine.

"Monique and I have talked about your emails. I would never speak to her the way you speak to me. Your emails are borderline rude and aggressive."

I chuckled and she asked, "What's so funny?"

"I've been called a lot worse. The funny thing is I have been neither to you. I will admit that I have been short and to the point. But in my defense so have you. You are extremely curt when you speak to people. I figured if you can do it, then you should have no problems being spoken to in the same manner. Just because I'm not going into details when you ask a question doesn't mean I'm being rude. You have to admit; I always answer your questions."

"What does curt mean?" she questioned. *Omg I wanted to laugh in her face.*

"It means being short with someone." I couldn't help but have a slick grin on my face.

"Oh," was her response. I figured she probably didn't hear anything else I said after I used a word she wasn't familiar with.

"You were very curt with me when I emailed you about the status of your level one audit report."

"Donna, you asked me if I was done. I replied yes. What else was I supposed to say?"

She was clearly frustrated, and I loved it. "You hadn't sent me the report. How was I supposed to know it was done?"

"I figured Biff would have told you," I said slowly to let the idea that supervisors should speak to one another sink in.

She raised her eyebrows in an 'ah ha' moment, but rather than acknowledge that would have made sense, she decided to take the conversation in a different direction. "You didn't even speak to me when you got back from your audit. You were talking to Melissa and as soon as I walked up you walked off. And then when you were in the copy room later that day you walked right past me and didn't speak that time either." *Come on! Where are the cameras? I have to be on some new reality show.*

I couldn't help but shake my head when I started to reply because she sounded like a whiny child. "You interrupted without saying excuse me. I figured it must be important so I walked away. As far as the copy room, if you felt you needed to say something to me I would I have listened. I didn't have anything to say." Monique knocked on the door and said their interview was supposed to start in a minute. *Thank you, Jesus!*

Turns out the person who they were interviewing never called in. Donna called me back into the conference room to finish up the conversation. *Are you serious? What else needs to be said? Don't you have any work you need to do because I know I do?*

She began a fifteen-minute speech about something or the other. I had completely tuned her out and was watching a group of college kids play hacky sack in the courtyard. After I read that scripture and realized it was going to impossible to have a true adult conversation with this woman, I decided to let what she was saying go in one ear and out the other.

"Is there anything you want to say?" Donna asked.

"No." *Why couldn't she grasp I had mentally checked out?* "I have a meeting with Monique in a minute."

"Wow. You are getting it from all directions today," she smiled an evil grin as I got up from the table.

I knocked on the office door that Monique was using.

"Come in. How are things going, Carol?" Monique asked as I sat down in a chair opposite her.

"Good."

"I guess we have a different idea of what good is," she replied with that infamous slick grin plastered on her face.

"I'm getting paid every day I'm here. That's good for me." I said as I crossed my legs.

"Donna has shown me the emails between the two of you. You are very disrespectful. Had it been up to me I wouldn't have hired you, but she saw something in you and fought to have you come on-board." *What did she think I was supposed to do with that little tidbit of information? These two women try to act tough, but they hold on to stuff forever. Let it go, that happened over ten months ago.*

"Oh really? Why wouldn't you have hired me?" I asked as I uncrossed my legs, placed my elbows on my knees, and rested my chin in my hands. I wanted to see if she would give me constructive feedback that I could use when I interviewed for my next position.

"I don't know. It was something about your aura," was her response. *Nope! Nothing valuable!* I leaned back in the chair ready for whatever nonsense was about to spew out of her mouth. "All of my supervisors are very qualified to perform their jobs," she began. *Was she trying to convince me or herself with that lie?* "Donna was a compliance officer back in Dallas. She has a wealth of knowledge that you should draw from. You and Donna need to work out whatever differences you two have. If she can't do her job and get you in line, then I will have to do my job." *Get in-line? Girl, bye! I was so proud of myself for sitting there so calmly. Did she really think that by saying do what Donna tells you or else was really going to scare me into submission? I wasn't going to do anything I didn't feel comfortable doing. I wish they'd try to 'fire' me. I had loads of documentation on Donna where she told me to do something that was incorrect or illegal. Bring it.*

After a thirty-minute one-way conversation about being black and working for the government and other mindless jabber, she stopped, "Do you have any questions?"

"Nope." I didn't hesitant as I got up and walked out of the office.

Inside I was livid. My head was pounding, and I could hear my heartbeat in my ears. This was the last straw. I grabbed Lori and said, "Let's go for a walk. I have to tell you everything that's been going on today."

209

When we got off the elevator in the lobby I started, "When I was talking to Donna about the hang-up incident she said you did the same thing to her. She called you back and asked why you hung up on her."

"Wait. What?!" Lori stopped walking. "She said I hung up on her? I would never do anything like that."

"Yea, I know. That sounded completely out of character. You are way too polite to hang up on someone, even a loser like her."

"If I would have hung up on her I would have gotten up and went to her office. I would've made sure she knew it was done accidentally. I can't believe she said I did that." Lori shook her head as she tied her hair back.

"I can. Donna is a liar."

Lori let me vent for thirty minutes. Needless to say, I was spent. I was able to finish the report for the coffee manufacturer and turned it in for Donna to review.

When I got home that evening I told Adam I was going to quit. My nerves were shot. I wasn't even remotely interested in this type of work. I realized at that moment that I could contribute to our family in other ways other than monetarily. I wanted to find out my audit results before I quit. I prayed that I had passed so it would be that much sweeter to give my two-week notice.

The following week Biff finally got in contact with me about my audit results. He told me I didn't pass. I was floored! *What happened to as long as the report isn't a case killer? Yet another lie. I guess God don't like ugly since He knew I wanted to drop the 'I quit' bomb after passing.*

He rattled off a list of things he felt I could have done better, and gave me the opportunity to rebut his findings. Towards the middle of the conversation, I knew he wasn't going to change his mind, even though the reason I did things a certain way were coming from either Donna or the compliance officer I had been working with during the inspection.

We ended the call, and I sent Donna an email saying I didn't pass. Failing sucked, but I knew I was done. I was mentally exhausted.

****

About two weeks after those meetings with 'frick and frack' I noticed a lump on my left side. *Another health issue...this job was taking a toll on me.* I went to a dermatologist and was told it was a lipoma. Normally, they can be removed in an office visit under local anesthesia but because this one felt deep I was referred to a plastic surgeon. The plastic surgeon confirmed it was indeed a lipoma and that it was deeply embedded in my muscle. I scheduled my surgery for June 1st. I planned the surgery perfectly because it was the Monday after I found out I hadn't passed. The doctor said the recovery time would depend on how deep the lipoma was. I requested three days off because that was the longest amount of time I could take off without needing to bring in a doctor's note.

When Donna approved my leave she sent me an email requesting a doctor's note. *Delete! I wasn't bringing her a damn thing because union guidelines stated a note was required if someone was going to be out more than three consecutive work days. She insisted on demanding stuff she was not privy to.*

While I was out Lori texted me.

> Lori: I didn't pass my audit. :(

> Me: What? I don't believe that.

> Lori: Too much to text. I'll tell u deets when u get back.

> Me: Ok. R u ok?

> Lori: I'm bummed but whatever. D said no1 can take leave cuz we didn't pass.

> Me: She needs to be reeled in. She's outta ctrl.

Donna didn't have the authority to disapprove leave as a form of punishment for not passing the audit. She should have punished herself for not providing us with adequate training. Prior to my audit, I had only performed three food manufacturer inspections. She had me do seven BIMO inspections to get the district's pending inspection numbers down. All level one audits are done at food manufacturers.

When I returned Thursday, she was out of the office. *Lucky me!* I was able to catch up with Lori on how her conversation with her auditor had gone. Lori's result was just as bogus as mine.

I emailed Donna:

Do you plan on being in the office tomorrow?

Her response:

Yes. Why? *Defensive much?*

My response:

I need to talk to you face to face.

"Good morning," I said as I knocked on Donna's door. "I can't lift anything heavier than five pounds for the next two weeks." I handed her the note from the doctor.

"Ok. I didn't need this type of note. I need one saying you were under his care for the past three days." *I totally ignored that dumb response.*

"I want to start off by saying thank you for hiring me. My last day in the office will be June 26th." Donna dropped her pen and gave me her full attention. *I really wanted to say today is my last day. See ya!*

"What's going on?" She started to fiddle with her hair, which was now in micro braids that were long overdue for a touch-up.

"I think it's best for me to take care of me right now. I've had a couple major surgeries since starting this job. You only get one body. I need to rest and take care of mine."

"If it's health related we can come up with an alternative work schedule to accommodate you. We have spent a lot of money training you. It

would be such a waste for you to leave now." *Like I care how much money was spent 'training' me.* "Don't make any rash decisions."
"This is far from a rash decision." I was sitting on the edge of the chair.

"If you tell me what's wrong I can call Monique and work something out." *Girl, bye! Like I want you two hens talking about my personal business.*

"God's got me. My last physical day will be the 26th. I plan on using my leave to carry me into July. I'll send you an email for your records."

"Ok. I really wish you'd reconsider telling me what's wrong so I can help." *She's probably scared to tell Monique I'm quitting. HA!* I had taken mountains of verbal abuse for nearly a year now, which had taken its toll on me. I was going to leave on my own terms, not in handcuffs due to punching her in the face.

"If possible, you may not want to send Jacob or Melissa to San Diego for their audits. Biff's personality is a bit intimidating."

"Is he that bad?" Donna asked. "I've never met him. We've only talked on the phone or instant messaged each other."

"It's not that he's bad, he just doesn't have a very warm personality, which might be a bit intimidating for those two."

"Ok," Donna replied. "I'll try to avoid sending anyone there if possible." She made sure to not look me in the eye when she made that last statement.

She continued to assign work to me: sample collections, undercover buys, recall audit checks, and training the two new guys. I guess she figured those things didn't require heavy lifting so she was going to make sure I earned my paycheck the last three weeks I was there.

Donna emailed me mid-June and told me that she was going to be out of the office for personal reasons. *Surprise, surprise!* She asked if I could make my last day July 6th versus June 26th. Donna made a lame excuse about having to get other people involved in the process. Rather than have multiple hands in the pot, she figured it would easier for her to handle everything once she returned on the 6th. I agreed - stupid me.

****

I arrived promptly at 7:00 am on July 6th. All I had to do was turn in all of my inspection equipment, computer, printer, camera, etc. *This will be quick – wrong!* Donna asked me to train Mark on how to do recall audit checks. I had just checked all my emails and noticed that Melissa had volunteered to do these, so why was she giving them to me? *Why not have Melissa train the guy? Oh yeah, that would make too much sense.* Mark and I met in the conference room where I explained the whole process. We finish up in about forty-five minutes.

I walked over to Jacob's desk. "Donna just emailed me and told me to get the recall audit checks that you are working on and finish them up."

"I just got them Thursday of last week, and Friday was a holiday. Does she think I'm that slow?" Jacob had a worry look in his eyes.

"Jacob, it doesn't have anything to do with your speed. She's just trying to keep me here all day, which isn't going to happen. When she asks you, can you tell her something like you've made head way on it and it would be more work for me to have to start over?"

He smiled and said, "Sure."

"Thanks."

Lori wasn't in the office long that day because she was heading to California to redo her audit. *You'll never guess where she was going, or maybe you've seen the pattern of how things were in this office. Yep, she was off to San Diego. Donna lied yet again!*

Donna called me around 9:00 am and told me to bring all of my inspection equipment to her office so that she could account for everything.

"There is a lot of stuff. It doesn't make sense to haul everything to our office. If you're worried about stuff being stolen, you can lock the equipment in the cabinets in my cubicle."

"Augh, ok I'm on my way," was her nasty reply. *Did she really think that I was going to bend over backwards to make this process easy for*

214

her? Please! I had already agreed to come in today. For the record, she had NO clue what she was doing. She was getting everybody and their mama involved in the process because it was the first time she out-processed someone electronically.

When she got to my desk, she brought a list of the equipment I had been issue (which I provided her a few weeks prior). As I was going through all the items on my desk, I noticed she wasn't even checking it off the list. At that point, I had nothing to lose and my temper was starting to flare up, "Everything is in either this drawer or that cabinet. Computer is on my desk. That's it."

She smacked her lips and said, "That's it?"

"Yep. I just need to shred these papers, and I'll be on my way."

"I'll get Antonio to do it." She proceeded to holler over the cubicle wall for him to come to my area. *Ghetto!*

"Antonio, shred these papers. Walk downstairs with Carol and get her parking decal." *A few minutes ago she was trying to get me to stay the entire day. Now she is trying to have me escorted out of the office! Thank you Jesus I don't have to deal with this woman ever again!*

"Since I'm leaving this early I'm going to put in leave for the rest of the day so I get paid the full eight hours," I said. *I wasn't trying to get jipped out of a full day's pay.*

"Don't worry about it," she replied.

"What does that mean? I'm going to get paid for the full eight hours?" I asked as I looked her dead in the eyes.

"Yes."

When I think back, I took a real chance believing that she was going to stick to her word, but I wanted to get out of there so badly I didn't care. I gathered my things and said good-bye to Jacob one last time. I walked through the copy room where Donna and Melissa were having a conversation and waved bye to Melissa. Antonio was right on my heels.

He was cool about the odd situation Donna had placed him. I told him not to get discouraged when Donna would go on her rants. He thanked me for the advice, and I was on my way.

Since my last day, I have met up with Lori, Jacob, and Melissa for happy hour gab sessions. I found out Jacob and Melissa didn't pass their audits. Thankfully, Lori and Melissa passed the second time around. Jacob and Antonio have since moved on to bigger and better things.

Never would I have guessed after twelve years of working for the feds that my fantasy gig would turn into a recurring nightmare. Each time I took a new position I went in with the hopes that things would be different. I was blessed along the way to encounter some true friends, as well, as grow into the woman I am today. Without the ups and down, I wouldn't have the appreciation for the few good people that are out there. *Nor would I have had enough material to write this memoir.*

I still feel like federal positions have the best perks, but I now know those perks don't outweigh my mental and physical well-being. Though I might be slightly jaded at the age of thirty-six, I still think my fantasy gig is out there. It's just not going to be with the federal government!

Made in the USA
San Bernardino, CA
27 June 2016